ARCANOS UNRAVELED

ARCANOS UNRAVELED

JONNA GJEVRE

STORYADOR PRESS

Text copyright © 2017 Jonna Gjevre
Cover art copyright © 2017 Kathleen Jennings
Cover design copyright © 2017 Stewart Williams
All rights reserved.

Published in the United States by Storyador.
www.storyador.com

Print book ISBN-13: 978-1-947990-00-5

Ebook ISBN-13: 978-1-947990-01-2

In memory of Michael Levy

CHAPTER ONE

When I return from the dungeons, there's a student leaning against the new cauldron. Not one of our Isthmus scholars, but a regular college student with a backpack and a red phone. Which is impossible. I've worked here since January, and no mundane student has ever set foot in our castle. It is, after all, invisible.

"Is there a Coke machine on this floor?" he asks, scanning the crates stacked in the mailroom. The shipping label from Ruskin's cauldron slowly drifts to the ground.

I freeze in place, wondering if I should (a) escort the intruder from the premises; (b) knock him on the head and dump him in the cauldron (which would make him Ruskin's problem, not mine, and would give me no small amount of pleasure); or (c) offer him tea.

As usual, I choose the least interesting option.

"Sorry, no Coke here," I say, ushering the student through the court and pointing to the stately building beside the Observatory. "Try Agriculture Hall."

He ambles off, at one point twisting his neck to look over his shoulder. His eyes widen, taking in the stone gargoyles flanking the entrance. "Whoa."

I'm not certified for memory work, and I can't afford any redirection charms, but I've learned to do my best with what I've got, and what I've got right now is a skein of enchanted yarn. I loop the handspun Shetland around my wrists and pull it taut.

You don't see that woman anymore. You have someplace important to go.

After an excruciating delay, during which the student wobbles back and forth like a fleshy marionette, the spell finally works. He tightens his grip on his backpack and strides purposefully toward Agriculture Hall. The skein flares briefly, then dissolves into ash.

Wrists stinging from the spell, I hurry down the steps to have a look at the castle. The entire building is flickering in and out of view. It's like a mirage, or an image reflected in a rippling pond. One of the windows facing the lake pulses in a rich spectrum, a tiny gothic rainbow hanging in midair.

Whoa, indeed. Clutching my skirts, I bolt back up the staircase to find the dean.

Perhaps you've heard about those secret schools of magic, the kind hidden away in places like the Scottish Highlands, where elite wizards stir potions and chant incantations. Someone is usually fighting evil, elegantly dressed in silk velvet.

That's not me. That's not my life.

It's true I'm the youngest professor at The Isthmus, and it's also true that The Isthmus is a prestigious college of magic. But I'm not an elite wizard, nor am I fighting anything particularly evil. I'm just an adjunct hedge witch, working part time. When I'm not avoiding a certain tenured faculty member, or teaching sophomores to weave flying carpets, I'm doing workaday knitting spells for the administration.

I race through the dean's reception hall and stumble into his office, setting off a musical series of detection chimes. Security has always been a big deal at The Isthmus, but this fall it's especially high. We have several members of the nobility on campus,

2

including Her Royal Highness Elena, Crown Princess of Carpathia, who is older than I am, failing my class on Enchanted Textiles, and giving the royal house of the East a very bad name.

Dean LaMarche stands with his fingers steepled together, silver hair gleaming, long nose tilted down in obvious disdain. Behind him hangs a huge painting of a strapless, red leather evening gown. No woman inside the gown. It's said that only those with the highest gift of sight can see the woman whose generous form fills out those scarlet curves. Personally, I think the dean's dress is, and always has been, completely empty.

"You're late for sound-proofing my curtains." His eyes narrow, moving from my curly ponytail and embroidered smock to my empty hands. "And obviously unprepared."

"Sir, I'm very sorry to say—"

"Where are your materials? Why haven't you brought them? Go back and get them now."

"But sir," I pause, just long enough to catch my breath. "The Drini shields are down."

If you've ever stepped into an elevator only to have your phone go dead, then you know how a Faraday cage works. The right kind of mesh or solid metal cage can keep a phone signal from penetrating a shielded room. Similarly, the right kind of Drini, or magical shield, can keep a stimulus from reaching an observer's brain. In layman's terms, a Drini makes things invisible, undetectable. Like the woman in the red dress.

Dean LaMarche scowls. "What do you mean, 'The Drini shields are down'?"

"I mean a student walked into the mailroom, stood right there in front of the mail portal, and asked for a Coke machine."

"What? Why didn't you say so at once?" The dean's nostrils flare, and his twin ravens launch from their perch. He pounds on his desk, and Ms. Nguyen comes running in.

"We need gargoyles! A noxious fog!" he cries, as the birds go flapping out. "Send word to the Regents and get Ruskin in here now. Tell them the shields are down."

A vein throbbing in his forehead, he darts a glance at the empty red leather dress.

"The Princess," he breathes, and fixes an eye on me. "Anya, you must make sure she's safe."

As it happens, I know exactly where Princess Elena is. She's in my chambers, and she probably wants a favor.

∽

Located between two lakes, The Isthmus is the only college of magical arts in North America. It's hidden within one of the largest mundane universities in the United States. The castle itself—Arcanos Hall—predates the ivy-covered buildings of the University of Wisconsin, which surround our campus on Observatory Hill.

My chambers are part of the old dungeons in the Arcanos cellar, where the steam tunnels under the floor keep my rooms in a constant tropical state. I'm a sweaty mess, most of the time. But I do have my own place.

Sometimes, when I'm making an invisibility cape or a large magical object, I'll drag my knitting up to the stone stairwell, where it's cooler. As I return from the dean's office, I find Princess Elena perched tensely on those worn steps, fanning herself with her gloves. She's wearing a leopard print caftan with strappy gold sandals, suitably informal for a Sunday afternoon, when no one's around. An ornate scattering of leaves forms a protective wreath atop her glossy black hair. I have no doubt the leaves are 22 karat gold.

"Really, Miss Winter," she says in her lush accent, "it's about time you came back. Are you done with the dean? I've been waiting and waiting."

She tugs on a glove. "How can you bear to work down here? It's like a prison."

I refrain from reminding her that this entire floor was used as an actual prison as recently as 1999. It's in the orientation booklet, and she can read.

"Your Highness, we need to go upstairs. There's been a security breach, and Dean LaMarche has ordered us to evacuate the lower levels. You must return to your chambers."

"Evacuate? Not until you promise to help me."

Help you with what? I want to ask, but the granite stairwell shakes, and the steam pipes begin to growl. "They're releasing a noxious fog. It's not going to smell good down here."

Princess Elena wrinkles her perfectly chiseled nose. "I can endure it."

I look at her gold sandals. The pristine soles are a distinctive, expensive shade of rose. Perhaps my best option is to lie.

"Very well, but you'll never get the smell out of your shoes."

Elena Gabriella, Crown Princess of Carpathia, leaps at once to her feet. "Bring some yarn for a shroud," she commands.

I gape at her. "A shroud? Are you kidding me?"

"Yes, a shroud. We've got a body to hide."

Most of the student dormitories in Arcanos Hall face an ugly modern parking lot, filled with the Volkswagens and Toyotas of UW-Madison's students and staff. But Princess Elena's suite features a breathtaking view of Lake Mendota and Portage Point.

"Don't you think we should inform the dean?" I pause to catch my breath, dumping my bundle of knitting supplies on the floor. There's no sign of a body anywhere, and I can't be certain this isn't a joke.

She gives me a look of terror. "Absolutely not! What if the

tabloids find out? Do you even realize what that would mean?"

She pushes aside a tall oak shutter and sinks onto her marble window bench, which perfectly matches her fireplace. Briefly, her fingers twitch. Then she frowns into her cheval mirror. "Good thing everyone's at the rugby match."

I'm about to make some reply about the importance of crowd control when she adds, "Otherwise they would have seen you."

Keeping her exalted status in mind, I consider how best to respond. With the shields down, there's a lot more at stake than her royal reputation. Under normal circumstances, mundane folk don't even feel the outline of our castle: all they ever see are the woods in the Lakeshore Preserve. But now that protection is gone, and every single one of us is at risk. We may have come a long way since the days of witch burnings and persecution, but no one wants the mundanes to know we still exist. They outnumber us a thousand to one, and their technology is toxic.

I open my bundle of yarn on the rug, which is Venetian, enchanted with detection spells, and completely soundproofed. Then I look around for the body she wants to hide, and that's when it hits me: she actually expects me to help her dispose of a corpse.

"Your Highness, I would say you have bigger problems than being seen in the dorm with one of your professors, especially if you want me to make you a shroud. I'm not really sure I can do this. It's against the law to conceal a crime."

Her cheeks flush. "It's not a crime. It was an accident, you understand?"

"Perfectly," I say, remembering (not for the first time) that the princess and I are nearly the same age. I wonder who cleaned up her messes in Carpathia.

"Where is he?" As I say this, I realize I probably shouldn't be assuming it's a guy, since the princess has never shown any interest in men.

She glances up, her eyes searching mine. Then she returns her attention to the mirror, making a dismissive gesture toward the French doors on my right. "He's in there."

As I step through the doors, the witch's wardrobe takes my breath away. I've always longed to enter the world of haute couture, to study an actual gown made by the magical couturiers of Old Vienna. Clothing like that is high art. It's not only priced beyond my reach, it's priced beyond my imagination. But now that world is literally at my fingertips.

I reach out to touch a jewel-encrusted length of soprarizzo velvet. It covers the gored skirts of a theatrical silver gown, the kind of ruinously expensive dress that demands a tiara and elbow-length gloves. The hem is edged with delicate lace panels, almost certainly knitted by indentured hedge witches in the Pyrenees. I wonder what kind of protection the lace confers—it's far too complex to read on sight.

Princess Elena glides over and tugs the gown out of the way, revealing a very dead corpse. "Such a pity," she says with forced bravado. "He wasn't bad-looking at all."

CHAPTER TWO

If you want to dispose of a body, you'll need three things. First, a standard invisibility cloak, modified to form a reality-altering shroud. Second, a place to bury or burn what's left of the corpse. Finally (and this is crucial), an ability to act swiftly and efficiently, untroubled by morality. I don't have that third thing, the untroubled moral compass, but two out of three isn't bad.

"Elena," I say, deciding right then and there that I'm not going to use her royal title anymore. Not if she wants me to cover up her negligent homicide. "We're going to talk about this."

A line forms between Elena's neatly groomed eyebrows. "What's there to talk about? It was an accident."

"Yes, but who is he?"

She throws up her hands. "I don't know. But we have to get rid of him. My father—you can't imagine what he'll do!"

Actually, I have heard nothing but terrible things about King Cibrán, the power-hungry tyrant controlling all the lands east of the Scandinavian Keel. I wouldn't want to be in Elena's fancy golden shoes.

Cringing, I inspect the body. Elena's accident is clean-shaven, mid-twenties, muscular build. He's wearing an ill-fitting jacket with silver epaulets, probably military orders. I'm guessing the orders are Alpine in origin, or maybe from the Cairngorms. His skin is a shade lighter than mine, his expression awkwardly caught between horror and surprise.

"Poor bastard," I mutter, wondering why his coat doesn't fit.

"Please." Elena's voice falters for the first time. "You've got to help me."

"Why? Why should I help you?" I wait for her to remind me she's a princess.

Her eyes widen with entreaty. "Because you're my professor?"

She can't possibly know she's said the one thing that will motivate me every time. I'm her professor. In spite of my lowly birth, my father's mundane status, my lack of formal training. In spite of all the ugly fallout from the Ruskin affair, I'm still a professor at The Isthmus. I still have a place in the world.

I manage a nonchalant shrug. "Fair enough. Bring me your invisibility cloak."

Returning to my yarn stash, I select a pair of ebony needles and a lustrous ball of handspun alpaca. Then I quickly cast on to create a light, resilient fabric. We don't have much time before the students get back, which means the gauge has to be right the first time around. When you're weaving or knitting enchanted fabrics, gauge is critical. Gauge—the relative density of the fabric—determines the degree to which a magical object can utilize or redirect fields of energy.

But magic often requires a mix of skill and sacrifice. It's not enough to knit a pattern without making a mistake: you also have to give up something of yourself. A heart shroud is a complex spell, filled with twisty cables mimicking the structure of the human heart. It requires considerable life energy, which means I have to use a delicate handspun yarn, strengthened at intervals with my hair. Yes, my hair.

I yank another curly strand from my ponytail, resentfully eyeing Elena's cascade of raven tresses. If this happens again, I'll end up bald.

I lift the knitted heart and test it for resilience. When it's grafted onto Elena's invisibility cloak, the dead man won't just disappear: his mass will be reduced to the size and weight of his heart. But only if the gauge is right.

"So," I murmur, ebony needles clicking too fast even for me to see. "How did you meet this guy?"

Elena averts her gaze. It's a very sad thing when you're stuck in an immense wardrobe with someone who would rather stare at a corpse than look you in the eye.

"It's not like you found him at the farmer's market."

She forces a tight smile, but says nothing. There's something about her behavior that isn't right, something I can't put into words. The man is dead. Surely she ought to be acting sad, or at least a little guilty. Instead, she's practically simmering with anxiety and rage. Whatever's happened, she can't talk about it, which means she'll have to lie. And if she lies to me, and if I accept what she says, then she won't have to lie to anyone else.

So I give her another opening. "I gather he's not from Wisconsin."

"No," Elena concedes, "he's not from Wisconsin."

I then get to hear the entire ridiculous story of how she posted an advertisement in *Cloak and Wand*, the popular society magazine, through which she met a young wizard who agreed to portal here from who-knows-where, lured by the promise of anonymous rooftop rapture with a mysterious masked enchantress.

This account is utter bullshit, of course. For one thing, I can't imagine haughty Elena of Carpathia arranging a romantic rendezvous with anyone, let alone a man whose coat doesn't fit. Furthermore, if this guy used the Arcanos portal, how did he get past the castle wards? But I nod agreeably and continue to work on my shroud.

"How was I to know he'd be hit by lightning?" Elena concludes, more aggrieved than apologetic. She toys with the feathers on a barracuda-trimmed mask.

"You staged a Rococo Love Pact? On the roof of a castle? Between two lakes? During the equinox?" I roll my eyes. "How could he *not* be hit by lightning?"

Seriously. She must have *wanted* the man to die.

I shove my knitting at her. "Don't touch the live stitches."

"What will happen if I do?"

"You'll explode." This isn't strictly true, but I don't want her messing up my work.

Seizing the lightning-struck corpse by the ankles, I drag him out onto the Venetian rug. Elena follows with her invisibility cloak and the half-knitted heart.

"Once he's covered by the shroud, he'll weigh a lot less. Let's search his pockets."

She stares. "We've already killed him. We can't rob him, as well."

"You," I correct, ripping off the man's silver epaulets. "You killed him. And we're not going to rob him, we're going to find out who he is. Don't you think his family deserves to know he's dead?"

For a moment, her face goes slack. Then she bristles, nearly stabbing herself with an ebony needle. "People who answer ads like that don't have families."

"Right." I seize the knitting before she can hurt herself. "And what about the people who place those ads?"

She turns away, unable to hide her bitterness. "They don't have families either."

There's not much I can say in response, so I return my attention to the corpse, finding a small leather notebook in the dead man's coat. It's filled with penciled scrawls written in Old Norse, which I can't read worth a damn. Still, I shove it into the pocket of my smock.

That's when I notice the corded tassel on my macramé bracelet was scorched by the memory spell I used on the student. Alarmed, I twist the precious bracelet around my wrist, looking for damage, but the chevron pattern seems unharmed.

Elena's voice drops to a whisper. "Thank you for helping me."

"It's alright," I say, after a pause. She's not the first person to find herself all alone in the world.

⌒

Whenever I do something out of a vague sense of duty or obligation, I always regret it. Why do I keep forgetting that?

A few minutes (and several dozen strands of hair) later, the shroud is done, and we're inching our way down one of the narrow back staircases, heading for the furnace room. It's almost dark outside. Elena has swapped her sandals for a pair of black flats, the delicate wreath of gold still woven through her hair. A lightweight parcel dangles invisibly from her gloved hand.

"Why do we have to use the furnace? Why can't we just dump him in my fireplace and be done with it?"

I'm about to explain the physics of concealment shrouds when a clatter on the stairs below causes us both to freeze. It's the unmistakable sound of stone claws, scraping against stone.

"They've released the gargoyles," Elena whispers, her face shadowy in the gloom.

"Perfect," I groan. "Bloodthirsty stone monstrosities."

Gargoyles are bound to the castle itself, designed to hunt down intruders. They almost never maul students, but we're carrying a dead intruder in our invisible shroud. Which makes us prime targets, and just as likely to find ourselves dangling from the bell tower as any mundane. If we don't make it, I really hope the gargoyles eat Elena first.

"We're trapped," she says, backing into me.

"Not yet." I grab her arm and tug her back up the steps to the Promenade level. "Gargoyles only monitor the perimeter."

Elena brightens. "Of course. The Grand Staircase!"

We hurry through the narrow servant's corridor that runs alongside the ballroom. Sliding open a wood-paneled pocket door, we step out onto the landing that overlooks the Great Hall. It's ghostly and surreal. The lamps have all been put out, replaced with luminescent emergency torches. Marble statues shine like ghouls in the eerie blue light.

As we're about to rush for the Grand Staircase, we're interrupted by the unwelcome voice of my bastard ex-boyfriend. "Your Highness! Please stop!"

We find ourselves facing James Ruskin: Distinguished Professor of Alchemy, legendary expert on magical potions, resident asshole of Arcanos Hall.

Ruskin executes an elegant bow. His teeth are white, his face suspiciously tan. His sideburns are perfect. His wavy hair, perfectly coiffed, is one shade too dark.

"Surely, Your Highness is not descending into that miasma," he says, gesturing at the yellow fog pooling on the tartan rug at the bottom of the stairs. He does not make eye contact with me, for which I'm grateful.

Elena's nose twitches at the word "miasma," but she inclines her head with swanlike grace, acknowledging his bow. I've long suspected her aristocratic hauteur is at least partly a protective strategy, a shield to keep people at arm's length. That being said, she's really good at it.

"Many find the fog disorienting," Ruskin continues, with a worried air. "It's designed to confuse and repel the mundane, but it may also affect witches. Perhaps my junior colleague here is not aware of the dangers, but in fact—"

"Thank you very much," she interrupts, tightening her grip on the invisible shroud. "I'm quite certain I'll be fine." She lifts her chin: a clear sign of dismissal.

Ruskin's focus shifts to her clenched fist, and for a brief moment his expression hardens. Then his lips split into a pleasant enameled smile. "Of course, Princess."

I escort Elena down the stairs, aware of Ruskin's questions burning into my back. He can tell we're hiding something, and I just hope he never guesses what it is.

As the fog reaches our knees, I shove an arcane handkerchief into Elena's free hand. I made these embroidered beauties to protect from electromagnetic surges. Never thought I'd have to use them indoors. "Cover your face. And try not to breathe."

We plunge into the fog spilling across the Great Hall, then duck into the sulfurous mailroom and creep down the staircase to the dungeons. The fog becomes so dense, we can hardly see. The stench and the confusion intensify, and for a few seconds, I can't even remember my name. Everything seems muffled and distant. Closing my eyes, I struggle to focus. *Your name is Anya Winter. You know where you're going. You know why.*

Then the fog dissipates, and my senses return. Above me, I can hear the din of students returning from the rugby match: they're choking, sputtering, cursing. But I can breathe again, and the air around me is clear.

Reaching forward in the dark, my fingers connect with the rough surface of a doorframe. We've reached the entrance to the steam tunnels. Dropping my knitting bag, I fumble about and find the torch mounted beside the door.

"What's between you and the professor?" Elena whispers into my shoulder. "Is he in love with you?"

"Ruskin?" I nearly choke on bile. Has he laced the fog with gossip extract?

Her voice turns mischievous. "It's so obvious. He couldn't even look at you."

I wince. It would be such a relief, just for once, to be able to confide in someone. I don't have anyone I can talk to, and sometimes it feels like the things I can't say are consuming me from within, gnawing up my organs, one by one. But even if Ruskin were other than what he was, I could never discuss him with a student, least of all the heir to the Carpathian throne. Still, I must disabuse her somehow.

"Gah!" I scoff. "He's the one who made this disgusting fog. Mind-altering potions are all he cares about." I struggle with my key and open the door to the Physical Plant. Our skirts slap against our legs as a rush of hot air sweeps past.

"Are you sure this is safe?" Elena grips my linen sleeve and follows me into the gloom, the door slamming behind us with an echoing bang.

I light the luminescent torch. "No, I'm not."

When I'm not in class, I'm usually knitting away in the cellars of Arcanos Hall, my hair frizzy, my body drooping from the heat under my floor. But I've seldom seen the source of the steam. Despite having faculty key access, I've only rarely visited the Physical Plant, where a magical fire burns, day and night.

It's currently a noisy, humid hell. We inch past the clanking gears of the Diffuser, where Ruskin's foul-smelling potions mix with the vapor being released into the ventilation system. The Diffuser's a giant steam-driven machine, with tentacles of copper piping that snake out from a giant cauldron, stretching across the ceiling. Over the sound of the gears, I hear water running, and the roar of a fire.

"Is anyone ever down here?" Elena asks, cautiously looking about.

"Just Rocco. He maintains the fire."

Rocco is a huge wizard from the Snowy Range. Four hundred pounds of muscle, hands as thick as oven mitts. I've never heard him speak, not even to answer a question, but he smiles at me whenever he comes up from the tunnels. I gave him some dried apricots once, and he practically inhaled them, so now I keep them on hand. Rocco always uses the narrow staircase near my chambers—never the Grand Staircase or the steam-powered elevators—since the dean doesn't want him to be seen in public. The real work in Arcanos Hall is kept out of sight.

Elena turns slowly in a circle. "Is Rocco here?"

"I don't see him." Rocco's loyal, but not necessarily to me. I don't want to know what would happen if he caught us burning a corpse. "He's probably tweaking the ventilation system. Let's finish this before he returns. Before the Regents get here."

Just saying the word "Regents" is enough to make me panic. They could easily arrive before nightfall. In the hot steam tunnels, the passage of time feels sluggish, but outside the castle, nothing is slowing down the sun.

We move past the rattling gears of the Diffuser to the main tunnel, its sloping surface littered with ash. A second passage branches out, shrouded in darkness. Something tells me the second passage leads to the Drinis, the legendary shields that protect our castle. But those shields aren't my responsibility: Elena is.

At last, a heavy metal gate is all that separates us from the furnace. The fire rages in a molten torrent of red and gold and orange.

Elena is dumbstruck. "I've never seen such a fire."

"Don't you have steam in Carpathia?"

"We do, but we use dragons for our heat source."

"Dragons?" I whistle. "We use enchanted peat."

Used properly, a small bale of peat can power a castle for a month. Used improperly, it can burn down a city in an hour. Believe me: we wizards play with fire.

She reaches for the gate latch, but I hold up my hand. "Wait!"

I haven't said much about my childhood, and there's really no time to discuss it now. Let's just say that growing up in an

16

abandoned missile silo can leave you with a constant itch of paranoia. "The gate could be enchanted. Booby-trapped."

"But it's just a furnace."

"Yes, but it powers everything, including the shields."

Elena frowns, thinking. I don't know why she's failing my textiles class, but it's not because she's empty-headed. "How do the shields work? Surely they're not just powered by peat?"

I study the carved hinges on the gate. No sign of a magical field. "That's above my pay grade. Only the dean knows how they work." Or how to fix them.

"My father won't tell me how our castle's shielded, either. He says it's best if I don't know." At the mention of her father, Elena tightens her grip on the invisible fabric containing the corpse. I don't know what happens to a princess who shames her royal family. But I do know what she's thinking: we have to get rid of the body, and fast.

I bend forward to examine the latch on the gate. There's no lock, no telltale spark.

Elena scans the door handle for traces of magic. "What sort of wizard is Rocco? What kinds of spells can he do?"

It's a good question. Rocco probably opens this gate at least once a day. But he's a hedge witch like me, and to the dean, he's probably nothing more than a servant. He couldn't possibly have access to any prestigious charms or spells.

I remember Rocco's muted gray eyes, and the stiffness in his huge hands. And then I know how he opens the gate, and it takes my breath away. He's part troll.

"Rocco's strong," I say, deciding to protect his secret. "And he has gloves."

Before Elena can process this, I grip the latch and press down hard. The gate creaks and swings open. At first, I imagine that I was wrong about the gate being enchanted. Perhaps I've gotten away unharmed. But then a ring of fire encircles my right arm and deepens into a painful vise, burning and burning. I sink to my knees, gasping as my torch falls to the ground and sputters out.

"Miss Winter!" Elena cries, watching me clutch at my arm. "Are you hurt?"

I bow my head, unable to speak. It's so much worse than I expected.

She tugs a gold leaf from the wreath in her hair. "Hold this. Please."

Without thinking, I close my fingers around the golden leaf, and at once a cooling sensation floods through my body. Moments later, the pain is gone.

I've heard of healing charms, and I have a basic understanding of how they work. But I've never been able to buy even the most rudimentary analgesic. You can ease magical pain only by experiencing it, and most wizards don't sell their agony at a discount.

I take a deep breath and open my hand. It's healthy and pink, the laurel leaf reduced to a dusting of powdered gold. "Thank you."

I've accepted a gift that's worth at least a month's salary. And that's just the monetary value. I don't want to know whose pain took mine away.

Elena offers me a polite smile, not guessing my thoughts. "I do have to start paying you back."

"You don't," I say, as a gust of hot air blows the powdered gold from my hand. "You don't owe me a thing." I'm a hedge witch. We don't believe in payback.

Elena pulls me to my feet, and together we step through the open gate, gazing up at the surging flames.

"Once the shroud starts to burn, your wizard will return to his original size," I warn. "Get him into the incinerator fast."

She nods, but doesn't move. Her focus shifts to the invisible parcel in her hand.

"If only we knew who he was," she says, unable to conceal the anxiety in her voice.

I think of the Norse-scrawled notebook in my smock. "We'll find out."

Elena inches toward the roaring furnace. I can tell from her gait that the hot floor is scorching her lightly shod feet. But still, she hesitates.

"Isn't it peculiar," she turns back to face me, "how someone's entire life can be held in another person's hand?" Her forehead glistens in the heat.

I step closer, afraid she's going to lose her nerve. "Elena, are you okay?"

She closes her eyes and murmurs an invocation. Then, with a sweeping motion, she flings the dead man into the furnace. The shroud sparks blue, and for a moment I see the body of the unknown wizard, silhouetted against the flames. It's strangely beautiful.

I'm about to collapse from relief when I hear a sharp intake of breath, coming from right behind me. Someone's watching.

In a panic, I stumble around, catching sight of a shadow moving in the narrow tunnel leading to the shields. My eyes strain into the darkened passage, an eternity crawling by as the furnace rages behind me. But there's nothing. The shadow is gone.

Pressing my fist against my chest, I try to calm my racing heart. Who was that? Why did they let us go? Then I'm galvanized into action. "Elena! We've got to get out of here."

Elena turns her back on the furnace. "It's done."

"Yes, and now we have to go." I'm about to tell her we're not alone, but for some reason, I stop myself. Maybe it's better if she doesn't know.

I remember the first lesson I learned from my paranoid, con-spiracy-driven father: *Never share information unless you have to.* Second lesson: *Always watch your back.*

I steer her to the gate. "I know that wasn't easy. But you did it."

Elena shakes her head, disoriented and disbelieving. "I did."

Everything has changed, but now we have to go back to the

way things were.

"Well, there's a lesson here," I say, gratefully taking refuge in clichés. "I certainly hope you've learned something from this."

I sound like a fussy old busybody, which might not be a bad thing, since fussy old busybodies are known to outlive everyone.

"Oh, yes." Elena manages an awkward smile. "There's definitely a lesson here. No more Love Pacts during the equinox."

I'm pretty sure that's not the real lesson she's taken from this incident, but I'm willing to let her have her secrets. After all, I have plenty of my own.

As we hurry through the gate, something slips free of the hinges and flutters to the ground. Something pale, almost translucent. I bend down to pick it up. It's nothing, really. Just a torn scrap of parchment, pockmarked with small round holes.

CHAPTER THREE

Why do we have to learn this stuff?" Lord Nigel Fob, heir to some dukedom I've never heard of, is not enjoying my class.

To be honest, I'm not enjoying my class either. The castle is in turmoil, I'm teaching in a makeshift classroom, and the Drini shields are still down. I've also hardly slept, I've been ordered to appear before the dean, and my chambers smell like sulfur. And it's Monday. And I haven't had any coffee.

"We need magic textiles to protect ourselves," I remind Fob, trying my best to sound neutral. "Look at the situation we're having with the shields. If we didn't have Professor Ruskin's wards protecting the castle, we'd all be sitting here wearing hats and scarves."

Mundane folk may not realize the limitless power of textiles, but we witches haven't forgotten how much arcane energy is twisted into the fabric of our lives. There's a reason why the first wands were based on spindles. With just a shaft and a whorl, an amorphous mass of wool or flax can be transformed into something that never existed before.

Magic or mundane, so much of our history depends on the simple twist of the spindle. Imagine a Viking ship, its sail swelling in the wind: now imagine that every inch of that hand-woven sail is made from thread spun by hand.

"Just because we need protective armor, doesn't mean we have to make it ourselves. This whole class is bogus!" Having made no effort to master the rudiments of spinning, Fob is now using his knitting needles to goose his classmates. There is no way he'll knit a functional item by the end of the term.

I produce an automated smile, focusing my attention on the iridescent charms holding Fob's elaborate coif in place. "Okay. Since many of you have already achieved your desired gauge, let's take a few minutes to review our objectives. What's the purpose of this class? What are we doing here?"

There's the usual shifting and grumbling, more than one averted gaze. Fob slides his rosewood needle through a gap in his knuckles, making it look like an extended middle finger. His cronies snicker, oozing contempt.

If you're female, and if the students you're teaching are nearly your own age, then you really can't afford to come from the working classes. Not if you want respect.

So there's very little hope for me. It's not just that I'm young: I'm also teaching an unpopular subject. Most students aren't interested in textiles, and they can tell I'm not a member of the gentry, even before I open my mouth. The only reason I'm even on the faculty is that old Zemlinsky died in January, and the dean needed an adjunct in a hurry. I'm just glad no one knows about my father. Not for the first time, I find myself wishing he'd been a magician instead of a physicist—it would have made my life so much easier.

"Anyone have any thoughts?" I feel horribly exposed, though not as exposed as I felt last night. Who was down there in the tunnels? Why didn't they confront us?

Bertha Bratsch starts to raise her hand, then puts it down again. This doesn't surprise me. Bertha's a scholarship student, the only one in the class. As a hedge witch, self-taught in herb lore, she doesn't have any formal training in applied magic. Every day, she sits in the front row, as far as possible from the door. She comes in before the other students arrive, hides her face behind a protective curtain of ginger hair, and leaves after everyone else has gone.

Bertha's tactic of avoiding attention is one I know all too well, since I often use a similar approach when I appear before the dean. Just thinking about him sends my stomach into turmoil. I only wish I knew why he wants to see me after class.

I breathe a prayer to Michael the Wise, tender guardian of academics everywhere. *Please, Blessed Elder. Don't let the dean's meeting be about the corpse.*

In the back of the oak-paneled classroom, strategically positioned beneath a large portrait of King Nestor, Princess Elena sets down her needles and raises a jeweled hand. "Miss Winter. I can answer your question."

This does surprise me. The princess never speaks in class, and I really didn't think yesterday's adventure would change that.

"Your Highness," I say, banishing thoughts of the dean. "Please enlighten us."

"In the last three weeks, we've mastered the use of the Turkish spindle," she begins, with a glance at Fob, "so we can spin our own yarn—yarn that's permeated with magical power. We've learned to cast on stitches and maintain a variety of enchanted fabrics through proper gauge. We've learned to install a lifeline, a failsafe in case we make a mistake. Soon we'll learn to bind off the live stitches, so that our spells won't unravel into chaos."

Nice summation. Perhaps Elena has been studying. Or perhaps she realizes how much she has to learn. Without my skill in arcane textiles, she'd still have a dead body in her wardrobe.

"Yes," Fob bursts out. "But why should we do that? There are hedge witches everywhere who will knit lace—even weave tapestries—for practically nothing."

A murmur of assent rises from the class. With the exception

of Bertha, they're all scions of wealth and privilege. They've all attended the best magical boarding schools. They all have ample money for charms. And they all can afford hedge-made armor—even Estonian Lace, the gossamer-thin fabric used to line mundane hats and clothes. They don't need to make their own armor. Which is why my other class, Enchanted Weaving, is much more popular. For young wizards, a flying carpet equals freedom. And when freedom is too expensive to buy in a shop, you learn to work for it.

Fob wrinkles his nose in my direction. "We could be learning alchemy right now, or building scaffolds for charisma spells. Stuff that's useful in the real world."

"You don't think it's useful to know how to protect yourself?" Elena bristles. "What would happen if—?"

"It's beneath our dignity," Fob interrupts. "I didn't come all the way to The Isthmus to do menial labor like some kind of hedge witch."

Hearing the word "menial" used in the same sentence as "hedge witch" sends a rush of crimson through my eye sockets, but I can't allow myself to be baited.

I take a deep breath and make my best attempt to look authoritative. "Lord Fob, if you would please allow the Princess to finish her statement."

"Yes, pardon me," Elena says with glacial froideur. "I was almost done."

Silence falls on the ballroom, broken only by the furtive clickety-clacking of poor Bertha Bratsch, who's trying to finish knitting her gauge swatch while following the conversation. Fob's iridescent hair flushes to a bright shade of red. He jumps to his feet, nearly knocking over his chair.

"My apologies, Your Highness," he mumbles to Elena, while making a cramped, nervous bow.

"Please continue, Princess Elena," I say, with an edge that astonishes even me. I'm angry, and I hate being angry. "Fob, sit down."

Bertha Bratsch stops knitting, her live stitches sparkling, her face round with surprise. Fob sinks into his chair, his focus shifting from Elena to me, then back to Elena. It's clear he doesn't know what's just happened. I'm pretty sure I don't, either.

As for the princess, she languidly straightens her diamond-encrusted bracelet, then brushes back a lock of gleaming black hair. "Magical armor is our first and best defense against the deadly fields of mundane technology," she recites. "At all times, we must shield our heads and hearts from toxic electromagnetic fields. If we want our magic to remain strong, we must learn to protect ourselves."

"Very good, Princess," I say, as Fob's sneer deepens.

"You certainly make an excellent point, Lord Fob," Elena says, flicking a sly glance at me before offering Fob her most indulgent smile. "But we must do our best to master these skills. We can't allow ourselves to be dependent on the lower orders."

Class dismissed, I stomp across the Promenade to the dean's office. I scowl at a row of ancient marble statues, and each one of them scowls right back. Having sacrificed nearly 50 strands of my own hair to make a heart shroud for Princess Elena, which she could never have made herself, I'm not at all pleased to hear her speaking of hedge witches in such a condescending, self-satisfied way. She didn't have to say "lower orders," but she did. She made a deliberate choice to identify hedge witches as her inferiors.

You sometimes make the mistake of thinking people are the same as you, simply because they need you. But the gulf is still there. You can't let yourself forget.

I console myself with the thought that my students are idiots and will all probably die before they graduate. Most likely in Ruskin's class.

As I round the corner, I nearly crash into Professor Inez Quissel, who teaches elite wand-craft and enjoys pretending I don't exist. She gives me a look of undiluted disdain, and then returns to her pretense. Storming into Dean LaMarche's reception hall, I throw myself into the closest chair, too angry to realize who's occupying the room. Then I look around as the dean's detection spells begin to chime, and my blood turns to ice. Surrounding me are the rich scarlet robes of the most powerful wizards ever to set foot on campus: the Inner Council.

If you're wondering who wields the power in any university, the answer is this: not the faculty, not the dean. It's the Regents who hold the purse strings, and it's the Regents on the Inner Council who set all the rules.

Gray-haired and patrician, the Marchioness of Lynch is dressed for serious business, wearing the Order of the Wild Rose across her sunken chest. Thin as a splinter, she's a tiny dowager with papery skin, a jeweled hatpin and a birdcage veil. Seated primly, nose in the air, she pretends not to see me. I'm guessing she's like Fob: she speaks to the lower orders only to get a cup of tea.

Simon Burke, on the other hand, stares openly, twisting his carnelian signet ring as he sizes me up. His dark beard is unkempt, his complexion red and carbuncular, his clothing carelessly askew. He sits with his thick legs sprawling, as if he's claiming all the space in the room as his own. Under his scarlet Regent's cape, I glimpse the embroidered outline of a phoenix, and I recall that Lord Burke's ancestors adopted the phoenix as their talisman after Fortress Burke was destroyed for the third time. They are one damn resilient dynasty.

He's a big, imposing man, as much known for his romantic conquests as for his clout in the realm of industrial magic. If the stories are true, he's probably trying to decide whether I belong in a sweatshop or a love shack.

"You there," he says, his eyes raking over the Ukrainian

embroidery embellishing the front of my blouse. "Are you the dean's new intern?" He says "intern" like it's a dirty word.

I stare levelly at him. *Oh, to be a basilisk.* "I'm faculty. Thanks for asking."

"Quiet, both of you," snaps Lady Lynch, just as the doors swing open, revealing the third member of the Inner Council.

This Regent is a somber wizard I've never seen before. Her black hair hangs in a long braid down the center of her back. She's flanked by two stony-faced soldiers: both pale and blonde, both dressed in brown. She does not speak, but whoever she is, her presence produces an immediate effect: Burke stands at once and bows, and Lady Lynch looks away, folding her thin hands across her lap.

Following Burke's cue, I acknowledge the new Regent, but she doesn't react at all. Silence hangs like a crooked painting. Then Ms. Nguyen arrives to show the Regents in, the gold embroidery on her dress shimmering. "The dean will meet with you now."

They file silently into the dean's office. But the Regent with the braided hair pauses and looks back at me, her expression inscrutable, her gaze lingering a moment too long. There's nothing in her heavy-lidded eyes: no warmth, no emotion, not even curiosity.

Then she turns away, and I realize I've been holding my breath, unnerved. Whoever this woman is, I can't read her at all.

"Don't just stand there, Anya." Ms. Nguyen peers at me over her glasses: not unkindly, but dismayed, as if she's found a moth hole in the middle of her best armor. "Go on in."

"But the Inner Council is meeting now," I stammer. Junior professors are never called into Council meetings—at least, not for anything good.

I dart a nervous glance at the soldiers, vaguely aware that someone else has entered the room. To my horror, it's Professor James Ruskin, legendary chemist and tongue-flicking reptile.

"Well, I hope I'm not late," he says, tossing off his cape with a flourish and making a slight bow. "After you, Miss Winter."

"Me?"

"Of course," Ruskin says, straightening his collar and looking impossibly smug. His perfect sideburns are freshly trimmed. "We're to appear before the Inner Council."

My mind reels. Why me? And why is Ruskin here too? Have they found out about the corpse?

It occurs to me that Ruskin could have been the shadowy figure in the steam tunnel. Perhaps he got his claws into Elena. That would explain her haughty behavior in class.

"Why do they want to see us?" I ask, beating down my panic. I don't have a poker face like the Regent with the long braid. If I'm unhappy, I can't hide it. With a chill, I realize the stony-faced soldiers standing beside Ms. Nguyen are wearing the brown uniforms of King Nestor's most elite military force.

Ruskin puts a brotherly hand on my shoulder, causing me to back up into the cloak rack, causing Ms. Nguyen to smile and turn aside. It kills me that the only professor at The Isthmus who's even willing to talk to me is the same one who tried to get me fired.

"There, there," Ruskin soothes, ignoring my retreat. "You mustn't be nervous, my dear colleague. I'm sure the dean will be as lenient as he can." His eyes are deep swimming pools of blue, overflowing with sympathy and concern. Or so he thinks.

Ruskin is good, very good. But I've learned to see through his chemically enhanced charisma, and I don't trust any of it. Not the soothing voice, not the lambent eyes, not the honeyed words. Not anymore.

"Lenient?" I echo, feeling like he's thrown incendiaries into the middle of the room. "What do you mean, lenient?"

"It's such a pity you aren't certified for memory work. You would have been able to do something about that intruder who got into the castle yesterday. But instead, you sent him merrily on his way, which is a complete breach of protocol. But how could you have known that, when you're so young and inexperienced?"

"But I used a Burning Web to cloud his mind." I thrust out my arms, showing him the scorch marks on my wrists. "I'm sure he doesn't remember a thing."

"Of course. You did the best you could," Ruskin says with an impressive display of emotion, appealing to Ms. Nguyen, who looks rather unsympathetic, but probably feels at least some pity, which is more than Ruskin has ever felt in his life.

"It's terribly unfortunate," Ruskin goes on. "With the Inner Council here, I fear the dean's hands may be tied. The other issues will undoubtedly come up—not to mention all those difficulties you had last spring."

"Difficulties that you got me into!" I snarl, giving way to fury. It was his fault I nearly lost my job. It was his fault I spent two days in magical confinement.

To protect his own reputation after the dean found out about our illicit affair, Ruskin accused me of stalking him and clouding his judgment with magic. Everyone on the faculty believed Ruskin's side of the story, because why would they believe a hedge witch like me? After everything that happened, it was an absolute miracle the dean allowed me to stay on campus. And he did so very reluctantly, citing "insufficient evidence."

Ruskin places a manicured hand on his chest. "I'm trying to help you, Anya. Believe me. I understand you're upset, but lashing out like this won't help. You can't allow yourself to be ruled by your emotions."

I stare at him, speechless. *You*, I think. *You are a snake.*

"I'll do what I can for you," he says with a sigh. "But now, we really must go in. They're waiting for us."

CHAPTER FOUR

As we enter the council room, Dean LaMarche is standing with the Regents, chatting with Lord Burke and Lady Lynch like they're his oldest friends.

Ignoring me, he nods curtly at Ruskin, then gestures to the new Regent with the long braid. "Professor Ruskin, Miss Winter: this is Captain Aradottir."

The name Aradottir means nothing to me, but it causes Burke and Lady Lynch to exchange a glance. Captain Aradottir bows, her oval face immobile. She removes her scarlet cloak, revealing a distinctive violet sash: the Order of the Arctic Cordillera.

So she's an Ice Captain, I think to myself. An intelligence expert. With a reputation that precedes her. From the chill in the room, I don't think anyone's happy that King Nestor has appointed this enigmatic soldier to the Inner Council.

We move to the mahogany table, Ruskin smiling in his bland, neutral way. His teeth gleam white against his tan, making him look like a rugby star, or one of those wealthy peers from the pages of *Cloak and Wand*. I used to think his lopsided smiles were charming, but that was before he tried to sell me down the river.

"Miss Winter," Ruskin says, pulling out an upholstered chair with exaggerated courtesy. "Please be seated." I sit down, and the chair slides into place like a deadbolt.

Simon Burke sits beside me and sprawls in his chair, his knee grazing my thigh. I move out of reach, and he spreads his legs even further apart. The embroidered phoenix gleaming on his chest, he leans close and whispers in my ear. "So, you're not an intern?"

Across the table, Ruskin sees this and smiles.

If Ruskin's here to see me dismissed, that would explain why he's practically gloating. But with the shields down and the castle defended only by secondary wards, shouldn't he at least be acting concerned? Shouldn't the shields be everyone's first priority?

A sudden fear paralyzes me. What if they think I'm responsible for breaking the shields? Treason of that kind is a Class One offense.

"We'll need to soundproof this room," says the dean, "and since Miss Winter was not able to repair my curtains yesterday, we'll require your assistance, Professor Ruskin." He frowns in my general direction, which doesn't help to alleviate my sense of dread.

While the dean lights the tapers on a silver candelabra, Ruskin bustles about the room, his glee at my apparent disgrace almost palpable. Ruskin also probably loves the fact that everyone needs his stupid potions and secondary wards right now. Come to think of it, he's probably making money off the shields being down.

I rub the scorch marks on my wrists and tug anxiously at my woven bracelet. Then I remember Elena's question in the steam tunnels. "Is he in love with you?"

They don't see it. None of them do. Whether it's through his charisma potions or by some other power, Ruskin has them all convinced of his earnest good will.

With a flourish, he uncorks a vial of green potion. Then he uses a delicate spritzer to seal the windows with a temporary air lock. With each spritzing of potion, the airy lace curtains deepen and turn opaque. Soon, the windows and the door are covered with a heavy shroud, each one as velvety black as the dean's ravens, who don't like the enclosed air one bit. Cawing loudly, they perch on the fireplace as Ruskin returns to his seat.

Rubbing his hands, Dean LaMarche glances up at the painting of the red leather gown. It's an odd quirk. It's almost as if his eyes are drawn to the immense canvas in times of stress. For a moment, I wonder if he can see the woman inside the dress. But as far as I can tell, no one can detect the woman in the painting, so why should he?

He clears his throat. "I'm sure you all know why we're here."

My heart sinks. Now that it's actually happening, I just want it to be over.

"Dean LaMarche," I blurt out. "I just want to say I'm so very sorry."

Ruskin's smirk deepens into a grin, which he immediately wipes away, replacing it with a look of studied concern.

The dean lowers his head, silver hair falling into his eyes. "Yes, Miss Winter. We are all sorry this has happened. But I, for one, am grateful you discovered the security breach when you did. And we're indebted to you as well, Professor Ruskin. Had you not been on hand to release the emergency fog . . . " He sighs. "I can't even bear to think what might have happened."

I open my mouth, then close it again. So this meeting isn't about me?

They don't know, I realize with stunned relief. They don't know about the corpse.

Ruskin's jaw works back and forth, as if he's trying to chew up all the smug words he'd been about to say. Finally realizing the dean is commending him for releasing the fog, he manages to sputter out a gracious response.

"Believe me," he says, "In a time of crisis, it's a great privilege to be of service. I'm very glad the fog was effective, and I feel certain that the secondary wards I've installed will render any additional use of noxious vapors unnecessary."

I steal a glance at the three Regents. None of them betrays any surprise. It's clear that from their perspective, this meeting has always been about the castle shields. But if that's the case, then what am I doing here?

"It's a damned mess," grumbles Lady Lynch, cracking her bony knuckles with an excruciating snap. "The sooner those shields are fixed, the better. We can't allow our alumni to lose confidence in The Isthmus. We're counting on their patronage."

"Yes, the repairs must begin at once." Burke nods and strokes his beard. "But how long will it take? And how much is it going to cost?" He stares pointedly at the dean.

Dean LaMarche pours himself a glass of sherry. "So. That's why I've called you all here. To talk about the shields. Sherry, anyone?"

I may be imagining things, but his hand appears to be trembling. It's almost as if he's steeling himself for something very unpleasant.

"Excuse me." Ruskin's voice resonates softly, like the purr of a kitten: a kitten with needle-like claws. "We are, as you say, indebted to Miss Winter for discovering the initial breach. But should she be present for this highly sensitive conversation? She's not a Regent, nor a senior member of the faculty. She's just a part-time adjunct. In fact, I'm given to understand that she's currently employed here on a probationary basis."

My face burns. Ruskin is just petty and mean enough to bring that up. He still hasn't gotten over the fact that he didn't manage to get me fired last spring.

"She's on probation?" If she had any pearls to clutch, Lady Lynch would be clutching them.

With an unconcerned air, Ruskin brushes his knuckles against the tanned smoothness of his chin. "I would never be one to hold her unfortunate parentage against her, but . . . "

What? I seriously want to die. I can't believe Ruskin's telling them this.

Lady Lynch stiffens and grips the carved armrests on her chair, her lips pursed together. "Parentage? What's this about?"

Now it will all come out. And it will be Ruskin's version of the story, including the part about how he discovered a stash of restricted potions hidden in my chambers, which I must have been using to cloud his mind. I want to sink into the enormous Navajo rug, never to be seen again. But then something happens that surprises me.

His expression neutral, Dean LaMarche slides the crystal stopper into his carafe of sherry. "Oh, that. Yes, we've learned that Miss Winter is the daughter of an Appalachian hedge witch, now sadly deceased, and a retired nuclear physicist."

"A mundane physicist?" Lady Lynch gapes at me.

Simon Burke sneers. "Is there any other kind?"

Ruskin allows himself a brief smile, but Captain Aradottir says nothing. Her dark eyes do not blink.

Dean LaMarche takes a small sip of sherry. "Along with her valuable skills in textile arts, Miss Winter also has some knowledge of mundane society, which we may at this point find useful."

I can't believe what I'm hearing. The dean is acting like it's no big deal that I have a mundane father. In fact, he's even implying that my background is some kind of asset. And he's saying this in front of the Regents. I allow myself to relax, deciding right then and there that if Dean LaMarche ever needs an ally, I will help him.

My new ally peers into his sherry, as if disappointed in its flavor. "So, to address your question, that is why Miss Winter is on this task force."

His face flushed, Ruskin looks around the room for support. Lady Lynch is all too happy to provide it.

She scowls in my direction. "I hope you know what you're doing, LaMarche. Can't say I'm pleased to be sharing a Council room with a hedge witch."

Dean LaMarche twists the stem of his sherry glass. "Your concerns are noted, my lady. Now, about the shields—"

"I have a question for the Council." It's Captain Aradottir, speaking for the first time, her accent modulated and precise.

"Of course, Captain," says the dean, giving her his full attention. He hasn't looked my way since the first reference to my background, which is probably a good thing, since one sympathetic glance might be enough to make me lose my composure. And I am not going to be seen crying.

Aradottir turns to address Ruskin, who at this point seems decidedly sullen. "How secure are the secondary wards protecting this castle?"

Ruskin holds up his hands. "They're fine. Wards and aversion charms are labor-intensive, to be sure. But they're absolutely sound."

I suppress a sigh. When Ruskin says "labor-intensive," what he really means is "exploitative." It will take hundreds of charms to keep those wards in place, and who will produce them? Indentured hedge witches, living east of the Scandinavian Keel. Without cheap labor, there's no other way it could be done.

The other Regents nod in hearty agreement. "Absolutely sound," Lady Lynch says with a complacent air. "Very good."

The dean appears strained, but he manages to smile, even puts his teeth into it.

"You're sure there's no danger of exposure?" The Ice Captain's tone is impassive, almost unsettlingly calm. "We are, after all, in a highly populated urban area. Mundanes are everywhere. Tens of thousands of them. The cost of containment—in memory charms alone—would be astronomical. And if containment should fail—"

"Trust me, the wards are sound," Ruskin repeats with a tight curve in his lips. He straightens a cufflink.

Aradottir presses her palms against the mahogany table and pushes back her chair.

"I mean no offense when I say I will not be trusting anyone. Instead, I will verify. King Nestor has authorized me to take any and all action necessary to maintain the castle's security. And now, I want to see the Drini shields."

The dean turns pale and fumbles his glass of sherry. "Now? You want to see the shields now?" Amber liquid spreads across the table.

I dig into my skirts for a handkerchief, and then it hits me: He doesn't know how to repair the shields. That's why Aradottir is here. That's why there's been a delay.

"I will see the shields now," says Aradottir. "And I will have a detailed report on everyone who has been near the shields in the last 48 hours."

"I'm the only wizard who has access to the shield rooms," says the dean, miserably shaking his wet fingers. "No one else can open the innermost door."

"No one?" Aradottir seems almost incredulous. She paces across the room, her long braid swaying, shoulders thrown back. The other Regents watch her, their faces uncertain. "This is the first time the shields have failed in over a century, and it has happened on your watch."

"I know, I know." Dean LaMarche cranes his neck, trying to get a glimpse of the huge painting hanging behind him. But he can't see the empty red gown without standing up. He slumps in his chair, desolate.

I reach across the polished surface of the table and press my woven handkerchief into his hand. Just a minute ago, I thought I was going to be fired. I thought the dean despised me. But he'd been protecting the secret of my background. He'd been protecting me—who knows for how long?

For a moment, I wonder if he was the one hiding in the shadows outside the furnace room. But that makes no sense. He would have confronted us.

"On your feet," says Aradottir, coming to stand behind the

dean's chair. "If this failure is a result of sabotage, you will have some explaining to do."

With a chill, I remember that Ice Captains aren't just intelligence workers: they're also arbiters of justice, appointed by King Nestor himself. Aradottir could have the Dean thrown in prison.

Lady Lynch jabs a bony finger at the Ice Captain. "You're out of line, missy. You can't be treating our dean as a suspect." The Order of the Wild Rose slides off her narrow shoulder. Impatiently, she shoves the sash back into place.

Dean LaMarche mops the spilled sherry with my handkerchief, unable to make eye contact with anyone. "The shields just stopped working. I don't know why."

"Captain Aradottir." Ruskin leans forward, oozing goodwill. "It's my understanding that the shields are partially driven by steam. If that's the case, then the steam technician could have sabotaged the shields by accessing the furnace. Theoretically, of course."

She frowns. "Who is this steam technician?"

A chill runs through me, as I realize what Ruskin's doing. He's turning suspicion onto kind, loyal Rocco, who works hard and doesn't speak.

"His name is Rocco," says Ruskin, in a poisonous tone. "Of course, Rocco's just a menial hedge witch, a dumb beast. I feel certain that he couldn't possibly—"

"Dumb beast or not, we will interrogate him," Aradottir says.

"No!" I blurt out a protest before I can stop myself. Then I add steel to my voice. "Leave Rocco alone."

Aradottir turns her cold gaze on me. I understand that the threat of sabotage is extremely serious, but there's something almost terrifying about the Ice Captain's intensity. "You have information about this wizard Rocco?"

"No," I say, clenching my fists. My eyes seek Dean LaMarche, who gazes mutely back. "I don't have any information about Rocco. But I know he's loyal."

"Hedge witches and menials," mutters Burke. He swings his knee back into contact with mine. "Always covering for each other."

"Should've kept them in their place," sniffs Lady Lynch.

Captain Aradottir is silent, as if calculating. Then she addresses the Dean. "You will take me—and only me—to inspect the shields."

Dean LaMarche nods, his cheeks as pale as his silver hair.

Aradottir casts her eye on the other Regents. "Lord Burke: you will find this steam technician and take him into custody. He will not leave this campus. Your Ladyship: the cost of maintaining the secondary wards will be your responsibility."

"My responsibility?" Lady Lynch is aghast. "Do you realize the extent—?"

Aradottir cuts her off. "Contact your cousin, King Nestor. Apprise him of the urgency of our situation."

Then she turns squarely on Ruskin, her expression menacing. "See to the wards, Ruskin. They must not fail. I personally will examine every spell, every ward. No classes will be held on this campus until I verify they are sound. We cannot place our students in danger."

"It will be done." Perhaps I'm imagining this, but Ruskin looks a lot less unhappy than I would expect. His lips are turned down, his countenance somber. But there's something fierce in his eyes, something I recognize. It's the same glitter of joy that shone through him whenever we were together. Whenever he was lying to me.

"Miss Winter," Aradottir says.

I realize I've been holding my breath. When her gaze falls on me, I deflate like a broken spell. "Yes?" I grip the fabric of my skirt, wishing it could make me invisible.

"Until the wards are verified, you will be relieved of your teaching duties."

In confusion, I wait for her to say something more. What does she want me to do?

Aradottir's expression is unreadable. "The dean will give you an assignment."

At this, Ruskin straightens in his chair, like a snake gathering itself up to strike.

"Sir?" I turn to the Dean, who's still clutching my handkerchief.

Dean LaMarche folds the wet handkerchief, then folds it again. "Yes. You'll need to help put the students under magical curfew and inspect their armor. After that—"

"My good sir." Ruskin's words come out like a hiss. "I hate very much to interrupt you, and I don't doubt that Miss Winter's contributions could be quite valuable. But perhaps we're forgetting about the incident yesterday with the intruder, when she allowed that mundane student to leave Arcanos Hall without receiving proper memory work. She herself admits she used only a Burning Web to cloud his mind. I hardly need remind you all that this is a complete violation of our security protocols."

The dean looks uncomfortable. Lady Lynch: triumphant. As for me, I can taste the bile rising in my throat.

Ruskin lifts a manicured hand, fingers trailing through sleek brown hair. "If only she weren't on probation. You'd be able to show our well-meaning colleague the leniency she deserves. But I hardly think King Nestor will agree to finance our security needs when he learns that the standard of defense at The Isthmus is not being maintained."

There is an awful silence. Cornered like a hare, Dean LaMarche looks entreatingly at the Ice Captain, waiting for some kind of response. But she says nothing.

The ravens caw in restless unison, and the tapers in the candelabra flicker. Meanwhile, my heart sinks, lower and lower, until it's lodged somewhere below my spleen. As usual, Ruskin has turned everything to his advantage.

But there's one thing I don't understand. Ruskin hasn't mentioned seeing me last night, heading down the stairs into the fog. Perhaps he's protecting Elena. Or perhaps he's withholding that information, keeping it back for another day.

Finally, Dean LaMarche clears his throat. "Professor Ruskin, you do make a valid point. Under the circumstances, it may be best if Miss Winter leaves the room for a few moments."

Oh, no. I sink into my chair and cover my face with my hands.

"If you would please step outside?"

My face burning, I shove back my chair and flee the room. Out in the reception hall, Ms. Nguyen pretends to busy herself with her papers. Aradottir's stony-faced soldiers stand at attention—one as round as a beetle, the other as lanky as a stick. No one speaks.

I pace back and forth, my chest beginning to ache. I can't bear the thought of being sent away. From the moment I first set foot on this campus, I've only ever wanted to be here, at Arcanos Hall. There was never anyplace else I wanted to be. I just wanted to be here—at the heart of magical scholarship in North America. I wanted a place at the table.

It sweeps over me once again: the familiar, strangling fear that I'll always be alone, that I'll never have a place to belong or someone to love.

"Miss Winter." Dean LaMarche's voice startles me. I look up to see him standing in the doorway, the painted red dress just visible behind him. "If you would please come in."

He seems to have aged immeasurably, his face weary and drawn under his silver hair. Holding open the door, he follows me back into the soundproofed room.

I take a deep breath, folding my arms across my chest.

Still seated around the conference table, Ruskin and the Regents look coldly at me.

The dean hesitates, then begins. "Miss Winter, I would like to assure you that the entire Council of Regents will review your case at the first opportunity."

"The first opportunity? But the full Council doesn't meet until next quarter!"

"In the meantime, I believe it may be beneficial for you to examine our current problem from outside the university." His forehead crinkles. "You will do this for me, won't you?"

"It's so unfortunate," Ruskin puts in, his voice as smooth as sour cream. "Truly regrettable. But I think there's no other choice."

Lady Lynch nods with prim approval and Burke runs a tongue over his upper lip. But Captain Aradottir shows no emotion, not even a flicker of interest.

"You want me to leave?" I stammer, ignoring Ruskin's elation. "Am I banished? If I'm banished, just tell me!"

Dean LaMarche won't look me in the eye. "Consider it a leave of absence, Anya. Surrender your keys and go outside."

CHAPTER FIVE

Back in my chambers, I fling open my cedar chest and rummage through piles of yarn, searching for my best lace. I need to find Rocco and warn him. But I'm not leaving without my yarn.

I've been thrown out before, so this shouldn't be anything new. At the age of eight, I was sent home from a mundane school in Oconomowoc after I refused to remove my tinfoil-lined cap for a hearing test. When I was twelve, enrolled in genteel sorcery classes at Rosewood, I was denied entry to the enchantment track because I couldn't afford any semi-precious stones for charms. And last spring, when Ruskin tried to get me fired, I spent two days in magical confinement, waiting to be cleared. Now I'm homeless, cast aside. Story of my life.

I grab a delicate lace shawl and tug it free from the skeins of yarn. Seeing the shawl calms my racing heart, if only a little. It was a gift from my mother, and it's the best proof I have that someone loved me once and wanted to protect me.

The horseshoe lace is made in the old Arcanos style, with fabric so fine the entire garment could pass through the center of a wedding ring. I know this, because my mother knitted it herself. When she gave it to me, she slipped off her gold band and pulled the entire shawl through the ring. The stitches glistened with power.

"Wear this and think of me," she said. "It will keep you safe."

I pull back my hair and wind the protective fabric tightly around my head. Then I grab all the yarn and gear I can carry, and I go to find Rocco.

In the steam tunnels, the damp air is almost too thick to breathe. Buffeted by the hot fumes of the Diffuser, Rocco is shoveling arcane peat moss into a wheelbarrow. He's a huge inverted triangle: sinewy arms, densely muscled shoulders and back. It's so clear to me now that he's part troll that I'm surprised I didn't see it before.

I wonder who else knows. No one, I hope. Or perhaps the dean has been protecting Rocco's secret, the same way he tried to protect mine. But why would he do that?

"Rocco, it's Anya."

Rocco lowers his shovel and turns around. His face crinkles with pleasure when he sees me. He's got a small, upturned nose, which seems almost out-of-place on such a big man. His hair— prematurely gray—is so short I can see his scalp.

"Urmph," he grunts. I've decided that Urmph means Anya.

"I shouldn't be here," I tell him, indicating my canvas bag. "I've been banished. They told me I have to surrender my keys. They're coming to ask you about the shields."

Rocco's eyes widen. He says nothing, but I'm sure he understands everything I say. Sometimes, I like to imagine that he lost his voice in a dramatic fashion: a magical duel, perhaps. Or maybe he sold his voice to an opera singer, so he could feed his sister's children. Maybe, at this very moment, Rocco's lustrous tenor is filling a concert hall in Old Vienna, soaring through an aria by Bellini.

I hold out a bentwood box. "I brought you some apricots."

With a silent nod, he takes the box of dried fruit. I wonder if there's anyone in his life—perhaps a nice troll from the peat bogs— or if he'll eat them all himself.

In the stairwell above us, there's a clang of metal striking metal. We both look up in alarm, and I glimpse a flash of light. There's nowhere to hide, and even if I did hide, I'd just be abandoning Rocco. So I dig in my heels, and I wait.

"The shields are here, Captain," we hear LaMarche say. "So is Rocco."

"I'll handle the menial," Burke growls. "Just leave him to me."

"He's not to be harmed. Take him into custody." It's Aradottir, her voice as cold as ever.

With a hissing intake of breath, Rocco clasps the bentwood box to his massive chest. Backing away from me, he retreats in the direction of the wheelbarrow.

"Rocco!" I can see the stark blue glare of a luminescent torch glancing off the walls of the winding stairwell. It looks like the dean, leading the way down.

"Miss Winter—is that you?" Dean LaMarche comes to a halt, silver hair gleaming in the eerie light. "What are you doing down here?"

"I'm just saying goodbye." The smell of peat and smoke fills my nostrils, and I feel Rocco gripping my shoulder. He spins me around and pulls me into a hug.

"That's enough! Let her go, Rocco."

Rocco releases me, but his eyes don't leave my face. With a big, clumsy hand, he awkwardly shakes mine, and I realize he's pressing something papery into my grasp. Whatever it is, he doesn't want the Regents to find it. I lean into Rocco and slip the paper into the pocket of my skirt.

LaMarche's voice is oddly frantic. "Anya, you must leave now."

"Yes, I'm ready." I pick up my canvas bag just as Burke arrives.

"There he is." Burke pushes past the dean and swiftly closes the distance between us. The blue torchlight illuminates his golden phoenix and massive signet ring—as well as the silver manacles gripped in his hand. Rocco holds his ground, his face hard and set.

"You mustn't hurt him," I cry, stepping in front of Burke. "He hasn't done anything wrong."

"We'll see about that." Burke brandishes his manacles as Aradottir reaches the bottom of the stairs.

"He has a right to counsel," I call out to Aradottir, who appears impassive, as usual. "He has a right to a fair trial."

If Rocco can't speak to defend himself, he'll need a lawyer. And that will cost money. Everything in this world costs money.

Burke bends down to whisper, his bearded face so close that my flesh crawls. "You insolent hedge folk and your talk of rights. You're lucky you live west of The Keel. A girl like you, in a factory town? You wouldn't talk so big."

"Miss Winter, you have your orders: you must leave The Isthmus at once. Give me your keys." LaMarche draws near, his torch flickering, his skin drained of color.

The dean's afraid, I realize. Even more afraid than Rocco is.

"But you need Rocco!" I snap, flinging my key chain at him. "How are you going to fix the shields? You can't even run the furnace without him. And he's done nothing wrong."

I direct this last sentence to the Ice Captain, though I have no idea what she wants or what she's going to do.

"Miss Winter." Aradottir approaches slowly, her expression neutral. "As Captain of the Arctic Cordillera, I give you my word: no one will be held at length without evidence. No one will be punished without a fair trial."

And somehow I believe her. She still scares the hell out of me, but I believe her.

She inclines her head toward the stairwell. "It's time for you to go."

I feel Rocco's thick hand on my shoulder, and I realize he's urging me to leave. Feeling lower than a snake's belly, I tighten my shawl around my head. Then I carry my belongings up the stairs, heading for the world outside.

Is there any way to measure the cost of what we do, leaving people behind? Surely, no matter what happens, I'll be haunted by what I've done. I'll see poor Rocco standing there with Burke, watching me walk away.

I lean against the door to the steam tunnels, aware that my eyes are stinging. Sometimes I think if I had the money for charms, I'd just buy a jade teardrop, and then I'd never have to cry again.

 Wiping my eyes, I check the contents of my canvas bag. I've got an invisibility cape, a change of clothes, and a rolled-up flying carpet. My woven bracelet, my best yarns and needles, a few silver coins. Everything I can carry is here, and now it's time to go.

I reach into my skirt pocket and inspect Rocco's gift. It's a rectangular piece of stiff parchment. Long, inky lines bisect the surface, dividing it into grids. The card is punctured (seemingly at random) with small round holes. It's just like the scorched fragment I found in the furnace room, only complete.

I can't imagine what it's for. It looks almost like a weaving script, but not for any loom I've ever seen. Why did Rocco give this to me? Why didn't he want the others to find it?

I shoulder my canvas bag and climb the last flight of stairs to the mailroom. I can hear people talking, but I don't give it a thought until I realize one of them is Ruskin.

"You know I have the utmost confidence in the dean," Ruskin says in his smooth, pleasing way. "But I fear he hasn't considered every contingency."

"What are you saying?" Unmistakably, it's Lady Lynch.

"King Nestor has the entire intelligence community searching for his missing queen. So what is that Ice Captain doing here? She ought to be hunting those bandits."

"Surely, the king doesn't think there's a connection," Lady Lynch says, after a pause.

Ruskin's voice drops to a whisper. "Surely not. But our truce with the East is breaking down, and the dean has been caught off guard. It may be necessary to take matters into our own hands. It's not just the security of The Isthmus at stake."

I plaster myself against the side of the stairwell and inch up the stairs. But their conversation fades out, and when I reach the mailroom, it's empty.

There isn't much that I'm sure of. I'm not the sort of person who goes around declaring my belief in things. But I know one thing: if Ruskin is undermining Dean LaMarche, then the dean needs my help, even more than I thought.

It's hardly escaped my attention how ironic this is. I used to be so nervous around the dean, in fear of the day he would declare me unworthy, throw me out of Arcanos Hall. And now that day has arrived in all its dreadful glory, and he's the only wizard I can trust to protect Rocco and my students. He's the only one I can trust to defend our home.

Passing the mail portal for what might be the last time, I make a promise to myself. If the university needs me, I will come back. Never mind that I could end up in prison.

What did the dean say, when he was forced to banish me? "Examine our current problem from outside the university." Fine. That's what I'm going to do. And Ruskin had better watch his back. Hauling my canvas sack over my shoulder, I cross the Great Hall.

A sneering voice pulls me up short. "Going somewhere, professor?"

It's my students. Fob and his wretched cronies are hanging over the edge of the balcony, smirking. Huddled a few steps away, her body half-sheltered by a statue of Michael the Wise, is Elena. There's something wild, almost desperate, written on her face.

"We heard you got fired," Fob continues. "So we took up a collection." He lobs a crumpled piece of paper over the railing. "Here's some homework for you to grade."

Milosz and Fryar—both of them muscle-bound idiots—join in the fun, pelting me with thick wads of paper. Elena watches, her jeweled fingers clenched.

"Thanks, boys," I say, stooping down to pick up the litter. "Just think: your homework is going out into the world, while you're stuck here under curfew, perhaps for the rest of the term. I'll make sure your homework sends you a nice postcard."

Fob's face darkens and his iridescent hair turns green. He pitches another homework bomb. "Rumor has it, you've spent plenty of time in the mundane world already. Go back where you belong!"

Then another crumpled piece of paper flies across the Great Hall and hits me right in the face. It's from Princess Elena.

"Well done, Your Highness!" Fob crows.

Elena extends her jeweled fingers with a bored air, allowing him to kiss her hand.

I pick up her paper. It's fine parchment, and heavier than paper should be.

"Thanks, Elena," I say. "Remember to work on your gauge."

With that said, I walk out the door.

CHAPTER SIX

Beyond the castle, veiled in fog by Ruskin's protective wards, lies the city of Madison, Wisconsin. Geographically, Madison's not a terrible place for wizards. True, it's not a remote mountain range, free of mundanes and filled with peaks of magical power. But it's much safer than some of the great isthmian cities of the East, like Tunis or Istanbul. If you're a wizard and you need to draw geographic power from an isthmus, Madison will do just fine. There's power here, where the ley lines meet between the lakes. There's power deep inside the earth.

Gingerly, I unfold the crumpled paper that Elena threw in my face. A heavy gold coin rests inside. It's old Ottoman work, featuring beautiful calligraphy in the shape of a sultan's seal. Embedded into the calligraphy is the strongest charm I've ever seen. A tiny hole punctures the top of the coin—a channel to release the sultan's command.

I shake my head. *I told you, Elena: you don't have to pay me back.*

She's an odd one, that princess. She wants to do the right thing. She just doesn't want to be seen doing the right thing.

Weighing the Ottoman coin in my hand, I realize I have

options I've never possessed before. The coin is charged with primal power, maybe even enough power to charm the ancient guardians protecting the gate.

Some people say the Arcanos wizards were the first to discover this narrow strip of land between the lakes of the Yahara, but of course that isn't true. These are the ancestral lands of the Menominee, the Ho-Chunk, perhaps even the Dakota Sioux. Long before them, unknown tribes lived on this isthmus, men and women who built effigy mounds on the lands held by the ancient guardians. On the grassy hill above Arcanos Hall, you'll find the largest of the effigy mounds—a bird in flight, and a rare, two-tailed water spirit.

As I leave the castle, it's toward the water spirit that I make my way. When you're banished, you don't just walk out of a warded castle and expect to come back. If you ever want to return, you have to get past the wards. At Arcanos Hall, you have to wake one of the guardians and command it to hold the gate. Which isn't just illegal: it's also extremely dangerous. But I don't give a damn. Banished or not, I have a responsibility to my students, even idiots like Fob. I'm still a professor at The Isthmus.

Surrounded by the liminal fog of Ruskin's wards, I approach the effigy mound from the only safe point of access: a mundane sidewalk that just cuts across the water spirit's tail. From the ground, the effigies look like long, grassy dikes. But if you're on a flying carpet, looking down, you can see what they really are. Over a hundred feet long, they stretch out across the ridge overlooking the lake, with broad wings and tails extended, like giant snow angels made of earth and stone.

It's a dangerous thing, waking the ancient ones. They live deep inside the earth, feeding off the power of the ley lines. I'm told they rise up hungry, demanding sacrifice, and I have no idea if Elena's precious coin will be enough.

Standing on the sidewalk by the water spirit's tail, I hold out the Ottoman coin, my hand trembling. I'm used to spinning my own spells, controlling everything myself with my yarn and gauge, not using ancient charms to engage with primal beings I don't understand. This had better work.

I release the sultan's seal, and power arcs out from the coin like a lightning bolt. My skin tingles all over, charged with magical fields. The ground opens beneath my feet, and the water spirit wakes with a strangled roar. He's ravenous.

"Swim far, old guardian. Remember to open the gate." The coin falls from my hand, and the earth greedily swallows it up. For just a moment, I glimpse gray scales moving like water through the earth, and a single green eye, larger than my head. Then the ground closes and the water spirit is gone, taking with it every trace of Elena's coin.

I sigh with relief as the fog abruptly clears. I'm still alive, and I've closed the gate. The blurry crenellations of the castle have given way to branches and blue sky, and there's nothing left of Arcanos Hall: just a faint shadow in the woods of the Lakeshore Preserve.

Beyond the threshold, the mundane world is startlingly bright. The sidewalks below the Observatory are nearly empty. A single student walks past me, eyes on her phone. Even if she saw me emerge from the fog, she will soon forget.

But now what? I have absolutely no idea what to do. Sooner or later, I'll have to find a way to live, and there's not a lot of work for witches in Wisconsin.

I know I'm better off than most. Thanks to my father, I actually have a birth certificate. With documentation, I could even get a job in the mundane world, though that's not as easy as it sounds, when you can't use a computer or a phone.

Fighting a surge of emotion, I make my way to a shaded bench on the edge of the Lakeshore Preserve. Banished or not, I can at least monitor the castle entrance. After all, Dean LaMarche needs my help. I'm halfway to my stakeout when I realize there's a man with a camera hiding in the bushes behind the bench.

Now, I'm no great judge of beauty. If I were, I wouldn't have been taken in by Ruskin's (obviously fake) smile, his (obviously fake) hair, and his (obviously fake) tan. Truth is, I don't date much. So what on earth could I know about men?

I know this much: the man lurking in the bushes next to my stakeout is quite possibly the most attractive human being I've ever seen. His profile is like an ancient Grecian coin. As for his physique . . . let's just say it's exceptionally fine. But he's also in my spot.

When a gorgeous male specimen is trampling the same bushes you were planning to use to stake out a castle, there's only one thing to do. You have to make him leave.

I march forward, ready for a fight. "You! What the hell are you doing?"

The stranger looks up in surprise, a large camera clutched in his hand. Not only is he carrying a mesh satchel with one of those revolting computers tucked inside, he's also wearing a silvery metallic hoodie with a nerdy embroidered logo that looks like a rocket. In other words, he's a dangerous technologist, and clearly not as handsome as I thought.

Nevertheless, his cheekbones are a sight to behold.

"Wait," he says, clearly confused. "What?"

I draw closer, jabbing my finger at the bushes under his feet. Fortunately, they're invasive buckthorn. But I'm willing to bet he doesn't know that. "Do you think you can just trample on the shrubbery wherever you please?"

"Look, I can assure you—"

"I saw you!" I fling my canvas bag onto the bench. The stakeout is now mine.

"Wait," he says again. Then his eyes grow wide. "You saw me?"

"Of course I saw you," I snap. "It's not like you're invisible." As I say this, I remember my invisibility cape. Since there's no law against using a cape outside the castle, maybe I should have put it on: I wouldn't be dealing with idiots like this guy.

"I see." Cheeks flushed, he grips the drawstrings on his metallic hoodie. Then he looks me up and down, eyes lingering on the lace scarf wrapped around my hair. "Please forgive me. I apologize unreservedly."

He inclines forward, as if about to take a bow. "Believe me, I became so interested in those surfers on the lake, I simply forgot where I was going." He waves a nervous hand in the direction of the lakeshore, where several bikini-clad college students can be seen windsurfing through a gap in the trees.

"Really?" I narrow my eyes. "You were taking pictures of women in bikinis?"

Clearing his throat in a display of embarrassment, he nods. "Um, yes."

This is obviously a lie, a completely unnecessary lie. Which is interesting.

He covers the lens of his camera with a metal cap. "Look, I'm very sorry. I didn't mean to step on the bushes. Quite the opposite, in fact."

"Maybe the spirit of the woods will forgive you," I sniff. "Or maybe not."

It occurs to me that I should get away from this mundane stranger with his dangerous computer and his ghastly metallic hoodie. I should go to the Observatory or to the Memorial Union, find a private spot, slip into my invisibility cape, and return to watch the castle. I should leave right now. But instead—for reasons that I can't explain—I stay. An uncomfortable silence falls.

There's something about this man that seems almost familiar, like a word on the tip of your tongue, or a song you're sure you've heard at least once before. It buzzes at the edge of the mind—an insight that's close at hand, but just out of reach.

"My name's Kyril," he ventures, as if looking for something to say.

"Huh." I'm not going to give him my name.

He notices my canvas bag lying on the bench and drops his satchel beside it. "Well, you're welcome to sit here, if you like."

I stare daggers. "*I'm* welcome to sit here? Do you think you own this spot?"

How can a man this attractive be this much of an idiot? He sounds as spoiled and entitled as Princess Elena, who's probably sulking right now because she's under magical curfew and hasn't got any lower orders on hand to do her bidding.

Kyril looks away, embarrassed. "I just meant I'd be glad to share it with you."

"Very well." With a haughty expression worthy of Elena, I take a seat under the trees and shove my bag into the center of the bench. Now I just have to make him leave.

"Great." Kyril sits down, stretches out his long legs, and sets his camera aside. Then he pulls his laptop out of his mesh satchel.

I stiffen with horror. Surely, he won't use that infernal machine while he's sitting next to me. Surely, he's not going to try to pick up some kind of WiFi or Something G.

He opens the lid, and almost immediately, a familiar tingling tells me that my protective lace shield is engaged. I draw a quick breath as a prickling sensation forms on my upper lip. Properly shielded with my mother's shawl, there's nothing to keep me from sitting this close to Kyril and his awful computer. Still, it would be better if I could make him go away.

I peer into my bag. There's enchanted yak fiber, coarsely combed and twisted by hand. It'll do just fine. A quick and dirty Field-Breaker's Noose, and Kyril's computer will go haywire. And the best thing about the field-breaking spell? I'll be able to reuse the yarn.

Kyril begins typing, his fingers flying almost as fast as I can knit. Two gold rings flash on his right hand. He's intently focused on his laptop screen, which radiates so strongly, I can hardly bear to look at it. Stupid mundanes and their stupid passion for stupid data.

"Nice computer," I say, pulling yak fiber onto my lap. "Is that an Apple?"

The corner of Kyril's lip tugs upward. "Something like that."

I weave my fingers through the enchanted yak fiber and begin to craft a rough I-cord noose, holding the tension in place with my thumb.

Over, Under. One stitch more.

Machines will fail, as the Norns make war.

Next to me, Kyril hums softly and jabs at his keyboard. I wonder if he realizes he's humming in tune with his computer.

"What exactly are you doing?" I ask, curious in spite of myself. There are no pictures on his screen, just rows of numbers and symbols. Which is very strange.

Kyril continues typing. "Same thing you're doing."

"Yeah, right." This moron has no idea he's talking to a witch.

He pauses, flexing his fingers. "At the most basic level, I am opening and closing a series of electrical switches."

I roll my eyes. "So, you're writing a computer program, even I know that. Hardly the same thing I'm doing." He must be one of those so-called coder geeks, completely in love with his obnoxious technology.

Kyril glances up in surprise. Then he returns his attention to his screen.

"I'm managing risk," he says, simply. "It's what I do."

You go ahead and do that. And I'll take care of some risks of my own.

Still looping my yak fiber into a noose, I scan the wooded acres between the effigy mounds and the lake. I can almost glimpse the shadowy door leading to Arcanos Hall. No one would ever know there's a flurry of activity behind that shadow: a campus under curfew, Rocco facing interrogation, the dean spending a fortune on secondary wards.

I wonder if Rocco is okay. Through the fabric of my skirt, I can feel the rectangular outline of the card he pressed into my hand. Something tells me it's important—perhaps more important than sitting here watching the castle. I need to find out what it is.

But now it's time to get rid of Kyril. My noose complete, I tighten my grip on the I-cord of yak fiber. I lift it into the dappled sunlight, pull it taut . . . and nothing happens.

Shocked, I watch the numbers scroll by on Kyril's screen. His computer should be crashing right now. The damn thing should be going down. Why didn't my spell work?

An anxious thought twists in my gut. There's nothing wrong with my spell. There's something wrong with Kyril's computer. That thought does not bear thinking about.

Abandoning the broken spell, I reach unsteadily for my canvas bag. I need to move away, get my invisibility cape in place, and find someplace to collect my thoughts. Time to regroup, as my father used to say.

"Gotta go," I say, shouldering the heavy bag. "Bye, now."

"What?" He closes his laptop and jumps to his feet. "But we've only just met."

"So?" I walk away, refusing to shake his extended hand.

Then I hear him call, "Please, you've dropped something."

I turn, scanning the ground for fallen yarn. But Kyril is standing by the bench, holding a rectangular piece of parchment. Rocco's gift.

I lunge forward, heart in my throat. I was sure that was in my pocket.

"I haven't seen a Hollerith card in a long time." Kyril examines the parchment, almost reverently, squinting at the round holes puncturing the surface. "Looks very old."

A spark of mischief flashes across his face. "So, what's it for?"

"Give that to me!" I snatch it from his hand. "It's mine."

"Of course." Kyril takes a step back, his expression puzzled. He starts to say something and stops, his eyes shifting from the parchment to my face.

"Thank you," I whisper, remembering my manners. I close my fingers around my treasure and walk away, aware that he's watching me go.

CHAPTER SEVEN

I follow the Observatory Path to the pillars of Bascom Hall, stopping on the steep edge of the drumlin ridge. Here by the statue of Abraham Lincoln, I can look down on State Street with its long rows of restaurants and shops. Only a mile away—at the very center of Madison's isthmus—looms the huge white dome of the Wisconsin State Capitol.

For me, this is familiar ground. But the paper in my hand is a mystery.

I haven't seen a Hollerith card in a long time. What did Kyril mean by that?

"Miss Winter, are you okay?"

I turn around to see a round-faced, narrow-shouldered student. She's armored with a faded green shawl, hideously tied babushka-style under her chin.

"Bertha?" I say, shoving the card into my cleavage. Then I realize Kyril's high-tech hands were recently touching the card. All the perfumes of Arabia won't make my bosom clean. "Bertha Bratsch! How did you get outside? There's a curfew going on."

She inspects her worn slippers, pale eyebrows knit together.

"You could have hurt yourself!" Breaking a magical curfew isn't just illegal: it's also foolhardy. I wonder if I need to run back to the effigies to check the castle. "How did you get past the wards? Did you leave the gate open?"

"No, never! I would never do that. It's just that Princess Elena said—"

"She said what?"

"We heard the dean was sending you away. So I waited for you on the threshold and followed in your wake."

Following the wake of another wizard through a sealed gate is a very dangerous thing to do, especially if you're poorly shielded, as I suspect Bertha is. You just don't do that sort of thing without decent armor. You could be caught up in the shield-spell, your mind becoming one with the gate forever.

"You realize that's dangerous? And against the rules?"

She looks away. "I had to get out of the castle. And you were the only person using the gate. I didn't know if I'd get another chance."

As a professor at The Isthmus, I should probably give Bertha a lecture and send her home. But I'm not exactly a professor anymore: in fact, I'm technically a criminal. I wonder if Bertha saw me charming the water spirit with Elena's coin.

"Bertha, why would you take such a risk?"

Her eyes are hooded, distant. She presses her lips together, shakes her head.

This drives me nuts. But I'm not going to force a confession out of her.

"Fine. What did Elena say?" I change tactics, but I'd make a lousy interrogator, that's for sure. Too urgent. Too desperate.

"She worried you might be in trouble."

Let her worry. "Well, as you can see, I'm not."

Bertha hesitates, glances back over her shoulder. "Who was that guy in the woods? The one with the computer? He looked kind of familiar."

I think of Kyril's rapt expression, holding Rocco's Hollerith card. An idea is growing in my mind, too vague and nebulous to take on a meaningful form. It's a rough outline on paper, with a dark-haired stranger in the center. He did look familiar. And yet he didn't.

"He's trouble. And you need a better shawl if you're going to get safely home. Come with me."

We hurry down the steep sidewalks of Bascom Hill, passing a tweedy mundane professor on the narrow pedestrian bridge. The earthy scent of tobacco floats beside him in the cool autumn air. I know it's just pipe smoke, not one of Ruskin's mind-altering vapors, but old habits die hard. Impatiently, I wave it off.

"How did you find out I was leaving?"

Bertha focuses on the cracked pavement. "Lord Fob went to the dean's office to complain that you were rude and disrespectful in class. But Ms. Nguyen said you'd already been asked to leave. So he came up to the dining hall to gloat about how he'd gotten you sacked, and Princess Elena had a complete fit."

"Really?" I say, not entirely sure I should be listening to all this student gossip.

"She said she wasn't going to let anything deprive her of her right to a liberal arts education. She said the dean had better find her another textile professor right away."

I smile at this. It's all very well for Elena to act high-and-mighty and to claim she's eager to learn, but there are only five magical universities in the entire Arcanos Empire, and Elena has reportedly been thrown out of four of them. It takes a lot for a Crown Princess to be thrown out of college, which makes me wonder what else she's done. Besides getting total strangers struck by lightning, of course.

We make our way along State Street, passing yoga studios and juice stands, Tibetan restaurants and hookah shops.

"I hope you'll come back to The Isthmus." Bertha instinctively tightens her shawl as we pass an outdoor café strewn with dangerous laptop computers. "Most universities don't even offer a textile curriculum. Hendorf is the only other one."

"Hendorf is surrounded by enchanted sheep," I say with authority, despite having never been there. "They'd be crazy not to teach fiber arts. Speaking of textiles . . . "

I come to a stop in front of a trendy boutique. Skeins of yarn hang from the rungs of a vintage ladder. Bright origami cranes flap their wings above a cauldron of rainbow fleece, and a sign proclaims, "A Fine Kettle: New Hand-dyed Rambouillet."

"Here we are: The Narrow Gauge." The only place in Madison we can get real help.

Bertha balks. "We're going in there? But it's a . . . store." She avoids saying "mundane," but I know what she means.

I can't help but smile. "That's what you think."

The Narrow Gauge smells deliciously of wool. It's a rich, oily scent that lures you in, convincing you that you have all the time in the world to craft your spells. There's a woman's voice on the gramophone, her throaty contralto singing of lost love and how the pain endures forever. I can't relate to the song at all, which must mean I've never been in love. Surely, getting screwed over by Ruskin doesn't count.

The front of the yarn store is filled with well-heeled ladies learning the art of needle felting. They glance up, make dismissive note of Bertha's rustic shawl, and return to their work. The shop attendant, who probably has no idea she's working for a witch, gives us a friendly wave as we pass the cash register.

We move deeper into the store, passing long tables of knitting books, racks of bamboo needles, and a wall of heathery Icelandic yarn.

The sooner I get rid of Bertha, the sooner I can find a way to help Rocco and Dean LaMarche. It's bad enough being banished from The Isthmus; I really don't need a curfew-breaking student on my hands, as well. Least of all, a student with secrets to keep.

"This is so soft." Bertha sinks her fingers into a skein of teal merino.

"Yes, but it's machine spun." I don't bother mentioning what Bertha already knows: machine-spun yarns contain absolutely no life energy, making them far too labor-intensive to use for spells.

We enter the empty classroom behind the shop. In front of the curtained window stands an antique spinning wheel. It's almost as tall as I am. Seeing the huge, primitive arc of wood, I can't help feeling a wave of regret: the plain little wheel I abandoned at Arcanos Hall was one of my greatest treasures.

I've left my whole life behind. Including Rocco, who needs my help.

Bertha draws closer, admiring the wheel's glittering silver spindle.

"Yikes!" She shrieks, nearly impaling herself as an old woman abruptly appears beside her. "Where did you come from?"

Monsita Olann is the oldest human being I've ever seen. Her face is so lined and cracked, there's no telling what she looked like when she was young. Her gray hair is hidden under her intricately woven kerchief, and her dress, embellished with Spanish Colonial colcha embroidery, is like a garden of desert flowers. As usual, she's arrived without warning, flaring up out of the ether.

"You've got a jumpy friend, Anya," she drawls, watching Bertha recover. She lifts an earthenware mug to her crinkled lips and takes a sip of what she calls tea. I'm sure it's bourbon. I don't judge.

She squints at Bertha. "Who might you be?"

Bertha looks like she wants to sink through the floorboards. "B . . . b . . . Bertha."

"Not the Bratsch girl?" Madame Olann brings her face inches from Bertha's. "Ah, yes. See it now. Got some of your granny in you. Good thing you didn't take after your ma."

At the mention of her mother, Bertha turns pale.

"Bertha's my student," I say, more to protect Bertha from being offered alcohol than to set the record straight. "Madame, this is Bertha Bratsch. Bertha: Monsita Olann."

Bertha, who has only just managed to pull herself together, draws a swift breath, her eyes widening once more. It's not every day you meet a legend.

"Monsita Olann?" she says, gaping at the shriveled eighty-pound woman whose impassioned leadership helped transform our society. It was because of Olann's work that King Nestor was moved to end debtor's prisons and extend full citizenship to the hedge witches of the West, allowing students like Bertha to study at The Isthmus.

"The same," she says with great aplomb.

Bertha flounders for words. "It's . . . it's an honor to meet you, Madame."

"Well, if you're looking for wool, you'd best come upstairs." Madame Olann waves a gnarled hand at the folding looms in the corner, and a wooden ladder plummets down beside them, falling from a hidden trapdoor in the ceiling.

On the floor above the yarn shop is another yarn shop, this one for hedge witches. To an untutored eye, The Narrower Gauge may look very similar to its mundane counterpart, but there are a few key differences.

First of all, everyone in this shop is wearing a scarf or a hat lined with lace. Second, there's considerably more fleece and roving than yarn, since most witches prefer to spin their own enchanted fiber. Spinning wheels clutter the floor like bicycles at a playground. The scent of lanolin mixes with fragrant herbs and foraged dyes: birch bark, madder root, logwood, cochineal, and meadowsweet.

"Lovely," Bertha sighs, admiring the freshly dyed fleece hanging by the fireplace. There's Karakul, Churro, rare Gulf Coast wool, musk oxen, tussah silk. There's even an exquisite shawl knitted from legendary white bison. For a hedge witch, the treasures in this shop are like the paintings in the Louvre. "Madame, may I touch the fleece?"

"Go right ahead."

I like wool as much as the next witch, but the only thing that captures my attention is the large floor loom positioned near the courtyard window. It holds a magic tapestry, nearly finished, of a dark-haired woman gazing into a well, her faced turned away from view. She has daisies in her hair, each flower painstakingly wrought with threads of gold.

"So," Madame Olann says. "You've got all your worldly goods on your back and the taint of technology in your hair. Reckon you've had quite a day."

I'm about to respond to this, when a young witch comes up the ladder, a black cat perched on her shoulder. With an agile leap, the cat launches itself at the loom and lands squarely on the magic tapestry. Dropping her teacup, Madame Olann reacts at once.

"Get that damned grimalkin out of here." She flings open the window facing the courtyard, and the witch hustles her familiar out. Hissing, it clings to the branch of a rowan tree.

"I hate cats," she says calmly, retrieving her fallen teacup from the rug. "Grew up on a goat farm in New Mexico, with two hundred head of Arcane Angora. Goddamn felines kept coming around, shredding our textiles, killing our baby goats."

She glares out the window, watching the cat paw at an orange clump of rowanberries. "Me? I'm gonna kill any cat comes near my loom. Kill it with my own bare hands."

Bertha's mouth falls open. I can tell she's never had a cat and has always wanted one. "Surely, magical kitties wouldn't kill baby goats?"

Madame Olann sniffs. "You can believe that, dearie. If it makes you feel better."

"Bertha needs better armor," I say, deciding the discussion of my banishment can wait. "She broke curfew and snuck out in my wake."

"Well," the old witch says to Bertha. "That weren't too smart. But I suppose you had your reasons. We all got our reasons." She jabs a bony finger at the chairs by the fireplace. "Sit down, girl."

Bertha sinks into a scratched leather chair, nudging a glossy stack of arcane tabloids out of her way. "I'm not going back. Not if I have to stay."

"What?" I take a seat across from her. "Bertha, you can't come and go as you please. Not from a shielded castle. Not in a state of emergency."

"Oh, I understand. You don't want any trouble, so you're siding with the administration." Bertha folds her arms across her chest. "If you're not going to help me, you can just say so."

"Hah!" Madame Olann's laughter rattles like a soup bone in a cauldron. "I *like* this girl."

Bertha's a smart witch; that's for sure. Not only has she accused me of blindly supporting the status quo, she's done so in front of a legendary hedge witch activist. Nice way to make me look bad.

I throw up my hands. "Bertha, I'm not supporting the administration. They just banished the hell out of me." Saying the word "banished" aloud, in front of these other witches, makes my disgrace so real, I almost lose my composure.

"You're my student, and I'm trying to keep you from getting killed. I don't even know why you need to get in and out."

Just for a moment, Bertha looks lost. "There's something I have to do."

"What could you possibly have to do?" I'm almost certain she's on a full scholarship, which means she's not allowed to have a job.

"Let the girl have her secrets," Madame Olann says, taking the white bison shawl from the rack above the mantel. "I know I have mine."

I glance at the magic tapestry on her loom, at the graceful woven figure with flowers in her hair. Beneath the woman's feet I can make out a series of magic symbols—possibly an old runic script, which almost no one on this continent can read.

Something tells me that the witch's secret is sitting out in plain sight, open to anyone who knows how to decipher it. But I can't read her secret, not any better than I can read Rocco's card punched with holes. I wonder, though, if there's someone who can.

Madame Olann holds out the exquisite bison shawl. "Tell you what, Anya. I've got a shawl Bertha can borrow. If you'll customize this piece, I'll let the girl travel with me."

Bertha scrambles out of her chair. "Really? Thank you, Madame!"

"Don't thank me. You're gonna help me carry my stuff."

Stunned, I take the bison shawl. "You mean you're going to The Isthmus?"

"Course I am," Madame Olann says. "They gave me your job."

"They gave you my job?" I'm too shocked and insulted to do anything but clutch at the shawl. *So they've already replaced me, the bastards.* "When was this?"

She inspects her empty cup of tea. "Weren't more than half an hour ago. Your dean sent one of his fat little ravens."

"He's not my dean," I say, feeling utterly desolate. "I'm unemployed."

She looks at me. "That you are. Want some tea?"

"Yes," I say, hoping the tea will be alcoholic. "Yes, I do."

Madame Olann crosses the room. Rather than put a kettle on, she extracts a bottle of small-batch bourbon from her armoire. Just as I'd always suspected.

I have to say: things are going great. I'm unemployed, useless to my students, unable to help Rocco, and having a drink in the middle of the afternoon.

"I could use some help with inventory," she says, filling an earthenware mug. "You could stay here and get things done. Just for a few days, of course."

I accept a generous portion of bourbon. "That would be lovely.

I'd be glad to help."

From the look of things, she doesn't need any help organizing her yarn stash. But when it comes to charity, we hedge witches have a code: don't burden anyone with obligations they can't repay, and don't place yourself in anyone's debt.

The mountains across the Atlantic are filled with exploited hedge witches, most of them bound for life by crushing debts and obligations. When you see an entire kingdom corrupted by indentured servitude, you learn to reject the very idea of debt.

Oblivious to our transaction, Bertha extricates herself from the stack of papers on her club chair.

"Oh my goodness!" she says, pulling one of the expensive tabloids out from under her butt. "It's Princess Elena. She's on the cover of *Cloak and Wand*."

"Let me see that," I say with an irrational surge of resentment. If Elena's in some overpriced periodical, I hope she looks like crap.

A glittering portrait of Princess Elena graces the cover of *Cloak and Wand*. She's wearing a huge kokoshnik-style tiara and a rather fussy coral evening gown. Which just goes to show that money can't buy good taste.

I page through the magazine in search of the article, momentarily distracted by a story titled "Nestor's Royal Vow: 'I'll Never Marry Again!'" It features a sad-looking image of King Nestor, still broken by grief over his missing queen. There's also a picture of Prince Dominic, awkward and blotchy as usual. The tabloids like to claim that the prince is much more attractive in person, but I rather doubt it. After all, pictures don't lie.

"School Bells or Wedding Bells?" is the cheesy headline for the Elena story.

Princess Elena has crossed the ocean! This fall the free-spirited Carpathian royal is enrolled at The Isthmus, the legendary college of magical arts in the Kingdom of the

West. "It will be a great honor to complete my education at Arcanos Hall," says the stunning beauty, who previously attended all four colleges East of the Keel. Elena's devoted admirer, industrialist Lord Burke, is said to be counting the days until the lovely heiress finally receives her degree. Could a June wedding be on the horizon?

"What?" I drop the tabloid into my lap. "Lord Burke is Elena's boyfriend?" There is absolutely no way that Princess Elena could be in love with Burke.

"Burke and Elena?" Madame Olann scoffs. "I'll believe that when the mountains fall into the sea. That princess has never had a boyfriend in her life."

This sounds about right. Which makes Elena's actions on Sunday even more puzzling.

"Who's Lord Burke?" Bertha asks, eagerly retrieving the magazine.

"One of our Regents," I say with a shudder. "He's on the Inner Council."

I don't bother to tell Bertha that he's a notorious lecher, an exploiter of hedge witches, and one of several people who sat around and sneered while I was banished.

A predatory gleam appears in Madame Olann's eye. "Is Burke on campus?"

I inhale the smoky aroma coming from my teacup. "He is."

"Oh, I can't wait to get there." From the look on her face, she's obviously planning to radicalize the student body, overthrow the Regents, and raid the liquor cabinet—in precisely that order. I wonder if the dean knows what he's getting into. Come to think of it, I wonder why she took the job. She *hates* the university elite.

Bertha pages through *Cloak and Wand* in hopes of finding another photo. "He's here at The Isthmus? Perhaps he's come to propose!"

"Right." I remember my confrontation with Burke in the steam tunnels, the way my flesh crawled at his touch. "Because he loves Elena so very much."

"Really?" Bertha is woefully unschooled in the art of sarcasm.

Madame Olann sighs. "Oh, honey, no. Burke doesn't love Elena, and for sure she couldn't love someone like him. But those aristocrats don't think about marriage the way we ordinary folk do. They've got empires to build. Love's got nothing to do with it."

I take a sip of bourbon, and it burns all the way down.

"Burke has my friend in custody," I murmur to Madame Olann, watching as Bertha locates another tabloid photo of Elena. "A hedge worker named Rocco."

She lifts her own teacup to her lips, and her eyes narrow. "Is that so?"

We're both quiet, thinking. Then I reach for the knotted bracelet on my wrist. The time has come to use it.

"May I borrow one of your ravens?" I've evaluated my alternatives, and I've arrived at a single, inescapable conclusion. "I need to send a message."

My dad's going to be so surprised to hear from me.

CHAPTER EIGHT

I wake with the taste of bourbon in my throat, a pickaxe pounding at the back of my head. *Rap, rap, rap.*

Rolling over, I recall crocheting a custom border around the white bison shawl. I remember Bertha insisting she had to go somewhere before nightfall. I remember something about the bourbon in the armoire.

The pounding in my head returns. *Rap, rap, rap.*

I pull myself upright and realize it's Madame Olann's raven, pecking at the window. It's after dawn. Cringing in the morning glare, I reach for my shawl and stagger forward. Somehow, I manage to unseal the window. The raven drops my macramé bracelet on the peeling windowsill, then departs with a noisy flapping of wings.

As I pick up the bracelet, blood rushes queasily into my head. Untwisting a coil of paper from the knotted chevron pattern, I find a message from my father.

Meet me at the Amish market. Noon. Bring a white chrysanthemum. Come alone.

In case you're wondering, my father is not Amish. Rather,

he's paranoid, compulsive about security, and unwilling to share his secrets with anyone. He owns numerous computers, but most have never been connected to the Internet. Others are so highly encrypted, no government in the world can crack them. Which is impossible, he tells me, unless you've applied encryption algorithms of profound mathematical complexity, increasing bit strength and adding elliptical curves to the algorithms over time.

I wouldn't know. I haven't actually seen the place where my dad works. I haven't seen him more than once a year since I was twelve. He doesn't trust me, which is why he wants me to bring a white chrysanthemum to the Amish market. So that he'll know it's me, or that I haven't been followed. Or whatever.

I rub my thumb across my father's message, and the ink smears off, leaving nothing but a blank scroll of white paper. Then I take stock of my situation.

I'm seriously hung over, for which I accept full responsibility, special bourbon notwithstanding. I'm also unemployed. I'm in a small attic room above The Narrower Gauge. There's yarn everywhere, dirty dishes in the chipped enamel basin. The room is impeccably shielded, with hand-woven batik wallpapers and lace curtains covering every window. My canvas bag rests next to the sofa.

Rocco needs me, and so does the dean. But what am I supposed to do?

Dean LaMarche wants me to explore the problem from outside the university. Well, I'm outside now, aren't I? And the problem isn't any clearer. I have no plan, no real allies, no idea of what he wants done or how. Seriously, why didn't he ask me to bring him a baby unicorn? At least I'd have a reasonable chance of finding one of those.

I empty my belongings onto the scratched surface of the pine table, trying not to resent Madame Olann for taking my job. Then I dig around in the kitchen and find some linden flower tea. There's nothing to eat but a mucilaginous porridge, which I reject utterly.

As the teakettle heats up, I take stock of things known and unknown. I've got one notebook, written in Old Norse. It was found on the stranger who died the night the shields failed. I've got one Hollerith card, whatever that is. Another card, this one a scorched fragment. Two military-style silver epaulettes. So much for things I know.

The things I don't know are far more numerous. Why did the shields fail? Were they sabotaged? And why doesn't the dean know how to fix them? Was he the one hiding in the tunnels the night we burned the corpse?

I make myself a strong, sugary cup of tea, realizing there are other questions that need answering as well. I just don't know if they're related.

It seems very strange to me that Elena's mysterious dead guy was mysteriously struck by lightning on the very day the shields mysteriously failed. Tabloids notwithstanding, if she thought he was a saboteur and she killed him to protect the castle, why didn't she contact the authorities? He couldn't possibly have been a romantic interest. Madame Olann said Elena didn't have boyfriends, and even if she did, it's hard to believe she could be attracted to a man whose coat didn't fit—much less, that she would help him sabotage The Isthmus. In fact, it's all rather unlikely.

What did the tabloids call Elena? Free-spirited. I'm guessing that's an editorial code word for "irresponsible." But irresponsible isn't the same thing as criminal. I'd probably be irresponsible too, if I were expected to enter into a *marriage de convenance* with the likes of Burke.

Come to think of it, I'm willing to bet Elena has been getting herself thrown out of college on purpose.

Sipping my tea, I reach for the scorched fragment I found in the furnace room. It's the same size as Rocco's card, but incomplete. Perhaps there were more of these, and they were destroyed.

Could they be linked to the Drini shields? From Kyril's reaction, I'm guessing the card is mundane, and very old.

Something about this Kyril guy has been bothering me. Not just his presence in the bushes next to my stakeout. Not just his willingness to lie about photographing women in bikinis. Not even the fact that Rocco's card was in my pocket, and then suddenly it wasn't.

Kyril's computer should have failed. There was nothing wrong with my spell.

∽

The Amish market is two hours west, as the crow flies. But I'm not a crow.

Wrapped in my invisibility cape, I'm cruising slowly on my flying carpet, breathing in the cool autumn air. Buffeted by gusts of wind, I tack back and forth to avoid leaving traces of magic. I'll probably be late.

When I launched this morning from the tiled roof of Madame Olann's shop, I deliberately avoided Observatory Hill and the Lakeshore Preserve. I didn't want to get too close to Arcanos Hall, didn't want to leave a magic trail. But now, heading away from Rocco and The Isthmus—it feels wrong to be leaving everything behind. I don't know how much my father can help, or even if he wants to help. I may end up with zero answers and a twenty-dollar bill.

Better than nothing, though. Much better than having no father at all.

When I was a child, forced to attend public schools wearing ugly caps lined with lace or tinfoil, I thought my dad was a complete freak.

I was right about that. He is a complete freak. But he also kept my magic alive. Many witches raised by mundane parents lose most of their magic by adulthood. Carelessly exposed to computers and cell phones, they don't have a chance to develop their powers.

Me? I was lucky. My paranoid father had no trouble believing my mother when she told him that repeated exposure to technology would irreparably damage my brain. Retired from his mysterious government work by the time I was born, he built us a home in an old missile silo, shielded the hell out of it, and made sure I never answered a phone. When my mother died, he wrapped one of her magic bracelets around my wrist and sent me off to a boarding school that he would never have a chance to see. He did so because she wanted him to, and she was the only person in the world he knew how to trust.

I arrive at the Amish market by 1:00 PM, a pilfered white daisy in my hand. My father is nowhere in sight. No one else is in sight either, but that's not surprising on a Tuesday afternoon. Apart from a hand-lettered sign that says Meat Raffle, the place looks abandoned.

I slide off the flying carpet and stretch my cramped legs under the cottonwood trees. I've been sitting cross-legged for far too long. Still draped in my invisibility cape, I roll up my carpet and cross the gravel parking lot, heading for the rodeo stands.

I've been to this market before. It's actually a county fairground, with an exhibition hall that serves year-round as an auction house. On Wednesdays and Saturdays, when the local farmers come to buy and sell, you'll find dozens of horse-drawn buggies and bicycles in the parking lot, alongside the usual SUVs and pickup trucks.

"Who goes there?" Ten feet away, my dad nearly scares the crap out of me. He's got to be the only person in the world who can catch an invisible woman by surprise.

"Dad?" I drop the white daisy, and it slowly falls into the visible world.

My dad emerges from the bushes next to the rodeo stands.

Still lean and muscular, even in his mid-seventies, he's wearing rustic overalls topped by a silver poncho. Under the poncho's hood, I can just glimpse his ears, the tips scarred by frostbite long ago. Above his scratched aviator sunglasses, his eyebrows are so long and unruly, a few bristly grey hairs are sticking out at right angles from his face.

"Didn't I teach you anything? You were crunching the gravel under your feet."

I sigh and fling back my cape. "Nice to see you, dad. Been far too long."

His craggy face softens, and he opens his arms for a hug.

"My little girl." His hands snag on my lace shawl. "Look at you, all grown up."

"All grown up?" My arms reach upward, and I return his hug, not sure what I'm feeling, not sure whether it's sorrow or surprise.

"Why the metal poncho? I feel like I'm hugging the Tin Soldier."

He straightens a stiff fold of silver fabric. "RFID-blocking, anti-drone wearable tech."

"So it makes you invisible or something?" I'm reminded suddenly of the weird metallic hoodie Kyril was wearing in the Lakeshore Preserve. Obviously a similar kind of high-tech camouflage.

"The fabric disperses my heat signature," he says with satisfaction. "And the reflective pattern near my face disrupts security cameras, undermining facial recognition."

"Huh." No wonder Kyril was so surprised that I could see him trampling the bushes. He thought he was invisible to computers, and he's probably the sort of person who honestly can't tell the difference between a computer and a human being.

We walk together beside the rodeo stands, heading for a papery expanse of dried-up field corn. A sign reads: Harvest Maze! Saturdays, 9-6. When I was a little girl, my parents brought me here every fall, so I could explore the corn maze. Eating apple cider doughnuts and running through the maze made me feel like a normal kid, if only for a while.

"Remember this place?" Dad says, with a broad gesture at the corn. "You'd spend forever hiding in this thing. Your mother always had to go in after you."

"I just wanted to find all the dead ends."

He snorts, catching me off-guard. I'd forgotten he even knew how to laugh. "The whole point of a maze is to find your way out, as fast as you can."

"But then the game's over. You're done. And you don't know how they made the maze."

He lifts his chin with fatherly pride. "You were never a normal girl."

I was never going to be a normal witch either, not with a mundane father. I do my best, but I'm not intuitively magical, which is why I never got any certifications. I'm mostly just a problem solver—good with numbers, good with patterns.

We enter the maze through an arching pergola made of dried cornstalks, and I hand him Rocco's card. It's a problem to be solved, and my father loves problems.

"I know it's called a Hollerith card," I say. "But what does it do? What's it for?"

He inspects the faded parchment, running his dirty thumb over its tiny round holes. "Why do you need to know?"

I open my mouth to tell him about the invisible castle and the broken Drini shields; about Lord Burke, who gloated while I was banished. But not a word comes out.

"Huhn," I say, and claw at my throat. Why can't I speak?

I try to breathe, and my nostrils fill with the smell of dirt and dried corn and more dirt.

"You can't tell me?" Dad takes off his sunglasses, revealing faded brown eyes.

"Urmph," I say, sounding uncannily like Rocco. I can't even tell my own father I've been enchanted.

Is this a side effect of being banished? I've never tried to talk to a mundane about The Isthmus before, so perhaps this enforced discretion is a condition of employment. Either way, the effect is clear: I can't speak about Arcanos Hall.

Reaching into my smock, I locate my fountain pen and the raven's blank scroll.

I've been banished, I try to write. But the ink stops midway through the letter *b*.

I open my hand, indicating helplessness, and point at Rocco's card.

A hard, grim look forms on my father's face. "They won't let you speak? You've been silenced?" He shoves his sunglasses back on and kicks at a clump of corn stubble. For a moment, I'm afraid he's going to lose his temper.

Then he breaks into a smile. "Damn! I wish I had security like that."

Typical. For him, this is just one more problem to solve.

"I'm sorry," I blurt. Apparently, apologies are allowed, as long as they're pathetic and abject.

"No apology needed," he says. "What did I tell you, when you were young?"

"Never share information unless you have to." My voice bursts free like a broken valve. I rub at my throat. That was quite a spell.

"Right," he says. "And always watch your back."

He tips back his head, squints at the dried tassels of corn. "It's better to protect the ones you love, by keeping them ignorant. Half a lifetime ago, I was doing work I still can't describe, for an organization that still doesn't exist. But I didn't have the burden of keeping my work a secret from my loved ones, since there wasn't anybody that I loved."

I follow his eyes into the rows of corn. "Not until you met mom."

I know why he loved her: because she had secrets even bigger than his own.

He grunts, and the thick folds of his eyelids seem heavier. Then he returns to what he does best: solving problems. "So, you can't tell me anything, but that doesn't mean I can't help. Early computers used these punched cards to encode data. You wouldn't have learned about them in your local grade school—years ago, they became obsolete."

He pauses. "Mostly."

"Computers?" That would explain why Kyril knew what it was. But what would a computer card be doing in Arcanos Hall?

My father glances my way, as if guessing my thoughts. "From what I understand, you folk don't use computers."

I open my mouth to say, "No, we don't," but my throat seizes up.

He peers up at the card, the rectangular shadow on his face pinpricked with tiny dots of light. "This card is very old. It predates any punch card I've ever seen. Almost looks like it was made for one of those jacquard machines, early 19th century. But this parchment is very thick—seems even older than that."

The word "jacquard" triggers a memory. "Like a jacquard loom? You mean that computers use the same kinds of scripts as looms?"

He laughs. "Sure do. That's where computers came from."

I've always thought of the Drini shields in terms of fiber arts, mainly because textiles were the only magical discipline I really understood. But I assumed I was using a metaphor, applying a familiar framework to something too complex to comprehend.

Maybe it's not a metaphor. Perhaps the Drini shields are actually giant textile machines, run by a computer-like code. Perhaps for hundreds of years, they've woven or knitted a giant shield around Arcanos Hall. But if that's true, then where can I find the rest of the missing code? And what on earth are they making into fabric?

I manage to force words past my lips. "Could this knit or weave something big?"

"How big?"

I gnash my teeth as the silencing enchantment kicks right in.

78

"Urmph," I say, then bite my tongue. Literally. "Ow!"

He can't help me. The realization leaves me perversely giddy. Every time I try to ask about deciphering the card, my throat seizes up, and I'm left staring at him, useless.

Even worse, I'm beginning to realize I won't be able to find anyone else who can help. With the silencing spell on my throat, I'm not allowed to speak to any outsiders or mundanes. As for seeking help from other wizards, right now my choices are few.

Perhaps Madame Olann could help. She's weaving something profoundly magical on her loom. I wonder, though, if I should trust her. She's never supported the university or its hierarchies. Besides, she has her secrets, and I have mine.

"You want my help," my father says, with a small shake of his head. "But you can't ask the questions you need to ask."

"Sorry, Dad." That's my second abject apology for the day.

He puts an arm over my shoulder. "Don't be. It's good to finally see you again."

A wave of sadness hits, and I feel like I'm twelve again, being sent alone into a world I don't understand. I wish I could talk to him. I wish I didn't feel so alone.

We return to the parking lot, and I glimpse an old bicycle hidden in the shrubbery near the rodeo stand. So he came here by bike. That's good to know. I wonder if he's still keeping any of his stuff back at the old missile silo.

His voice breaks through my thoughts. "Do you need anything? Can I help?"

Grateful, I open my drawstring purse and produce a few silver coins. "Trade?"

He digs deep into his overalls and withdraws a grimy wad of paper money. "It's a deal," he says, eyes crinkling behind his aviator shades. "Take it all."

"Are you sure?" It's a lot of American money.

"I'm sure, Anya. And don't spend all your silver, if you can help it. What have I always told you? Hard currency is hard to find."

I nod my thanks. "I'm going back . . . if they'll let me. I have to find my way back."

"You came from Madison, didn't you? On that thing." He indicates my rolled-up Persian rug. "Are you sure it's safe?"

I open my mouth to answer, but nothing comes out. Silenced by the spell, I just look at him, and I wonder how he knew I was in Madison, or how he knew my kilim was a flying carpet. He and my mom kept a lot of secrets, even from each other. But he's always had a way of finding things out.

I resort to clichés. "When you're flying, the probability of survival is equal to the angle of arrival."

He produces a wry smile. "You young people. When I was in Madison, in the early seventies, I didn't even own a car."

I roll my eyes. "I suppose you had to walk to class, a mile each way in the snow."

"Not at all," he says. "When the weather was bad, we just went underground."

I try to imagine my father as a young man, navigating a subterranean campus. But my mind rejects the thought. He has always been an old man.

He clears his throat. "Look, I know you can't talk to me, not any more than I can talk to you. But that doesn't mean we don't care about each other."

He pushes back the sleeve of his western-style shirt, revealing a blurry green military tattoo. Below the tattoo is a frayed macramé bracelet, identical to my own.

"If you need me, send another message. I'll find you again."

"Thanks, Dad." I give him an awkward hug, and unroll my flying carpet.

I'm about to pull my invisibility cape over my head, when he says one last thing.

"There's a building in Madison that looks just like your card.

I used to take engineering classes there. It was built in the sixties, when punched cards symbolized everything we knew about computers."

"A building?" I don't know why he thinks this information will help.

He smiles, and reaches for my hood. A moment later, he's staring at nothing.

"All roads lead to Engineering, Anya. Every tunnel does, as well."

∽

When I get back to the attic above The Narrow Gauge, I find Monsita Olann dyeing fleece and complaining about my students. A magical ventilator hums above her stove, and the air smells like wet musk oxen.

"May the Norns forgive me," she says, shaking her head. "I wanted to kill them all. What a bunch of spoiled brats!"

Using a pair of tongs, she inspects a clump of the tea-colored fleece in her cauldron. "You're a saint, Anya. How'd you put up with those kids for all these months?"

I prop my flying carpet against the wall. "I just want to help people learn."

"Bah!" She isn't having any of that. "Can't you see they don't care? They're just going to get their fancy degree, step on our backs, and take their place at the top."

This is her great refrain. She sees the university as part of an antiquated system that perpetuates inequality. It keeps hedge witches in sweatshops, elite sorcerers in power. Maybe she's right. But that doesn't mean The Isthmus isn't worth saving. It has to be worth saving. It's my home.

"And so ignorant," she continues with a scowl. "All they know about is East versus West. Never heard of anything magical outside the Arcanos Empire. Never seen a weaving from the Andes. Can't name a single mountain range in all of Africa. Haven't got a clue about the different kinds of magic outside their own little world."

This comment makes me a bit uncomfortable, since I'm not particularly knowledgeable about the forms of witchcraft practiced outside the former Empire. In my defense, I have tried hard to find things out.

"And that princess of yours," she turns on me, almost accusingly. "Worst knitting I've ever seen. Gauge so tight, her fabric stands up like a soldier's dick. Like a—"

"How's Bertha?" I ask, interrupting her rant. "Did everything go okay?"

This gives her pause. She turns off her peat-fueled stove and sets her tongs aside. "Well. At least I've got one good student." It's clear she's not going to say anything more.

I spend the evening earning my keep, sorting through Madame Olann's inventory. She has yarn and roving of every fiber, every color. She has angora, enchanted cashmere, and mulberry silk. She has mordants, dyes, and herbs. I make a huge chart of her stash, cross-referencing everything by fiber, color, ply, and weight. Her finest yarn, I notice, is reserved for the magic tapestry stretched across her loom.

It makes me wonder how the Drini shields could actually be run by a code. I've seen plenty of mundane looms with chains of coded charts attached to the dobby. But mechanically produced fabric has no magic, no life energy. None at all. The whole point of textile magic is that you draw upon your own power to enact the spell. You store your life energy in the loose fiber as you twist and spin it into yarn, and then you embed additional energy into the fabric with every stitch you make. That's why machine-spun yarn can't be used to knit shields or armor. That's why a machine-woven rug can't simply be enchanted into a flying carpet.

The power has to come from somewhere. So does the thread.

"Do you want a separate category for the energized singles?"

I ask, holding up a springy batch of single-ply Karakul. Energized yarn continually twists back on itself, so when it's knit, it creates a deliciously warped fabric.

"Always." Madame Olann lifts the yellow-gold fleece from her cauldron and lays the wet roving on an old towel. "You can't get a more devious yarn."

"What do you use it for?" I wonder if she'll actually reveal a secret.

But she ignores my question. "There's an Ice Captain on campus."

I pause over my piles of yarn. "Her name is Aradottir."

"Kirsten Aradottir, yes. I knew her parents, may the Elders bless their journey. She's running evacuation drills."

"Evacuation drills?"

"In case the wards fail."

"But the wards are sound," I begin, and then stop. It was Ruskin who told us the wards were sound. The same Ruskin who screwed me over and sold me down the river. And why on earth would I believe him?

"You better hope so," she says. "I was demonstrating a picot bind-off when your friend Aradottir sprang the alarm. She gave the students two minutes to get to the portals on the roof. Lord Fob, that trumped-up little aristo of yours, was late. She told him to his face that he would have been left behind."

"Left behind?" Much as I dislike Fob, this sounds unreasonable. Aradottir is completely ruthless.

She rolls her fleece in the towel and gently presses down. "Puts me to mind of the story they tell about the Phoenix dynasty. How Burke destroyed his own family fortress, back in 1891."

"Burke?" Must have been Simon Burke's great-grandfather.

"Threat of detection, they say. Villagers getting too close to the truth. So Burke took his infant son and torched the entire castle. Left his lady and all the servants to burn."

I feel sick. If they have only two minutes to evacuate, they're not going to rescue a prisoner from the dungeons. "Would Aradottir really burn down Arcanos Hall?"

Madame Olann's look tells me she's seen it all. "To save us all from exposure? Believe me, people like her will do whatever has to be done. Her whole life is about protecting her community."

For some reason, this makes me think of my father.

She continues, as if reading my mind. "Her father's people came from the far north, where witches once lived peacefully with the mundane. But times changed, and whole villages were wiped off the map. You live with the legacy of something like that, and you learn to guard against disaster. You learn to eliminate every threat so innocent people can sleep at night. That's how the young captain has lived in the world. That's the kind of person she is."

I reach for the inventory charts, my stomach churning, my face carefully neutral. I have to go back tonight. If the wards fail, Aradottir will destroy Arcanos Hall. And she might not risk waiting for anyone. If she has to, she'll leave Rocco behind.

CHAPTER NINE

The Engineering building reeks of data transmission. Two blocks south of Observatory Hill, it's an ugly, cement rectangle, with an exterior grid punctuated by tiny windows. Lit up at night, it really does look like Rocco's Hollerith card.

I have to find Rocco before it's too late. If Aradottir really is prepared to torch The Isthmus, then she's also probably willing to accept collateral damage. But Rocco isn't collateral. He's my friend.

All roads lead to Engineering. Whatever my father meant by that, the answer must lie below, in the UW steam tunnels. Surely, the tunnels must run close to Arcanos Hall, perhaps even connecting at some point. If I'm going to get into the castle undetected, my best chance is going underground.

I land on the roof of Engineering and burn through the access door's alarm with a Muzzled Beast spell, annihilating a piece of Celtic cable-work knitted in the shape of a dragon. Then I step inside. My mother's shawl crackles and sparks, indicating dangerous technological fields.

With my invisibility cape trailing behind me, I glide down the stairwell. When you're invisible, the world seems hyper-real. Light is polarized. Yellow is vibrant. Blue is more blue. You're wholly in this world, but you're seeing it through a vivid filter.

The entrance to the steam tunnels is simple enough to find. I break into the custodian's closet in the basement, and right there by the fire alarms and electrical boxes is a sign that says Steam Tunnel Access. How easy was that?

Too easy, perhaps. I'm about to knock open the battered metal door, when I realize it's unlocked. In fact, it's propped open with a twelve-pack of beer: cheap, disgusting beer made by brewers who should have stuck to milling flour.

The skin on my arms prickles with unease. The tunnel door should not be ajar. UW-Madison has security concerns like any mundane university, and a ten-mile network of tunnels connecting every building on campus is a security nightmare. I'm just hoping the cheap beer belongs to some kids having a party.

I retrieve a luminescent torch from my satchel and peer into the tunnel. It stinks of mold and rodent droppings. I really don't want to do this. But Rocco needs me, so there's no choice.

As I inch down the metal ladder, waves of scurrying insects dart in every direction. Having grown up in a missile silo, I'm not as disturbed by underground gloom as most people are. Still, I could have done without the cockroaches.

I drop to the ground and brush the cobwebs off my cape. A long insulated pipe stretches out in both directions. The pipe is bigger than the abdomen of a horse, far larger than any of the copper tubing in the steam room at Arcanos Hall. Flanking the pipe is a huge network of power lines and data cables, old and new. Just seeing them makes me wince. A pressure gauge rises like an antenna above the belly of the steam pipe, its dusty clock face showing a PSI of 1200.

Great. I'm in a tunnel with a giant pressurized tube carrying superheated steam, and I'm probably not alone.

If you're going to break into a meandering system of tunnels to find something that was built over a hundred years ago, you should probably have a map or a good sense of direction. If you don't have either of those things, then your best bet is to move in the direction of the oldest masonry. After wandering through several damp, overheated concrete corridors, breathing in the odorous fumes of cat piss and mold, I finally stumble upon old brick and even older stone.

I find myself in an underground room with an arched brick ceiling. Dusty brackets hold tubes of fluorescent lights. Detritus litters the floor: metal tools, crushed beer cans, lengths of white plastic pipe. Before me looms a giant, abandoned boiler. My torch illuminates a cracked pressure gauge and a faded sign: "Legacy Boiler System. Agriculture Hall."

I allow myself a faint smile of relief. Of all the buildings at UW-Madison, Agriculture Hall is the closest to Arcanos Hall, separated from the castle only by the effigy mounds on Observatory Hill. The two-tailed water spirit must be right behind the boiler.

This may actually work. But only if the water spirit opens the gate.

Huge and round, like the oversized hatch on a submarine, the cast-iron boiler door blocks my way. Setting my torch on a molded plastic chair, I reach for the best yarn in my satchel, only to freeze when a loud, echoing boom shakes the entire boiler. Dust lifts from the boiler room floor and hovers like mist above the ground. I watch in horror as the rusted metal wheel on the boiler door groans and trembles, then slowly begins to turn. The door abruptly swings open, revealing a looming, hooded figure, his torso flickering with reflected light.

I scream aloud, causing the man inside to jerk backward and bang his head on the overhanging doorframe. "Argh!"

I glimpse dark hair, knife-sharp cheekbones, and an aquiline nose. Unmistakably, it's Kyril. He pokes his head again through the door, driving his knuckles into the bruised section of his skull. His huge black pupils focus on my abandoned torch. "Who's there?"

I back away from him, looking for a weapon, any weapon. I was careless yesterday, far too careless. I assumed Kyril's presence in the Lakeshore woods was a coincidence. I assumed he was just a geek with a laptop and a high-tech hoodie. Wrong, wrong, wrong.

I pick up a filthy broom and brandish the bristles at him. Then I remember I'm still invisible. Dropping the broom, I retreat into the steam tunnel.

Kyril removes his hand from the back of his head, his fingers velvety wet in the luminescent light. He's bleeding. Limbs trembling, he struggles out of the boiler hatch before collapsing onto the ground.

I glance behind me. The tunnel to Engineering is empty.

If there's anything I've learned from my father, it's to withhold trust. Last spring, I chose to ignore that advice, and I ended up being screwed by Ruskin, falsely accused of all manner of treachery, and placed on probation. Lesson forever learned.

However, Kyril is not Ruskin. And he's lying on the ground bleeding.

It's not in my nature to trust anyone, but it's also not in my nature to leave a beautiful man to die. Kyril's eyes are closed, his breathing shallow. Burgundy-black and viscous in the eerie blue torchlight, slick ribbons of blood trail down the side of his neck. His silver hoodie flickers with reflected light, and gold rings flash on his hands.

I inch closer, holding my breath. But when I'm close enough to see his eyelashes, Kyril strikes, faster and more sudden than a poisonous snake. Hurling himself into my chest, he pins me to the grime-encrusted floor and tears off my invisibility cape. A ripping sound tells me my cape is ruined.

"You!" His eyes grow perfectly round.

"Let me go," I hiss, struggling to get out from under his weight.

His jaw hardens. "Tell me who you are!"

"None of your business."

He seizes my arm and pulls me to my feet.

"Get your hands off me," I snarl, shaking myself loose. Kyril abruptly lets go, and we stare at each other, panting like dogs in the sun.

Kyril's gaze rakes over me, starting with my lace headscarf and the Persian rug coiled on my back, pausing briefly at the ball of angora clutched in my hand.

He picks up my torch. "You have one chance to tell me who you work for."

"Or what?" I back away from him, retreating toward the Engineering tunnel. "You're going to kill me?"

Kyril takes a step closer. Then another. "You won't remember."

For some reason, this frightens me more than being told I'm going to die.

His face is dark with menace. "Where did you get this torch?"

"It's university property," I say, which is not exactly a lie.

Kyril takes this in, about to ask another question, then throws up his arm to protect his eyes as all the fluorescent lights suddenly flash on, hitting our faces like staggering strobes. Voices boom in the steam tunnel.

"Damn!" Stumbling in the glare, I seize my satchel and invisibility cape. The cape is unraveling into chaos, completely ruined. A sharp, metallic taste stings my tongue.

Kyril throws my torch into the boiler and grabs the door. "If you want to live, get inside." He slips into the boiler so fast, it's hard to believe he was ever here.

I now have two choices, and neither one is good. Either I can stay here to be discovered by security (or whoever is coming through the tunnel), or I can climb into an abandoned boiler with a man who just threatened me.

He attacked me when I was invisible. Then told me I wouldn't remember.

Computer notwithstanding, Kyril is obviously very powerful, which means he's way more dangerous than any doughnut-fed security guard coming down the corridor.

I'm about to take my chances with campus security when the metallic taste returns, this time flooding my entire mouth. I inhale, smelling nothing but mildew and rat droppings and cat piss and decay. But the coppery taste in my mouth can't be denied. It's like the bite of ozone that accompanies a lightning strike. It's the coming of a data storm.

We all know that electromagnetic fields can be toxic to witches. But it's one thing to lose your magical powers slowly over time, through the constant drip of exposure to cell phones and WiFi; it's another thing entirely to lose your magic all at once, from a massive poisonous blast. Some witches are simply injured by storms, unable to use charms or create spells. But others are completely broken. They end up dead-eyed and shattered, wandering in the streets, forever trying to grasp that they were meant for something more.

"Wait!" I dive for the boiler with my gear, just as Kyril is pulling the door shut.

He lets me in, then tugs the door in place as I glimpse several figures at the mouth of the tunnel. The first four are heavily cloaked figures, their faces obscured by densely knitted cables. But the last one—long arms dragging something massive—is huge and misshapen, his rough skin as red as clay.

"A golem," I gasp aloud, past caring whether Kyril knows if there are monsters in the world or not. Only later do I realize that if Kyril were truly mundane, the silencing spell thwarting my voice would have kept me from telling him that.

Kyril tightens his grip on the door. "He's about to unleash a data scourge."

"A data scourge?" Completely lethal to witches, scourges are so rare I only know about them by reputation. They release storms of toxic fields, leveling entire magical communities. Has this scourge been brought to destroy Arcanos Hall?

"We can't go out there," Kyril says. "If the soldiers don't kill us, the scourge will poison us in minutes."

"Can you lock it?" I have no idea whether I should trust him or not. What was he doing in the boiler in the first place? Was he the one who sabotaged the castle shields?

Kyril grits his teeth, clinging to the inside of the wheel joint. His fingers are covered with jeweled rings. Blood soaks the neckband of his reflective silver hoodie, wet and real and close enough for me to touch. Outside the boiler, a deafening thud shakes the ground as something heavy falls.

Then a man's voice grates in our ears, harsh and cruel, like stone scraping stone. "Release the storm."

CHAPTER TEN

Just three days ago, my concerns in life were few. When I wasn't knitting my fingers raw, I was avoiding Ruskin, saving my silver to buy enchanted wool, and fretting because my students and colleagues despised me. How ridiculous it all seems, considering I'm now banished, trapped in an abandoned boiler with an exceedingly dangerous man, and menaced by a heartless golem, a deadly data scourge threatening to destroy me forever.

I tighten my shawl around my head. The metal walls of the boiler are helping to block the electromagnetic fields, but I can tell I'm being exposed to dangerous levels of technology. The taste of copper grits across my tongue.

Kyril's nails dig hard into the rusty rivets holding the door in place. The small moonstone cabochon on his index finger shines brighter, as if it's being illuminated from within. A star gleams in the center of the stone. Abruptly, the stone cracks.

"Locked," he whispers, shedding the ring into his pocket. He slumps against the wall of the boiler and wraps his arms around his knees.

Relieved, I pick up the torch and examine our new home.

Green-tinted rust peels from the curved interior of the boiler walls. Narrow steam vents are visible near the top. As far as I can tell, this boiler (and the coal furnace below) hasn't been used in decades.

Kyril's computer rests on a tripod in the middle of the boiler, its screen flickering with patches of white and gray, like a blizzard at dusk. Something tells me it's malfunctioning. Above it, a stream of blue light twists and coils like an incandescent worm.

Outside the boiler, I can hear the golem stomping around the furnace room. Bound to obedience and crafted from living clay, golems have no hearts, no minds of their own. They exist only to follow orders, and they kill anything in their way.

The heavy object the golem was carrying emits a low, humming sound. If it's a data scourge, then the golem must be completely contaminated by now. There's no armor in the world that can withstand prolonged exposure to fields that strong. The golem was sent here to die.

Beside me, Kyril is quiet, as seemingly defenseless as he was earlier, when lying sprawled on the ground. With his eyes closed, he appears almost childlike. I wonder how good his senses are, whether they're better when his eyes are closed.

Kyril's no ordinary mundane. He may be able to use technology without suffering harm, but he clearly wields magic as well. That moonstone cabochon on his finger was an asterism, one of the most valuable gemstone charms. But what kind of wizard is he? I've never heard of a mage who could use technology. The whole point of using shields and armor is that magic and technology are antithetical.

A sudden pounding outside the boiler causes my ears to ring. The curved walls begin to quake, a sickening vibration pulsing through the metal with every blow. The noise penetrates to the very center of my chest.

"The golem is digging into the wall," Kyril whispers, his body not moving.

Why? I mouth the word, not willing to trust myself to speak.

Kyril opens one eye. "To amplify the storm."

I try to remember what I was doing before Kyril appeared inside the boiler, before the golem arrived with his toxic transmitter. I was trying to reach Rocco. I was trying to find a way into The Isthmus. I was going to call upon the water spirit guarding the gate.

"There's power here," I whisper, as bricks continue to fall. "Deep in the earth."

Kyril nods and pulls away from the boiler wall. "The guardians are holding the reins. I tried creating a worm to penetrate the firewall, but the castle wards wouldn't let me find any vulnerability to exploit. My spells all went to pieces." With a sigh, he closes his computer and slips it into a mesh satchel. The glowing blue worm flickers out.

I don't know what a worm or a firewall is, but wards and spells are words I understand. I don't trust Kyril, and I'm certain he doesn't trust me, but at least we're speaking the same language. Mostly. "Why were you trying to break in?"

"I wasn't trying to break in. I just wanted to see if it could be done."

"Why would you do that?"

Kyril rubs his eyes with his fists, a gesture eloquent of fatigue. "I manage risk. It's what I do." He doesn't say whose risk he's managing, which makes me wonder.

"Well, if you couldn't get in," I whisper, "the golem shouldn't, either. That means the wards are working."

He shakes his head. "The golem isn't trying to get in: he's trying to flood The Isthmus with toxic fields. All he needs for that is to draw upon the ley lines."

Ley lines? And he said The Isthmus. I pause for a moment to let that sink in.

Who is this man, and how does he know so much about our community?

The pounding outside continues. Golems have fists like jack-hammers. I take a breath, deciding that limited, short-term trust is the only thing that will keep me alive, or save my friends from the data storm.

"Whoever made this golem sent him here to die," I tell Kyril. "Which means they were willing to sacrifice a priceless weapon to compromise the castle."

Kyril arches an eyebrow. "Technically, a golem is not alive."

I give him a dirty look. Pedantry does not please me. "If I can make a web portal, I can get past the wards. The water spirit will open the gate for me. We can get inside, warn everyone to evacuate, find some help."

This surprises Kyril, and for a moment his weariness drops away, and I glimpse a trace of the playful man I met in the woods of the Lakeshore Preserve.

"The guardians will open the gate for you?" He favors me with an almost sunny grin. "You must be very special."

"You'd better believe it."

I'd rather not tell him I'm a banished professor, and at this point a criminal.

Kyril gestures toward the steam vents in the back of the boiler. "Those vents don't lead anywhere. A few yards in, the pipes have been pulled out, filled with clay and stone. The ley lines are close. If it's even possible to create a portal, that would be the place."

I rise cautiously and peer up at the steam vents. They look uncomfortably narrow. Kyril has broad shoulders, and I've got my share of curves.

"I don't know," I whisper back. "Can we fit into the vents?"

"I did when I tried to open a back door." Kyril pauses. "We can't stay here. Sooner or later, the golem will dig as far as the ley lines. And before that happens, those vents will be exposed to open air. We'll have nothing—no metal or stone—protecting us from the storm outside."

He doesn't need to say more. I know what the storm could do to us. In vain, I try not to think of the homeless witches I once saw in Minneapolis. I try not to think about their beaten, empty eyes. For a moment, I'm paralyzed by fear. Then I make a decision.

I reach for my precious ball of angora. I've held onto this yarn since I was twelve, because there never was a spell worthy of its power. Unknit, yarn is infinite with possibility, coiled with delicious potential. But now the time has come to use it.

"All right," I say. "I can create a web portal. It might just work. But I'm going to need a gemstone to stabilize it, if you're going to travel in my wake. And you will owe me a ball of yarn."

"You can make a portal with just a ball of yarn?" Kyril is shocked. "Is that possible?"

I glare. "Just a ball of yarn? My dying mother spun this yarn by hand from angoras she raised herself. Do you have any idea how hard it is to groom a magic bunny?"

I jab an impatient finger at his glittering array of jeweled rings. "If you want me to get you past the wards, you will give me the best gemstone you have left. You will owe me a ball of yarn. And you will agree to be in my debt."

There's a moment of silence as he takes this in. Whoever he is, he apparently knows enough about hedge witches to recognize he's facing a critical moment. Hedge witches never place people under direct obligation. Not unless they mean to call in the favor someday, in a very big way. The golem pounds into the wall as Kyril searches my face.

"I accept your terms," he finally says. "I will owe you a ball of yarn, and I will agree to be in your life debt." He reaches under the bloodstained neckband of his shirt and withdraws a gold chain. Hanging from the end of the chain is a star sapphire ring.

He snaps the gold chain and thrusts the ring into my hand. "This was my mother's ring. Now get us out of here."

The star sapphire is the most magnificent cabochon I've ever seen. It's an old stone, elegantly set with split prongs in a platinum bezel. Larger than a hazelnut, the sapphire is a perfect asterism. Linear threads within the stone form a lustrous, translucent star. Those threads are going to come in handy.

I swiftly measure the outline of the steam vent and cast on to make an airy spiral web, using my largest rosewood needles. A web portal is a primitive, dangerous spell, and I've never actually made one before. The prospect terrifies me.

When I was a girl, my mother told me once how she crafted a web portal to escape a sweatshop in Appalachia. This was before she met my dad, before King Nestor wrote the edict freeing the indentured hedge workers of the West. It was a wrenching, primal spell, drawn directly from the chaos in the earth, but she had to do it. She had to get free.

Kyril is quiet and unusually patient, watching my needles fly. There's no time to put in a lifeline, no time to check my gauge. The noise from the digging is still audible, but the boiler doesn't shake as much, because the golem is now deep into the rock. I'm worried this means the toxic fields from the data scourge will reach the steam vents and the ley lines before we do. But worrying isn't going to help. Right now, all I can do is build a web.

"You used a Fibonacci sequence," Kyril abruptly says when I'm done, his voice a harsh whisper. I look up at him, surprised. Then I slip my needles free and thread his star sapphire through the center of the web, breaking the yarn with my teeth.

"I thought those lace spirals were random," he said. "But you were adding up the sum of the last two repeats, every single time. Do you really think this can work?"

I shrug. "We're at least thirty feet underground. If the web breaks, we'll die instantly, crushed by the weight of the earth."

His lips curve into a smile. "How comforting."

"Right," I say, bracing against the boiler wall as I get to my feet. "Let's do this."

I'm not a claustrophobic person. I can handle living in a windowless dungeon, in a converted missile silo. I can handle being trapped in a boiler with a dangerous stranger. But wedging myself into a steam vent with said stranger is really the last straw.

"I don't think we can fit," I gasp, as Kyril boosts me up into the steam vent and climbs in behind me. My flying carpet lies abandoned beside Kyril's computer, and the luminescent torch is uncomfortably wedged into my cleavage. "I can't breathe."

"It's probably better if you don't breathe," Kyril hisses, shoving me forward. "More room for me. Tell me when you reach the end of the pipe."

The end of the pipe abruptly appears right in front of me. It's a wall of compacted clay, inches in front of my nose. "Here," I whisper, unfolding the angora web. "It's here."

Illuminated by my fading torch, a deep crack begins to forms across the clay surface. A deafening thud shakes the steam vent, and the fissure in the clay deepens.

"We have to do this now," Kyril says. "The golem has almost reached the vent."

"But it isn't going to work!" I struggle to stretch the web spiral across the fracture in the earth. "There's not enough stability to ground the web."

"Can you make it through without me?" Kyril's voice is unnaturally calm.

"Of course I can," I snap, beginning to panic. "But that wasn't the deal we made. You're supposed to travel in my wake. You have to be able to reach the stone."

There's a long pause. I have no idea what Kyril's thinking.

"Then I'll reach the stone." He snakes forward in the steam vent, his masculine body uncomfortably close. He smells like blood and metal. I feel myself flattened against the flaking, rusty wall. I can barely draw a breath. I'm pretty sure I'm going to suffocate.

Kyril barks out a strangled laugh. "I'm afraid I'll have to put my arms around you. If that's alright."

"If you must," I manage, the words barely coming out.

Kyril inches forward, one silver-clad arm slipping around my waist, the other curving behind my hair to reach the stone.

"At the very least," he says, "It will be an interesting way to die."

I want to tell him to shut up, but I can't breathe at all. My peripheral vision sparks and unexpectedly fades out. I close my eyes, and then all at once the path before me becomes clear. I see threads of power lying deep inside the earth—long striated ley lines of magical fields, endless and perfect. Then the web portal opens, and the bird effigy and the water spirit both rise up to greet me, tails stretching toward the lake, wings reaching for the night sky.

We land with a crash in the steam tunnels of Arcanos Hall. We're in a dimly lit room, perfectly oval. Towering in front of us is an ancient machine.

Kyril pushes himself away as if I were somehow poisonous. "Are you all right?"

"Fine," I say, too distracted to be bothered by his behavior. My eyes are on the machine in front of me. It must be the legendary Drini that shields The Isthmus.

The Drini is not a loom. It's not a mechanical knitting device, either. But it's obviously some kind of textile machine. It's a giant contraption, with a single enormous needle poised above my head, like a deadly rapier caught mid-thrust. A clockwork carriage device connects the Drini to the copper pipes leading to the furnace room. The carriage is scorched with peat ash and smoke—clear evidence that it's been set on fire from within. But there's no sign of yarn or thread. And why is there only one needle?

I'm still trying to sort this out when a woman dressed in black storms into the shield room, clutching a polished wooden staff. A long black braid swings about her shoulders.

It's Kirsten Aradottir.

"On your knees," she shouts, aiming her staff at my chest.

I drop to the ground, certain that this is the end, the absolute end. But Kyril hurls himself against Aradottir, knocking the Ice Captain off balance. "Stop!"

Aradottir immediately jumps back into a fighting stance, about to blast Kyril to bits. Then she drops her weapon with a resounding clang. "You!"

Dumbfounded, I stare at Kyril, who has fallen to his knees, both hands raised above his head. It's clear that he and the Ice Captain know each other. But how?

"I surrender," he says, lacing his fingers together. "I'm unarmed."

She scowls, taking in Kyril's jeweled rings and metallic jacket, not to mention the dried streaks of blood on his neck. "What are you doing here? How did you get in?"

Kyril's face is grim. "The castle wards are collapsing. There's a golem in the steam tunnels to the south. He's breaking through with a data scourge."

"A data scourge?" Aradottir blanches. "How much time do we have?"

"An hour, no more."

She wavers, eyes filled with sorrow, as if caught up in a memory. Then she steels herself. "I'll take care of it."

"You can't!" Kyril cries. "You have to evacuate the students. You must find volunteers."

I realize with horror that the volunteers in question will have to destroy what's left of the golem and defuse the data scourge. Even with the best shields, the toxic exposure could cost them all their magical power, possibly even breaking their minds.

Resolute, she retrieves her staff, points it in my direction.

"This woman. Is she your collaborator? Or your captive?"

For one blissful moment, I imagine that Kyril will morph into some kind of hero. He'll say that he took me captive, that he forced me to help him enter the castle. Or he'll say that I'm innocent, that I helped him detect the golem. He'll beg Aradottir to let me go.

But Kyril doesn't do any such thing. "I found her trying to break in."

Aradottir flicks her staff toward the door. "To the dungeons, witch."

Her focus shifts to Kyril. "You were never here. I want you outside the castle. Now."

"What?" Anger bubbles up like an overflowing cauldron. "I'm going to the dungeons, and he's free to leave? You bastard, Kyril! You're in my debt."

Kyril stands and flexes his fingers. "I'll remember that. Later."

Again, she brandishes her weapon. "Get moving, both of you."

"I'm out of here." With a final glance at the scorched Drini, Kyril hurries out of the room.

"You can't leave like this!" I shriek as he disappears into the corridor. "You owe me a ball of yarn!"

CHAPTER ELEVEN

Okay, so now I'm in jail, thanks in part to that treacherous idiot Kyril. Unfortunately, imprisonment is the least of my problems. Kirsten Aradottir has sent her men to evacuate the castle, which will soon be flooded with toxic fields, which means I'm still in mortal danger. So is Rocco. Across the dungeon corridor, he peers out through the bars of his cell, his face covered with gray stubble, his eyes bloodshot from lack of sleep.

Aradottir slams the door to my cell. "You'll stay here until I can find a volunteer to take out that golem."

"Urmph!" Rocco cries, a thick hand gesturing at the lock on his cell door.

She regards him dispassionately. "Are you trying to volunteer?"

"No!" I cry, but Rocco doesn't seem to hear me. He nods his head up and down.

The Ice Captain considers, her gaze flicking skeptically over his massive form. I can see that she's weighing the risk of releasing him against his obvious physical strength.

"You understand the dangers?" she finally asks. "You'll be provided with charms, but they may not withstand the data storm."

"Urmph!" Rocco grips the bars of his cell.

"No!" I cry. "You can't do this!" Trolls are fully magical beings. The storm will kill him for sure.

She holds up her key. "You'll be released on one condition only: you must destroy the golem and contain the storm. Will you perform this task?"

"Urmph!" Rocco nods vigorously, gripping the bars of his cell.

"Come with me," she says, unlocking the rusty door. "And prepare to take a vow."

I extend my arms through the bars. "Rocco?"

Rocco's calloused fingers scratch against my skin, his hand closing around mine. I gaze up at him, too exhausted to speak. Rocco is leaving—possibly to his death—and there's nothing I can do.

Then a familiar voice breaks the silence. "I'll take over from here, Captain."

Her braid swinging in an arc, she snaps around to face the new arrival. It's the dean. Accompanied by Aradottir's pasty-faced guardsmen, he's dressed for dangerous work: his silver hair covered by a thick hood, a HazMat cloak with heavy knitted protection cables hanging from his stooped shoulders. He's carrying a roll of parchment and a carved box, most likely filled with powerful charms.

"You and your men must evacuate the students at once. I will deal with the storm."

"You're sure about this?" Aradottir's voice betrays the barest hint of an emotion. It might be surprise: it might even be respect. She darts a glance at the shorter, beetle-shaped guard, who acknowledges her with a curt nod. Like the dean, he's heavily shielded.

"Very sure," says Dean LaMarche. "See to the students, and leave Miss Winter behind bars."

"Leave me?" I can't believe what I'm hearing. Neither can Aradottir.

He ignores this. "Leave her. Let it be known she's in custody."

For a moment, no one moves. Then Aradottir inclines her head in a formal bow. "As you wish. But if you fail to contain the storm, you know what I must do."

His face is grave. "Understood."

Her gaze shifts to Rocco, a slight frown on her face. For a moment, she hesitates. Then she sprints up the stairs, leaving silence in her wake. Her soldiers follow in asymmetrical unison, one hurrying on short legs, the other as gangly as a stick insect.

Dean LaMarche hands Rocco the coil of parchment. "Retrieve my treasure, and bring this report to King Nestor. Do not be seen."

"Urmph!" Rocco grips the parchment and departs, the dean reaching up to touch his arm as he goes by.

I exhale, not sure what just happened. "Sir, did you just let Rocco go? Does Aradottir know—?"

"Anya," says Dean LaMarche, his voice dropping to a whisper. "I may not see you again, so I need to tell you this now. Rocco's heading south to the Sandia Mountains. I'll take care of the storm."

This is impossible. The dean is an old man. He shouldn't be volunteering for any mission, let alone a single-handed encounter with a golem and a data storm.

"But what about your magic? Your sanity! Have you thought about what the storm could do to you?"

"Never mind that. I have access to the most powerful weapons in the world. I must use them to protect . . . what I love. I've failed in every other way."

"Sir, please don't talk like that. You haven't failed." I don't know why I'm consoling him, when I'm the one who feels betrayed.

Dean LaMarche sighs, the lines on his cheeks deepening into furrows. "Let me tell you what happens when you get old. You become complacent. You take it all for granted—the security and the freedom you worked so hard for when you were young."

"You're not old, sir." This is obviously a lie, but the dean could use some cheering up. I mean, really. I thought I was depressed.

"I'm not talking about myself. I'm talking about The Isthmus. We've grown careless here: we've felt safe for too long. You must find a way to fix the shields, Anya. You have to turn this around. But first, tell me everything you know."

In a rush, I describe what I saw in the steam tunnels. But for some reason, I decide not to mention Kyril. Not because I feel any loyalty. Certainly not. It's just that I need to keep something in reserve.

"But what about me?" I conclude, belatedly aggrieved as I realize I'm still behind bars. "Why did you tell Captain Aradottir to leave me here?"

"Never mind that." He produces a delicate silver key. "Take this, and use it when the time is right."

I reach through the bars for the key. "How will I know when the time is right?"

He laughs, a strained mixture of bitterness and mirth. "When you know who's trying to tear this university apart."

"But what about you? What about your magical powers?"

He gives me a weary smile. "They're gone, Anya. As good as gone."

He hurries away, his thick black cloak flapping soundlessly in the narrow corridor. I watch him go, trying to understand. *They're as good as gone.*

As soon as the dean is out of sight, I slip his silver key into the corroded clockwork lock on my cell door. It doesn't fit. I try to think about what's just happened, and it's all too much. I want to help Rocco and the dean, but I don't have any spells. I don't have any yarn. I have a key, but it doesn't work. This is Kyril's fault, whoever the hell he is.

Actually, that's not fair. Kyril isn't the problem. Someone else is trying to destroy Arcanos Hall, along with everyone inside. And by doing so, they're trying to destroy the university itself—The Isthmus and all it represents. The shields were clearly sabotaged, and no one knows how to fix them. Ruskin's new wards are deteriorating, which should not be happening. And this data scourge is the dirtiest, cruelest weapon of all.

Who would do such a thing? If I stay here in prison, I'm never going to find out.

I stare at the dean's silver key, wondering what I'm supposed to do with it.

I don't know who Dean LaMarche is. That's a very strange realization to have. I don't understand what motivates him. There's so much about him that doesn't make sense, like his obsession with that mysterious painting of the empty red gown. Or his willingness to help me, to help Rocco. Surely, he's left me in this cell for a reason. I just wish I understood why.

Exhausted, I collapse on the bench. It must be two o'clock in the morning, maybe even later. I'm hungry, and tired to the bone.

Just when I think my mood couldn't possibly get any worse, the scent of sandalwood fills the air. His sideburns as sharp as dueling blades, Ruskin breezes into the dungeon. He's dressed for evacuation protocols, wearing a long, hooded cloak and a slouchy newsboy cap. He has a fine, Turkish-made carpetbag tucked under his arm.

I lean back against the granite wall and plant my feet on the floor. "Get out."

"My dear Anya," he breathes. "I'm ever so sorry to see you in this state. Kirsten Aradottir is threatening to blow up the university—she doesn't have any faith in my wards. And she says she's just going to leave you here. Poor girl! I came as soon as I could."

"I have no complaints," I say with a shrug. "These dungeons are clean and dry—pretty nice compared to my chambers down the hall. In fact, if I ever get my old job back, I'm going to see if I can move into the prison wing."

He grimaces elegantly. "How can you be so naïve? You're not going to get your old job back. Not when you're suspected of committing sabotage."

"Sabotage?"

"The dean and I have tried our best to be advocates for you. But the students are evacuating, the faculty in a panic. Aradottir is determined to find a scapegoat."

"A scapegoat? Like Rocco?"

This pulls Ruskin up short. Uneasy, he makes a half-turn in the direction of Rocco's cell. "Where is Rocco?"

"Don't know," I say, without a trace of emotion. "The dean took him away."

Ruskin pauses, and then reacts with impressive pathos. "That's *terrible*. And now that you've defied your banishment, it's only a matter of time before they punish you, as well."

"You know what? I don't care if they punish me."

"But *I* care. What is it about you that makes me want to break all the rules? Against my better judgment, against all my instincts, I must set you free."

"Are you kidding?" That sounds too good to be true. "I'm not going anywhere with you. I'd rather be flogged at dawn." But if I stay here, the data storm could destroy all my magical powers. It could even break my spirit.

Ruskin rests a manicured hand on the bar of my cell. "You mustn't blame me for my role in sending you away. I didn't trust that Ice Captain. I was afraid she'd put you in prison—perhaps even send you to some awful chain gang in the Rockies. My dear Anya, she's obsessed with magical security. She's looking for any excuse. To protect our community, she now wants to burn the castle down. She might even leave you here to die, and I couldn't bear that."

I narrow my eyes. "What about Rocco? Could you bear seeing *him* die?"

Ruskin shakes his head, miserable. "I can't save everyone. Sometimes you have to make the hard choices." He extracts a small crystal vial from under his cloak.

"What's that?" I push away from the bench and approach the door. "Poison?"

"Poison? You *wound* me. I would never do anything to hurt you."

He unscrews the silver stopper, and at once a distinctively clean, juniper scent fills the stale dungeon air. "*Angelica archangelica*. The Holy Ghost, they call it. Harvested from a fairy glen on the Lofoten Islands."

Astonished, I suck in my breath. *Angelica archangelica* is the most magical of potions, named for the highest of angels, and devilishly hard to distill.

"Just drink this potion. You'll dissolve into the ether. Undetected, you can follow me to safety. Do you remember my cabin in the woods? Do you remember how you once loved me?" His eyes grow glassy and moist. "We had such plans, Anya. Please tell me you haven't forgotten."

Damn, but his charisma spells are good.

I inhale the clean, gin-like scent, considering. "How much time do we have?"

His lips curve seductively. "Once you're free, we'll have all the time in the world."

"I mean, how much time before I have to decide? Is Aradottir really going to torch Arcanos Hall? Are you *planning* for your wards to fail?"

Ruskin frowns, uncertain about this line of conversation. He closes the stopper on his vial, and the scent of gin and freedom fades away.

"You seem determined to believe the worst of me."

"And you seem determined to send me away from The Isthmus. All that bullshit last spring—trying to get me fired? And now this?"

"Yes," he says. "And now this."

Something happens then that I don't expect. Ruskin's glossy hair fades to a muddy brown, and his burnished skin grows rough and ashen. I've never seen him this way.

He draws a ragged breath and looks into my eyes. "I'm not perfect, Anya. And I know I haven't always treated you right. I shouldn't have tried to send you away last spring. I should have told the truth about our relationship and accepted the dean's reprimand. I'm a selfish creature. I realize that. But I do love you."

"What?"

He rubs his forehead, which seems more worn and weathered than it did before. "I didn't always love you. I mean: at first I just wanted to use you. And then I got rather attached to lying to you, which was an amazing turn-on, believe me."

He frowns a little, as if surprised. "Now I just want you safely out of the way."

All I can do is stare. Ruskin's legendary charisma has been stripped away, replaced by a real person who apparently really loves me, which is completely screwed up.

Either that, or he's the best con artist I've ever seen.

"You're a terrible person, Ruskin." As I say this, I realize that his shoulders are relaxed, his manner unhurried. He's not counting every minute; he's not desperate to leave. Which means that whatever else he's done, he couldn't possibly have unleashed the golem and the scourge. He doesn't know how close the storm is.

"Terrible?" Ruskin smiles breezily, his charisma spells sliding back into place. "Oh, yes. I know." He stoops down and nudges the vial of *A. archangelica* through the food slot on the floor. "You don't have to come away with me. But if Kirsten Aradottir decides to destroy Arcanos Hall, please drink this potion and find your way out. Before it's too late."

Curled up on my prison bench with the potion and the silver key tucked in my smock, I'm still reeling from Ruskin's attempt to break me out of prison, when yet another unscrupulous man arrives to break me out of prison. This time, it's Kyril.

He rushes in, too edgy and urgent to appear entirely self-possessed. He's a bloodstained mess, but his jeweled rings flash in the dim light. He's carrying something new, obviously supplied by Aradottir: a large canvas rucksack with long Icelandic words printed in block letters.

"Anya Winter," he says with a decent attempt at insouciance, leaning back against the bars of Rocco's empty cell. "Daughter of a hedge witch. And a scientist."

It's all I can do to keep from rolling my eyes. "Not just a scientist: a goddamn physicist. And if you're going to give me a bad time about my parentage, you should know right now that I don't give a damn."

He dangles a gold locket from a chain. "Thought you might want to call in your favor."

"Jewelry? Are you kidding me?"

"It's not a trinket; it's freedom."

"If you think you can get out of your life debt simply by letting me out of prison, you're very wrong. I'm staying here, and you're going to owe me a favor."

Kyril folds his arms across his chest. "That could be risky. The data storm is dangerously close, and the castle wards are collapsing. If they fail, Arcanos Hall will be unshielded, completely visible to mundanes. You know Kirsten Aradottir will never let that happen. She'll destroy The Isthmus first, along with everything inside."

"I'll take my chances." I'm still wondering who Kyril is, how he knows all this. "But you took a huge chance, agreeing to be in my debt, because I'm not in a forgiving mood. Your pal Aradottir just sent my friend Rocco into danger. Because apparently hedge workers like me and Rocco are expendable."

Uncrossing his arms, Kyril takes a step closer. "I'm truly sorry about that."

"Sorry isn't enough. Do you know what what's going to happen

110

to you if Rocco doesn't make it safely back?"

"I'll spend the rest of my life repaying you." His voice grows so soft, I have to strain to hear. His head droops, eyes in shadow. "You must love this Rocco very much."

I understand suddenly why the dean left me locked in this cell. It's the person behind the bars who has all the power.

"You can pay me back right now. Tell me who you are. Tell me how you know Captain Aradottir. And tell me who sent that golem here with the data storm."

Kyril's head jerks up, his features grim with fury. "If I knew that, I'd be hunting the villain down. I wouldn't be wasting my time with you."

"So I'm a waste of time, am I? And what exactly are you?"

His face closed off, Kyril thrusts the locket through the bars of my cell and lets it fall. "I'm done here, Anya Winter. That's what I am."

Alone in my cell, I contemplate my options. Frankly, I'm finding imprisonment rather interesting. I have a key, a vial of potion, and a gold locket, and I've only been in jail for fifteen minutes.

Above my head, I can hear the muffled pounding of footsteps on the Grand Staircase. They must be sending my students to the roof: Princess Elena, Baron Fob and his cronies, Bertha Bratsch. I wonder if Bertha is actually here, or if Madame Olann helped her sneak off-campus, yesterday after class.

I pry open Kyril's locket and peer inside. It contains a mechanical scarab: expensive as hell and ugly as a redcap, but ideal for eating the metal out of a magical lock.

I close the locket and reach again for Ruskin's crystal vial. Kyril may have amazing cheekbones, but it's Ruskin who wins first prize in the fancy gift department. Gingerly, I unscrew the vial, and once more the clean, juniper-like scent floods my cell. It really is *Angelica archangelica*, the most marvelous of potions, and Ruskin really did give it to me. One sip of the distilled herb, and I could be as free as a leaf, floating in the ether, drifting for up to a hundred feet before I regain my corporeal form. I mean, what else could the potion be?

That question pulls me up short. For some reason, I'm reminded of my father and his wearisome bedtime stories about The World Of Technology And Its Many Dangers. He once told me a story about a computer virus that was invisibly embedded into a helpful program designed to destroy other viruses. The experts couldn't detect the hidden virus, because they didn't know how to read the helpful program down to the lowest levels of its code. Stupid experts: their computers all died. The End.

I had such a great childhood.

Slipping Ruskin's potion back into my smock, I pace in tight circles around my cell. I don't know how to analyze potions at all. Just because something looks and smells like *A. archangelica* and promises to transport you safely into the ether, doesn't mean there isn't something else in the potion as well. Only Ruskin would know that. Only he knows how to analyze a potion down to the deepest molecular level.

He did say he wanted me safely out of the way. He just didn't say what that meant.

As for Kyril's scarab, I can't be sure that will work properly, either. I'm not an expert in clockwork. What if the scarab doesn't eat the metal out of the lock? What if it crawls up my nostril and eats my face instead? Scarabs have been known to do such things.

My father always said you have to watch your back. But you also have to watch your nostrils, if scarabs are around. Dad just didn't know about those.

I tug the dean's silver key out of my pocket, snagging it on the rough linen fabric. Of the three men who just gave me gifts, only Dean LaMarche is trustworthy, and I already know his key doesn't work. But he didn't say it was for getting me out of prison.

He wanted me to stay here until I learned the truth.

I'm still trying to process this thought when yet another person arrives to break me out of prison. This time, it's Princess Elena.

CHAPTER TWELVE

Anya!" Elena comes rushing in with a rustle of taffeta. She's wearing an exquisite chain mail cap with sharply pointed cat ears, knitted from delicate strands of gold. "I've come to help you escape!"

Once again, it's all I can do to keep from rolling my eyes. "Really? Who told you I was in prison? And why aren't you on the roof with the rest of the students?"

The princess digs into her purse, and a jumble of charms and gemstones spills to the ground. "Ruskin told us you were here. He said you tried to sabotage the university. Is that true?"

I have to hand it to the dean: he's far craftier than I ever thought. Every wizard in Wisconsin is coming to the dungeons to confront me.

"What do you think?" I say, determined to find out what Elena knows. "If it's true, then I'm a dangerous criminal and you really shouldn't be offering to help. Use your brain, Elena. If you've even got one."

Her aristocratic veneer returns at once. "Ungrateful witch!"

I curl my upper lip with scorn. "You sound just like Lord Burke."

The cold hauteur vanishes, replaced by a flash of fear. "Lord Burke?"

"But shouldn't you be calling him Simon? Since the two of you are getting married and everything."

"Please," she begs, her voice edging into panic. "Please forget I called you names. You must let me help you."

"Why?"

"Because I'm in your debt, you idiot!"

"You've already helped me enough. You gave me the sultan's coin, and I used it to break in. We're even." I shake my head. "Seriously, you don't want to compromise yourself any further. You should be on the roof right now, ready to evacuate. Go away."

Elena sinks to the dungeon floor and bursts into tears. I don't know what I expected from her, but I certainly didn't expect this.

"No!" she wails, shoving the charms into her purse. "I can't do this! Don't make me do this!"

"Elena? In case you haven't noticed, I'm in a dungeon, trapped by a magical lock. I'm not in any position to make anyone do anything." As I crouch down, she reaches through the bars and grips my hand, like it's her only lifeline.

A wave of desperation crashes over me as well. Maybe I should accept Elena's help. I'm not sure I can get out of here on my own. If the dean can't take care of that data scourge, I could end up compromised by technology. Once broken, my magical powers will stay broken forever. Even worse, I could go mad. And that's assuming the castle isn't blown up, with me locked inside.

Elena continues gripping my hand, and her shoulders shake. "I can't marry him. I *won't*. You don't know what it means to me, this shabby little college with its horrible students and its nasty, overcooked food. The Isthmus—it's all I have left."

She lifts her head, her eyes welling. "Now they're on the roof, leaving in groups of ten. Soon he'll realize I've gone. I've got no place left to go. He'll try to make me go back with him."

She takes in a hissing breath. "So I'm running away, and you're coming with me."

I tug my hand from her grasp. "Do you realize how selfish you are? The university could be destroyed. People will be homeless. Every magical volume in the library will be gone forever. And you're worried about your own problems?"

I know I'm being cruel. In my heart, I pity Elena. I can't imagine being a princess, expected to marry a malevolent creep like Burke. But I must find out what she knows.

She winces. "Yes, I'm a selfish person. My own problems matter more to me than other people's problems. Is that so wrong? Is that so strange?"

To be perfectly honest, that's not so very strange at all.

"Why does King Cibrán want you to marry Burke?"

"Why do you think? Money! The monarchy is bankrupt, and Burke has been financing everything. We've got to pay him back somehow."

"You don't have to pay him back: your father does. This is the twenty-first century. Why can't you choose your own spouse?"

"It's impossible." Elena's face closes off.

"Why is it so impossible?"

"It's completely impossible. It's easier to imagine the end of the world." She digs her polished nails into her temples, briefly closing her eyes.

Then she takes a breath. "There was someone I once knew, who really understood me, who saw me as more than just Cibrán's heir. And I thought that if I ever . . . but it wouldn't have worked out, you see? Because things don't work out for me. And I thought I was okay with that. But then today I saw her again, and it all came back."

"What are you talking about? Who did you see?"

"Never mind. The point is that it wouldn't have worked out, because of who I am, because of what she does. She works for the royal house of the West, and I will never be anything but an Eastern princess. I have this life that I'm living, and it all looks so glamorous, but none of the good parts are real. What's real is that I have responsibilities and I don't have any options."

"Elena, you always have options."

Before she can respond, a metallic clang reverberates through the stairwell. Someone's at the top of the stairs, tugging open the heavy door. "Elena!"

Elena turns pale. "It's Burke. You have to get me out of here!"

"I thought you were going to get me out of here."

"He mustn't find me!"

"Your invisibility cape!"

"We used it for the shroud. I didn't buy a new one. And now it's too late!"

I reach inside my smock, retrieving Ruskin's vial. The magical potion glistens through the crystal facets, treacherous and inviting. Hesitantly, I slip it through the bars. "Ruskin gave me this. He claims it's *A. archangelica*."

Her eyes widen. "*A. archangelica*?"

"So he says. But he could be lying. He's betrayed me before."

Elena seizes the vial and unscrews the stopper. The scent of juniper floods the dungeon. "I'll drink it."

"But we don't know . . . "

"Ruskin loves you. He may be a conniving jerk, but he loves you. I can tell."

She tips back her head and gulps the entire potion down. Immediately, she fades into the ether, and I'm left staring at a shuddering black-and-white afterimage that's completely uncharacteristic of *A. archangelica*. Flowing locks of silver have replaced Elena's raven hair, and a honeycomb of shadows with cat ears flickers where her gold beret had been. Then there's nothing left.

Burke storms into the dungeon. His beard is unruly, his gloved hands clenched into fists. Gone are the scarlet robes of the Inner

Council, replaced by a heavy black cloak, the kind you wear for a long-distance portage. A densely cabled hood hangs from his shoulders. I don't have time to think about what that means.

He strides toward my cell, his movements urgent, his face suffused with rage.

"Where's my princess?" he snarls, waving an impressive ivory wand.

"Don't know," I say, slipping my hands into my skirt pockets. "She just left."

"Tell me where she's gone! Tell me what you know, and I'll let you live."

The floor buckles, and a flash illuminates the entire dungeon, both clear signs of a powerful Stone Maelstrom spell. Which should be impossible to cast within these walls, unless . . . unless he knows the wards protecting the castle have already failed.

"I don't know where she went!" I repeat, fumbling for Kyril's locket. That damned scarab had better not eat my face. "She disappeared. I can't tell you what I don't know!"

He raises his wand to cast a killing spell, but I flip open the locket and brandish Kyril's scarab with all the menace I can muster. "If you strike me, this scarab will detonate, killing us both."

A smile tightens Burke's lips. "Fine. Stay here and rot."

The stones beneath his feet abruptly collapse, tipping him into a swirling vortex, as the entire dungeon corridor becomes a narrow funnel of swiftly moving stone.

"Goodbye, little witch." With a triumphant leer, Burke pulls the cabled hood over his head and disappears into the vortex.

CHAPTER THIRTEEN

We often imagine ourselves in moments of moral crisis, wondering if we'll have the strength or the courage to do the right thing. Would you risk your life to save a lost princess? Would you jeopardize your health to save a priceless castle from ruin? You're probably hoping the answer to both questions is yes. You're probably hoping you're brave enough to make the right choice. But the truth is, most moral crises come with complexity attached. We're forced to choose which one to save: the princess or the castle.

Watching the dust settle from the Stone Maelstrom, I realize that blisters are forming on the inside of my mouth. It's toxic radiation from the data storm, seeping up from the tunnels below. Automatically, I tighten my shawl around my ears, feeling the fabric crackle and fray. I need to get out of this prison cell fast, before my armor fails, before I lose all my powers, before I go mad. But what to do after that?

Elena has been spirited away into the ether, and not just for a short hop. Only Ruskin would know where she's gone. But the dean is in the steam tunnels alone, facing the data scourge. Which one of them needs me more? I don't just need the courage to do the right thing: I need to know what it means to do the right thing.

I press open Kyril's locket and release the scarab. I don't like machines at all—not even clockwork charms. But I don't have any other options. This had better work.

The scarab twists inside its locket, fixing me with its cold, mechanical gaze, as if trying to decide whether it should eat the lock or aim for my nostrils. I take an anxious breath, hoping for the best, suddenly aware of the profound silence in the castle.

The students are gone. Aradottir got them all out.

Desperate, I nudge the tiny metal scarab over toward the door of my prison cell, and it quickly shimmies down the corroded surface and dives into the keyhole. Then I hear the faint, scraping sound of the scarab's tiny steel teeth gnawing on the charms inside the lock. Moments later, I'm kicking open the heavy iron door and racing for the stairs.

You did all right, Kyril. But you still owe me a favor.

Upstairs, the Great Hall is empty and desolate. The air tastes cleaner than in the dungeons, free (so far) from the data storm. But the massive doors are propped open, and the marble statues of the Elders stand forlorn in the gloom. Hesitantly, I step outside.

Ever since the Drini shields failed, The Isthmus has been cloaked by a liminal gray fog—courtesy of Ruskin's wards. But now there's no fog anywhere to be seen. Instead, the stately buildings of UW-Madison are illuminated by distant streetlights. In the foreground, his jeweled rings flashing under the full moon, is Kyril.

He paces across the lawn, just below the outline of the effigy mounds, unrolling a string of magical charges. The charges look just like those pale lights that mundane folk drape over their houses during the holidays. Except for this: they're not twinkling, but burning.

"Kyril!" I race down the broad stone steps. "What the hell are you doing?"

He doesn't even bother to look up. "Managing risk."

"You're blowing up Arcanos Hall?"

"I've got my orders."

This absolutely will not do. I don't know what's happening with Ruskin's wards, and I have no idea whether the dean will be able to dismantle the data scourge. But I'm not going to give up on The Isthmus so quickly.

I'm not going to abandon the priceless volumes in the library, the magical fleece in the weaving studio, the ancient clockwork portal made by goblins. They say that each of the statues in the Great Hall channels the spirit of one of the Arcanos Elders, who founded the university centuries ago. I'm not going to leave them all behind. I love this place.

What did Dean LaMarche say when he left me to face the data storm? "I have access to the most powerful weapons in the world. I must use them to protect . . . what I love."

With a flash of dismay, I remember the huge oil painting hanging on the wall in the dean's office—the red leather gown with no woman inside. I remember the way his eyes would turn to that empty red gown in moments of stress.

And then my heart nearly stops as I realize the truth. The dean doesn't just love The Isthmus. There's someone trapped inside that painting, someone he loves. And he doesn't have the means to set her free. Whoever she is, I can't let Kyril destroy her.

I rush forward to seize the magical charges, but Kyril simply raises his hand, sending a gust of wind straight into my knees. I tumble to the ground, tasting bitter soil and dried tufts of grass. What a dirty trick.

I struggle to my feet. "I don't know who you are, and I don't really care. But I won't let you do this. You have to give the dean more time! He's going to contain that storm."

"He's failed, Anya. The secondary wards have collapsed. It's three o'clock in the morning, and this castle is completely visible to anyone who walks by. How long before some mundane person spots these towers standing in the moonlight? And how long before every witch in Madison is compromised by the aftereffects of the storm? Destroying the castle is the best and fastest way to protect our secrets and take out the storm."

"But Arcanos Hall isn't empty! The dean's painting is still inside."

"Painting?"

"Were you just going to leave me there to burn? The same way you're going to leave the woman trapped in that painting?"

Kyril drops his string of sizzling charges and closes the distance between us. His eyes flash. "I wasn't going to leave anyone, Anya. I'm not some trigger-happy saboteur. I've been waiting for Kirsten to get everyone out. She would never sacrifice anybody, not unless she was the one being sacrificed. But we have to be ready. We have to be willing to do the right thing. It's not just The Isthmus at stake."

With a shudder, I remember hearing that phrase before. Ruskin said that very same thing to Lady Lynch when I was banished. But it probably meant something very different to Lynch and Ruskin. People have very different ideas about what's at stake.

Maybe I didn't know before, what it meant to do the right thing. But I do now.

"Kyril, there's a life at stake. If you have any kind of skill with machines, you will help me repair that Drini shield. And you will do it now, before Aradottir returns."

"It's not safe to enter the shield room. It's too close to the storm."

"The dean won't let us down. He *will* contain that storm."

"But how can we—"

"I'm calling in my debt."

This has the surprising effect of completely silencing him. He stares, mouth open.

"Let's go," I say. "Unless you've sworn some kind of oath to serve Aradottir."

He doesn't move.

"Have you?" I ask, wondering if he will actually honor his debt. "Have you sworn an oath to serve her?"

"I have not." He leans close, his voice dropping. "You don't know what you're doing, and you're going to get us both killed. Even worse, The Isthmus will be visible to mundanes, while that data storm has time to spread across this city, weakening every witch between these lakes. But, as you say, I'm in your debt. So let's not delay getting ourselves killed, shall we?" He turns his back on me and marches toward the wide stone staircase.

"Kyril—" I begin, but he cuts me off.

"Don't even talk to me. Kirsten Aradottir is setting charges near the lake. When she reaches the front of the castle, she'll go down to the dungeons to retrieve you, and then she'll connect her charges to mine and burn the place down. So that's exactly how much time we have."

We cross the Great Hall and race down the stairs to the dungeons. The nearby door to the steam tunnels stands propped open. The stench of hot metal rises up from below.

I peer down the darkened stairwell. Instinctively, I tighten my shawl around my head, even though I know it's not strong enough to protect me.

Kyril raises his hands, and I realize that the gemstones on his rings are all glowing. They're creating a soft halo, like the golden light that burnishes the evening sky. The air around us becomes humid and thick.

He steps past the heavy iron door, and our protective halo bulges forward into the stairwell, like a misshapen balloon. "I can't believe I'm using up every heirloom in my arsenal, just to go on some fool's errand with you. Not to mention risking my life."

"Shut up, Kyril." I give him a shove, and together we rush down the stairs to find the Drini shield.

❧

123

Here's the thing about knitting, what differentiates it from other art. You don't need any special tools or fancy equipment. All you need are two sticks and a single piece of string. If you run out of yarn in one skein, you simply splice it to the next skein. Theoretically, a single thread could go on forever. Two sticks. One piece of string. That's all you need.

Surrounded by Kyril's fragile halo, I gaze up at the legendary Drini machine. It's not a traditional loom or knitting machine. There's only one needle—a huge spike that's longer than my torso. But I know absolutely that the Drini has been knitting a shield around The Isthmus for centuries. Drawing upon the ley lines— the threads of power deep inside the earth—the Drini has formed a protective mesh around this castle, a magical Faraday cage shielding it from danger, hiding it from view. The thread is still there. It goes on forever. But how do we access the ley lines? And why is there only one needle?

"This is obviously some kind of textile machine," Kyril says, looking up at the giant needle. "You just need to fix it."

"Are you kidding?" I wave a hand at the scorched gears on the Drini's carriage device. "This is obviously some kind of computer. *You* need to fix it."

"I'm not here to provide tech support," Kyril sniffs. "And that is not what I would call a computer." Still, he slides his lean body under the carriage device, examining it from below.

The gears connect to a barrel-shaped panel, studded with tiny metal spikes. Despite being burnt, the steam-powered carriage device seems newer than the rest of the Drini, almost as if it had been built for a different reason, at a different time.

"The Hollerith card," I say, slipping Rocco's card out of my smock.

Kyril reaches for it. "It's definitely part of a code to run this machine."

"So we just have to make the machine accept the code."

"Easier said than done. We can't install any code until we've rebooted this thing."

"Rebooted?" Once again, Kyril is talking and thinking like a total mundane.

He tugs at a metal device, his body twisting slightly from the effort. "If this is the card reader—then it's completely fused together."

"But what have we here?" He pulls open a soot-stained panel and reaches upward. "Looks like a control panel. And a keyhole."

"The dean gave me a key!" Nervous with excitement, I hand him the silver key.

Maybe the key is all we need. Could it actually be this easy to fix the Drini?

"It fits!" Kyril installs the key, and for a moment, nothing happens.

Then, the machine abruptly shudders into motion, sending its pointed spike lunging through the air like the feints of a swordsman on a cliff. The giant needle swings up and down, silent as a hawk dropping from the sky.

I stumble backwards, and the halo surrounding us trembles, its delicate shell nearly breaking. Horrified, I realize that Kyril's gemstone charms are nearly spent. My feet grow cold, and every stitch in my clothing feels pronounced, scraping roughly against my skin. The storm is coming through. Soon, it will poison us both.

"Stay close. Don't break the halo." Kyril edges his way out from under the carriage device. He hands me the Hollerith card and we stare up at the machine.

"It's operational," Kyril whispers in my ear. "Awaiting some kind of command. But I don't think your card is going to do us any good. The part of the machine that reads the card is completely melted. It can't process any code."

I feel desolate, physically sick. I'm trapped underground with a stranger, unable to help the dean, likely to lose all my powers. "But can't we . . . don't you *write* codes?"

Kyril shakes his head, a strand of his dark hair grazing my cheek. "Not like this."

The thick, humid air of our protective halo punctures all at once, giving way to sharp, metallic fumes. I inhale, breathing in the storm. We're running out of time.

"No!" I can feel my lace armor sparking, overcome by toxic fields. It's too late to flee. In just a few minutes, it will all be over. The dean wasn't able to contain the storm.

I gaze up at the ancient, useless Drini, imagining that its jolting needle and absent thread should somehow cloak all the bodies of the dead. And then I realize why there's only one needle. "Kyril, we need to stop the machine!"

Without pausing to question me, Kyril lunges forward and seizes the sides of the needle with his bare hands, stopping the deadly spike mid-thrust.

I grasp the giant needle, and the gleaming metal moves easily in my hand. I pull it towards me, then loop it back down. Again, I pull it towards me, then loop it back down.

Kyril stares. "What are you doing?"

"I think I'm casting on." Which conveniently requires only one needle.

A luminous thread of power begins to glow, shimmering, golden, and clear. It's the ley line. Surely, the thread was always there, caught up in the machine, waiting for the technique that would call it forth. A shining thread catches on the giant needle as I swing it around. It forms a translucent chain of gold. The worm-like chain extends and grows, penetrating the granite wall. Then the Drini takes over, moving of its own accord, using the same looping motion I'd begun. The stone floor opens seamlessly, and a second giant needle joins the first. Noiselessly, they bind together an unbroken chain of golden light.

"It's working! We've fixed the Drini!" Overcome, I throw my arms around Kyril, realizing too late that this could be very awkward, since I'm not even sure if we're friends.

"Too late for us," he mutters hoarsely, pulling me into his shoulder. "But we can die happy."

"Happy?" I whisper back, dizzy with toxic fields.

"Happy enough."

The warmth of his skin seems both otherworldly and entirely real, as if we've been caught in the space between two realms. The air crackles with power, and I realize with appalled horror that I'm clutching at the fabric of his silver hoodie. It's all I can do to stop myself from kissing him. Clinging to Kyril's bloodstained clothes, I realize that he's breathing hard. Then I realize something else as well: my mind is clearing, the metallic taste is fading. Could the Drini shields be protecting us already?

"The dean," I mumble into Kyril's collar. "He took out the data storm."

He lifts a hand to straighten my scarf above my ear. It's an odd gesture. "The old man did all right. Who would've thought he could?"

I'm still trying to comprehend this, still trying to process the fact that we aren't immediately going to go crazy or die, when the giant needles churning beside us abruptly disappear, taking the ley lines and the curving walls of the shield room with them. A faint golden light hovers in the air, then fades out.

"Anya," says Kyril, releasing me and slowly turning. "*Where is the castle?*"

I stare at the jumble of stones where the castle walls had been. "Did Aradottir . . . ?"

"No, she did not. We'd be dead."

The ground beneath my feet feels rocky and uneven. I lift my eyes to the ceiling, seeking the graceful arches of Arcanos Hall. But I see only a patch of starlight and a full moon. *What have I done?*

CHAPTER FOURTEEN

Surrounded by boulders, we're trapped in a narrow crevasse, the moon above us illuminating a sliver of sky. From a distance, a woman is calling. "Kyril! Kyril!"

"It's Aradottir," I say, not sure whether I should be relieved or terrified. If the Ice Captain is still here, then we can't be completely dead. And this can't just be some kind of twisted dream. But what has happened to Arcanos Hall?

Kyril's voice is grim. "Make yourself scarce, before she finds you."

"But Dean LaMarche," I protest, stumbling over a rock the size of a corgi. "He might be hurt. I have to find him. I have to help him."

"You can't help anyone if you're in custody. I'll take care of the dean. Aradottir mustn't know you're here."

"But what's happened to the castle?"

"Damned if I know. You've got some seriously messed-up magic, Anya. Making an entire castle disappear." Kyril tugs me over to the darkest corner of the crevasse and shoves me behind a boulder. "Hide here. Do it now."

"Kirsten," he yells, and clambers onto a jumble of moonlit rocks. "Can you hear me?"

I crouch behind a jagged boulder. "Kyril, the data storm—"

"Quiet!" he hisses. "Do you want to be imprisoned for sabotage? Again?"

"Kyril!" Aradottir is closer this time, her tone thick with relief. "Are you hurt?"

"I'm not hurt." A luminescent torch brightens Kyril's face as a rope falls, flooding his features in blue and silver light. "Get me out of here."

I hide in the darkness until I'm sure they're gone. Then I slowly claw my way up the side of the crevasse, my skirts tucked up into my waistband, splintered fingernails digging into the rough surface of the rock. It takes freaking forever. Twice, I lose my hold and slide back down.

It would have been nice if Kyril had left me the rope. Even better if he'd been willing to advocate for me with his pal Aradottir. But no, instead he left me in a bottomless pit to fend for myself, all of my favors all used up. What kind of a mage is he, anyway? And how do he and Aradottir even know each other?

"Hey there, are you all right?"

Clinging to the wall of crumbling mud and stone, I somehow manage to look up. It's a woman in her forties, with black-framed glasses and spiky salt-and-pepper hair. She's crouching on the edge of the crevasse, her faded jeans stretched tight across her knees.

"Fell in," I manage to grunt, reaching for her extended hand.

"You're lucky you weren't killed." She digs in with her thick boot heels and pulls me out. "Where the hell did that sinkhole come from?"

I lie on the cold grass and struggle to catch my breath. It's almost dawn, the eastern sky traced with pink and gold.

"You sure you're okay?" Her face wrinkles with concern.

"Fine." I roll over and pull myself upright, giving way to coughing. "Just fine."

"Sorry, but you don't look fine. Your legs are scratched up. Let me take you to the hospital." She produces a small black device, and points it at a shiny new car parked on the edge of the road, its lights flashing.

"I don't have insurance," I say. And there's no way in hell I'm going to a high-tech hospital in a computerized car. I'm about to crawl away when I see something entirely unexpected, something that changes my mind. It's a small brown truck going north on Observatory Drive, heading for the hospital. Kyril's in the driver's seat, his eyes intent on the road. There's an old man propped upright in the battered truck bed, his face as pale as his silver hair. *It's Dean LaMarche. Kyril got him out.*

"On second thought, take me to the hospital."

The medical campus is just a mile or so north on Observatory Drive. When the woman with the oddly quiet car drops me off at University Hospital, I realize very quickly that I don't have a plan. I can't be certain the dean is even here. I don't know how badly hurt he is, or how much time I have before the rest of the magical community finds him. Plus, I don't have an invisibility cape, which means I'm in no position to sneak around. My best option is to be direct, and to lie through my teeth.

Fortunately, I was raised by people with secrets and thus have some experience with falsehood. Quelling my anxiety, I march right in and approach the front desk.

"Excuse me, my dad was just brought in. May I see him? Did you check him in?"

"Your dad?" the sallow-faced clerk inquires.

"Tall and thin? Mid-sixties? Silver hair?"

"Uh huh. And who exactly are you?"

"My name's Anya." I reach into my torn skirt pocket and retrieve one of the most magical talismans I own: a pristine blue

U.S. passport. I've never actually shown it to anyone, never actually used it for ID, but it's my ticket-out-of-jail card, tangible proof that I have a place in the mundane world, whether I want it or not. It says: *I belong here.*

The clerk thumbs through the passport and inspects my photograph, acting like she's never actually seen a passport before. "The man you describe was left outside the ER. Just a few minutes ago."

"Left *outside* the ER?" I barely contain my rage. If that's Kyril's idea of a rescue . . .

"No papers with him. You say he's your father?"

"My stepdad," I say, aware that I'm probably committing some kind of mundane medical fraud. "He's the dean—his name's Dean LaMarche."

The clerk looks at me appraisingly, and I instinctively tighten my shawl around my head. Despite all the machines and devices on display, the hospital doesn't reek of technological toxins. In fact, the air feels far less poisonous than I would have thought. Perhaps mundanes don't use their ubiquitous cell phones in places where people are sick.

Minutes later, I'm being ushered into an examining room with heavy vinyl accordion walls, where Dean LaMarche is lying on an ugly paper-covered table, pale and disoriented but very much alive.

"Looks like your dad was injured in a fall," says the dour, businesslike nurse. She's attached some kind of clear tube to the dean's exposed forearm. "Does he live all by himself?"

"I beg your pardon?"

The nurse regards me with disdain. "He's confused. He doesn't even know his own name. Given the state he's in, you really ought to have him in a facility." She sweeps out of the room, with an expression that says: You are a terrible excuse for a daughter.

"Dean LaMarche," I whisper, leaning close. "Sir, are you okay?"

His eyelashes flutter, then drift shut. "Anya."

I grasp his cold hand. "I've got to get you out of here. You need

131

healing charms."

"Won't help," he murmurs, his eyes still closed. "Better to stay here awhile."

"But these doctors—"

"Can't hurt me," he finishes. He turns his head on the pillow and weakly squeezes my hand. "Someone's coming, Anya. Better go."

For someone whose mind has probably been broken by a data storm, the dean possesses extraordinary gifts of perception. I slip out of the examining room and peer into the hallway just in time to see the scowling nurse shaking her finger at the newest visitors to the hospital: Captain Aradottir, Professor Ruskin, and Lady Lynch.

Aradottir is still dressed in her cloak and boots, looking very much out-of-place in the mundane hospital. Ruskin has made a decent attempt at camouflage, a ridiculously boyish Bucky Badger hoodie pulled over his university clothes. But Lady Lynch looks exactly as she always does: patrician, snobbish, overdressed. A small boy hangs over the back of a waiting room chair, gaping at the millinery excrescence atop her head.

"Family only," the nurse is saying. "You can see your friend when Dr. Sen is done. Mr. LaMarche's daughter is with him now."

"Is that so?" Aradottir drawls. She slowly turns her head in my direction, and I dart behind the accordion-shaped room divider. "I don't recall being told he had children."

Wrapping myself inside the folds of the heavy vinyl divider, I do my best not to breathe.

"Where exactly is this so-called daughter of his?" Lady Lynch's clipped vowels seem to pierce through my eardrums. Her heels clatter swiftly on the linoleum floor, rounding the corner into the examining room and coming to an abrupt halt. "Oh, my poor old friend!"

"There now, my lady." It's Ruskin, oleaginous and slithery as ever. "Please don't distress yourself. Our dean is in good hands."

"But look at him," Lady Lynch says, completely aghast, "His

face is as blank as a farmhand. He's devoid of all magic. His wits have been scrambled. He's undone!"

"Your Ladyship, this is not the time or the place," Aradottir begins, but Lady Lynch is gathering her oratory powers, on an absolute roll.

"Oh, that I should live to see this day," she wails. "My ancient alma mater destroyed—(and that was your doing, Captain. You *know* it could have been avoided)—and my poor old friend brought so low. And why was he brought to this awful place?"

"You're going to have to leave," a woman puts in. "Ma'am, this is an urgent care facility. We're seeing patients here."

"Are you Dr. Sen?" Ruskin's charisma potions spice the stale hospital air with the scent of lavender. "Please excuse my friend. She's distraught, of course. We're so grateful for your help. So very grateful. If we could just sit here for a while . . . "

"Of course," Dr. Sen says at once, in the placid, easy manner of someone who's just been subjected to a massive dose of compliance compound.

I suppress a sigh, convinced that I'll be trapped inside this gray vinyl room divider until I asphyxiate. Either that, or I'll be caught.

"Have you seen a young woman?" Aradottir asks the doctor in her slow, deliberate way. "His daughter? Did she have any—how do you say it—ID?"

"Um," says Dr. Sen hazily, still under the influence of Ruskin's charms. "The nurse did mention something about a girl. If you would come with me." She and Aradottir walk away, the doctor's clogs clomping loudly, the captain's boots as silent as falling snow.

"Well," Lady Lynch bursts out, clearly glad to be free of Aradottir and the doctor. "This is a disaster! The Isthmus is gone, destroyed! Dean LaMarche is reduced to an empty shell. So much for our plans!"

"All my formulas," Ruskin says, his voice unexpectedly raw. "A lifetime of research—gone forever." The anguish in his voice

133

surprises me. I hadn't expected him to feel so strongly about his potions. Surely, he can just make some new ones, right?

"But we must rally ourselves," Lady Lynch says, her tone resolute. "With the dean gone, the young people will look to us for leadership."

"Indeed," Ruskin says with an effort, clearly trying to rally himself.

"Naturally, there will be many who will second-guess the Ice Captain's decision to destroy the castle, but that wasn't *our* decision, it was hers—we'll make sure everyone knows that. We'll have to move to a new campus, and *someone* will have to become the new dean."

"Are you thinking—?"

"That's exactly what I'm thinking. Inez Quissel may have seniority, but she lacks political clout and she knows it. She'll get the rest of the faculty behind you. Burke and the other Regents will support your candidacy—for a price. As for Aradottir, her only concern is security, and we can supply all the protective wards she needs."

Ruskin sounds uncertain. "But Aradottir is loyal to King Nestor, and you know Nestor will never accept being dependent upon hedge-produced Eastern charms, not when—"

"Nestor is desperate," Lady Lynch cuts in. "His truce with the East is hanging by a thread. Besides, he's an old man, his powers failing. Surely he's thought about succession. He can't remarry because he refuses to believe his wife is dead. If he wants any preference at all for that morganatic son of his, he'll agree to our terms."

Concealed within the accordion room divider, which undoubtedly off-gassing all kinds of nasty chemicals, I feel a terrible urge to sneeze. My nostrils tremble, and my chin inches higher and higher as the sneeze continues to build. I'm about to panic when the grouchy nurse returns.

"Family only," she grunts. "Like I said. You're going to have to leave."

"We're so sorry, ma'am," Ruskin begins, obviously about to unleash another wave of compliance compound. But Lady Lynch is ready to go.

"We've seen enough, Ruskin. He's not himself anymore." As they file out of the room, she says one last thing. "We've got an Assembly to prepare for."

Untangling myself from the accordion doors, I find Dean LaMarche lying prone on the examining table, his face slack as an empty shopping bag. When I burst out with an impressively loud sneeze, he doesn't even flinch.

"Sir," I whisper, touching his shoulder.

He opens a single eye. "Are they gone?"

CHAPTER FIFTEEN

Y ou'd better go, Anya." The dean's chest rises and falls, as if speaking just a few words is a terrible effort for him.

"But you need to get out of here! They might run tests on you. This place isn't safe."

"Captain Aradottir will help me when I'm able to travel. But she can't be everywhere at once."

"What does that even mean? And what's going to happen when the hospital staffers tell her about me? She'll know I'm here, and then she'll—"

With a weak gesture, he dismisses this. "Tell me what happened. How did I get here?"

The last thing I want is to tell Dean LaMarche that I made the castle disappear. But there's no point in concealing Kyril's existence at this point. "A mage named Kyril helped Aradottir set the charges around the castle. He brought you here afterward."

"A mage named Kyril?" Recognition flickers. "You must help him."

I groan. "Must I? Really?"

He clasps my hand. "Do this for me. Now go."

Outside the hospital, the morning sun seems ridiculously bright and cheery. Why should the sun shine on such an awful day? Desperate and exposed, I make my way back to Observatory Drive and hurry toward Arcanos Hall, trying not to think about the fact that it's gone, completely gone.

It's my fault. When I initiated the cast-on to restore the shields, I set something else in motion, something I didn't expect. Because of me, the entire castle was spirited away.

I'm about to cut across Walnut Street to get to the secluded Lakeshore Path when I realize a small brown pickup truck has pulled up beside me.

"Want a ride?" Kyril asks, patting the backrest of the passenger seat. It really is unfortunate, how handsome he is.

I approach the car, eyes blazing. "Even if I wanted to be hauled around in some nasty mundane vehicle, do you think anything could induce me to accept a ride from you? After you dumped the poor, helpless dean outside the hospital, like he was a bale of hay? Do you call that taking care of him?"

Kyril raises a perfect eyebrow. "Dean LaMarche is not poor or helpless. He's one of the most powerful wizards in the world."

"He's lost all his magic," I say, forlornly. And who knows what else that data storm did to him.

"That doesn't mean he's helpless." Kyril speaks with conviction, as if he knows something about magic that I don't. "Get in the car, Anya. You can't be standing here in the middle of the street. It's not safe."

"I don't want your help," I tell him, skirting the front of his truck, and then I'm hustling down the center of Walnut Street, heading for the safety of the woods. "And I'm not going to ride around in your gas-guzzling monstrosity," I yell over my shoulder.

Kyril yells back. "I'll have you know this vehicle runs on used cooking oil."

I put my nose in the air. "So that's why it smells like a burger shack."

"Wait," Kyril says with a smile, driving alongside me as I stroll toward the woods. "You're sure you won't let me help you?"

"Nothing could convince me." Not even the dean's request.

"Not even this?" Stopping the truck, he holds up the torn fabric of a gossamer-thin invisibility cape. He must have retrieved it from the tunnels when he rescued the dean.

"Not even that," I say, snatching it from his hand.

Kyril shakes his head, still smiling. Then he drives off in a cloud of oily fumes.

♋

Let me tell you something about knitting, something amateurs don't know.

A knitted item is almost never beyond repair. If you find a hole in a knitted garment—magical or otherwise—you probably have a chance to fix it. But when it comes to repairs, many knitters and witches are doing it wrong.

If you're dealing with a non-magical fabric, you could perhaps weave or darn a patch over the hole, or perhaps use *boro* techniques to stabilize the fabric, but the patch will affect the fabric's texture and subsequently compromise the gauge. And gauge is everything. With a magical fabric, you never want to patch, and you never want to tie a single knot. What you have to do is unravel, to strip away the damage until you reach the point where the spell is still uncorrupted and clean. Then you rebuild.

If I'm going to repair my invisibility cape, I'll need the rest of my gear. Specifically, I'll need the delicate bone needles my mother made when I was a girl. Why? Because the gauge has got to be a perfect match.

But that means I'll have to take a chance on someone I don't

138

really know.

Wobbling precariously on the fire escape, high above the orange berries of the slender rowan tree, I knock on the door to Monsita Olann's attic apartment. I still have her key, but it seems rude to let myself in when I'm a wanted criminal. Actually it would probably be rude to let myself in anyhow, whether I was a wanted criminal or not. But I wouldn't know about rudeness, having been raised in a missile silo, which isn't much better than being raised in a barn.

"Anya?" Madame Olann pokes her head out, the delicate fabric of her kerchief snagging on the doorframe. Moving more swiftly than anyone that hunched and decrepit should, she slips out onto the fire escape and closes the door behind her. "We thought you were dead."

The metal balcony sways under our weight. "Well, as you can see, I'm not dead."

Barefoot and clothed in a yellow housedress, she looks me up and down. "I can't let you in, dearie. I've got students downstairs, camped out on the floor of the yarn shop, all scared out of their wits. They think you're a dangerous saboteur. And dead, of course."

"Are they all here?"

"The Bratsch girl's on her own. We divided the others into groups and found them shelter. But the princess didn't make it."

"She didn't?" I try to sound concerned, but my question comes out sounding false and disingenuous. I remember the vial of potion I gave to Elena, and the way the afterimage of the pointed ears on her cap continued to flicker, long after she'd disappeared. She can't possibly be in the ether. So where did Ruskin's potion send her?

"You're not worried about your princess? Even though she could be dead?" She raises her eyebrows. "Anything you care to tell me?"

For a moment, I consider trusting her with an account of what happened last night in the dungeons, and afterward in shield room. But my father's advice comes back with the force of a mandate.

Never share information unless you have to.

"No," I say, my gaze falling to the old woman's knobby feet. "I must be in shock or something." A long silence, punctuated by the brittle tones of a redwing blackbird.

"Well," Madame Olann rustles her fingers together as if she's knitting with invisible yarn. "If you're not dead, then perhaps the princess has survived as well. Wouldn't that be nice?"

"Yes," I manage. "That would be nice."

She lets out a sigh, but I can't tell if it's annoyance or relief. "From what I've heard, the princess has some good reasons to be hiding. She's been in love with the same person for nearly five years. The king won't accept her choice, and he's threatened her with all kinds of horrors if she disobeys. Poor thing is in a bind."

"I'm in a bind, too," I blurt, without thinking. "I mean I—"

She cuts me off. "I don't want to hear about your troubles. This isn't about you. I've got students to protect. I've got problems of my own. I'll get your yarn and your things."

"You don't have to help me," I begin, but she's already slipped inside. When she returns with my big canvas bag, there's something new in her face.

She looks me up and down. "You're alive."

"Obviously."

"But Arcanos Hall was destroyed."

"It's gone, yes." I'm a mediocre liar, but this is not a lie.

"So how did you get out?"

I pitch the bundle of yarn and gear over the side of the fire escape and make my way down the ladder. When I'm at eye level with her gouty, twisted toes, I leave her with a parting gift. "Magic."

⌒

A few blocks away, my father's thick bundle of U.S. dollars proves useful for the first time. I slip into Steep and Brew, peel off a bill to pay for tea and a scone, and sit in the back, next to the students with their ubiquitous laptops and noxious phones. No witch in her right mind would set foot in this place, even if she did have money for tea and scones. I'm lucky, I realize. I have enough money to live on, enough money to hide.

A bearded hipster squeezes behind my chair to plug in his phone, muttering something about online banking. I marvel at these mundanes. They entrust all their wealth and all their secrets to strange devices whose inner workings they don't fully understand. Not one in fifty knows what happens inside those diabolical machines. They just blindly trust that it will all work out. And yet they claim they don't believe in magic.

Safely anonymous, I unpick the torn edge of my invisibility cape. The spell embedded into the fabric has already unraveled into chaos, but that doesn't mean I can't slip in a lifeline, frog the damaged portion, splice the torn threads, and ravel it back again. Pulling the gossamer yarn loose, I wind it around my left hand. Then I reach for the needles made of bone.

Lady Lynch mentioned an Assembly, which must mean the Regents—not just the Inner Council—will gather in one place to determine the fate of students, the future of the university. Lord Burke will be there, and Captain Aradottir.

They'll all know about the data storm by now, and the dean's heroic sacrifice. They'll also know the princess has gone missing. But only Burke knows that Elena was in the dungeons before she disappeared. And I'm the only one who knows that Burke knew about the storm in advance.

I'm almost certain it was Burke who sent the storm to destroy the university. But why would he do that? Elena said he was financing the Eastern monarchy, expecting an alliance with Elena in return. If Burke is helping to consolidate Cibrán's power, by quashing the hedge witch rebellions in Scotland, perhaps he could also be working to destabilize Cibrán's opponents, by compromising the only university in the West.

It occurs to me that it's dangerous, being the only person who knows someone is guilty or complicit. In the lurid crime novels I read as a teen, people who kept knowledge to themselves invariably died before they could share what they knew. I should probably talk to someone. But whom could I trust?

Kyril? Madame Olann? Kirsten Aradottir?

With Dean LaMarche incapacitated, I don't have a lot of choices.

Somehow I doubt that Aradottir has told anyone that the Isthmus was spirited away before she could destroy it. Sharing such information would create unnecessary panic. I also doubt that Aradottir has told anyone about Kyril, whoever Kyril is. For all her coldness, the Ice Captain seems to be a woman driven by the need for absolute security; she shares information only when she has to. Not unlike Kyril, to be honest.

What was Kyril always saying about himself? "I manage risk. It's what I do."

If everyone thinks I'm a saboteur, then I'll definitely have to manage some risks of my own. Specifically, I'm going to need to be invisible. I take a sip of gritty tea and straighten the fabric of my invisibility cape. Sliding a glittering row of live stitches onto my tiny needles, I begin to rebuild.

CHAPTER SIXTEEN

The problem with sitting in a marsh when you're invisible is that you invariably leave indentations in the foliage. So I have to keep moving.

With Arcanos Hall gone, there's really only one place in this part of Wisconsin that's suitable for an Assembly: Portage Point, the narrow, marshy peninsula that stretches out into Lake Mendota. Nearly a mile long, and studded with effigy mounds that go back several hundred years, Portage Point is shaped like a narrow, beckoning finger. I'm betting the Assembly will be held near the portal at the tip, most likely just after sunset. If I'm wrong, then I'll have gotten my feet wet and been eaten by mosquitos for nothing.

Carefully avoiding both the gravel footpaths and the effigy mounds, I do my best to stay between the Narrows and the Point. After circling for two hours in the damp, muggy marsh, I'm almost about to give up, when I realize that someone else is hiding in the reeds. It's Kyril.

He doesn't have an invisibility cape—instead, he's concealed in a muddy canvas duck blind piled high with decaying reeds.

He's got a camera pointing out of the blind, and I can just see his Grecian nose and the black arches of his eyebrows.

Drawing closer, I realize Kyril's duck blind is actually resting on a canoe. Midges swarm busily around him. I inch close enough to glimpse the sweat glistening on his cheekbones, and then give him a scare. "Used up all your charms, huh?"

He starts, and the reeds laced to his canoe tremble. "What the hell! Anya, is that you?"

"Let me guess, you're managing risk."

He sinks back into the blind. "I see you fixed your cape."

"You don't see any such thing," I say, squatting beside his canoe. My shoes sink ten inches into wet marsh. The air smells like rotting vegetation.

"Don't be so proud of yourself. Want to know why I'm in a duck blind and not wearing an invisibility cape?" He stares straight into the tiny glass window on the back of his camera, not even bothering to look in my direction.

"I'm guessing you don't have a cape."

"You'd be guessing wrong. I'm in this blind because King Cibrán is coming tonight, and his security team will arrive first to sweep for concealment devices and other forms of magic. Your cape is going to make you a sitting duck."

"Are you kidding? *The* King Cibrán? Princess Elena's father? Doesn't he need permission from King Nestor to enter the West? And how do you even know this?"

"Tell you what," he says, letting the camera hang from his neck. "In the spirit of collaboration, I'm going to be a nice guy and share my hideout with you. You won't even owe me a favor. But you'll have to put away that cape."

Disappointed, I tug off the cape and roll the airy lace into a neutralized coil, slipping it inside my bag. "You know I spent the last ten hours repairing this damn thing."

Kyril pulls aside the canvas flap. "I know you did. Get inside."

I squeeze past him and crawl into the blind, dragging all kinds of mud with me, nearly tipping the wobbly canoe. We sway precariously. It's dry inside, but not much bigger than the claustrophobic steam tunnel we shared last night. I'm practically sitting on Kyril's lap. The brittle silver fabric of his metallic hoodie scratches against my arms.

He drops the canvas flap, plunging us into absolute darkness, and unaccountably, my heart begins to race. Sharing a tiny canoe-sized tent with a mysterious stranger may sound quite romantic, especially when the mysterious stranger happens to be particularly good-looking. But nobody's good-looking in the dark.

"Do you have any . . . non-magical sources of light?"

"Can't risk it," he whispers in my ear, his voice oddly husky. He leans close, smelling deliciously of fresh citrus, and I realize I'm holding my breath. This won't do.

A bloodthirsty mosquito buzzes past, and I swipe hard, hitting Kyril's face instead.

"Do you mind?" he asks, sounding aggrieved.

I'm about to apologize when we hear a great rushing sound, like a hundred geese launching themselves from a lake. Flying carpets. Many of them.

Kyril's hand closes on my shoulder. "Cibrán's entourage. Deactivate your scarf."

I quickly roll up my armor and slip it into my bag. We're miles from any strong WiFi or other toxic fields, but I still feel naked and exposed.

A narrow sliver of fading light enters the blind, and I realize Kyril has nudged aside just enough of the canvas flap to poke his camera lens through the reeds.

"If they sweep for technology, they'll find your camera."

"It's not digital," he whispers back. "And it's just for show. Like my bird-watching books. In case we get caught." He seems ridiculously confident.

"Maybe you don't realize King Cibrán has imprisoned people for months at a time, without a trial. Or maybe you do know that, and you're just being cocky."

He shrugs. "I *am* being cocky, but I also know more than you do. Cibrán controls the East, but he has no authority here. He's been allowed to bring in a small security team because his daughter is missing, but he won't risk doing anything that will anger Nestor."

"Well, if it's just a security team, then how will they secure the area?" I wonder if Kyril's ever spied on a royal council before. Something tells me he has.

"After they sweep for magical weapons and devices, they'll allow the Regents to enter. The King will come through the portal at the last minute. Then they'll close the portal and put a ward around the entire Point. No magic allowed, nobody in or out."

"But we'll already be here." I say with a smile, feeling rather smug, despite my wet shoes, empty stomach, multiple mosquito bites, and sense of impending doom.

"Exactly," Kyril says in the darkness, and it sounds like he's smiling back.

Security is a tricky thing. It's tricky, because one of the most dangerous things in the world is thinking you're secure. Case in point: King Cibrán's security team.

After they finish sweeping the peninsula and patting down all the Regents, they seal off the Point with powerful wards. Then their job is done.

They've locked themselves in an airtight bubble without magic, without technology. Completely secure. Nothing to worry about. They may as well be putting their feet up. Which is why Kyril and I are able to paddle close enough to witness the historic Assembly.

Torches flicker, and the full moon casts an eerie glow. At the very tip of Portage Point, Lady Lynch has chosen the highest ground. She's seated primly on the picnic table that marks the portal, her bony legs pressed together, feet resting on the rotting bench boards. Unable to use magic, she's waving away mosquitoes with a delicate paper fan.

Ruskin hovers at her side, his attention divided between her and the King, whose makeshift dais is draped with delicate mosquito netting. The netting is clearly non-magical, but it creates an almost invisible barrier between the King and the twenty Regents. The message is clear: "You're not on the inside."

On the inside is King Cibrán, a regally dressed man who looks very much like a toad. How he managed to father anyone as beautiful as Elena is completely beyond me. You really have to wonder how much royal blood is actually royal at all.

Ready to begin, Ruskin nods to Lady Lynch, who nervously clears her throat.

"My dear friends," she intones. "We are gathered here to mourn the terrible loss of our ancestral alma mater, Arcanos Hall. We are all terribly sad."

"So sad!" Ruskin laments, as a mournful threnody echoes through the faculty.

Lady Lynch continues. "It grieves me that Captain Aradottir saw fit to destroy our precious university, though she *claims* she was only doing what she must."

"Where is Aradottir?" growls Simon Burke. Unshielded, with his hood thrown back, his hair is almost as unkempt and disheveled as his beard. He scans the long row of Carpathian soldiers, as if searching for Aradottir and her men.

There's an awkward pause. Apparently, no one wants to be associated with Aradottir, and no one wants to bring up the fact that the King's daughter is missing. Given Cibrán's reputation, I wouldn't want to be the one to mention Elena's disappearance, either.

"Aradottir is managing security for the students," Ruskin finally says, with a wary eye on the royal dais. Apparently, this comment isn't nearly neutral enough for His Majesty, because King Cibrán explodes.

"Not *all* the students," he roars. "Where is Elena? Where is the heir to my throne? And where is that Ice Captain? This is not the first time she has tried to undermine me. Let her show her face!"

"Your Majesty," sputters Ruskin, clearly wishing that Aradottir were around to take the blame. "We have no news of the princess. We fear . . . "

"Fear? I'll show you fear. You don't know a thing about fear."

Cibrán's voice is so menacing, I instinctively recoil, then realize I'm clutching Kyril's knee. Half-hidden by darkness, Kyril puts a finger to his lips.

Burke steps into view once more, his posture stiff and resolute. "With the exception of His Majesty the King, no one feels more distress than I do. The princess is my cherished fiancée, and my heart is in agony. But I refuse to believe she's dead."

I can't believe he's calling Elena his fiancée. When we were in the dungeons, she made it clear she loved someone else. Burke really must think she doesn't have a choice.

He gestures deferentially to the King. "Does she not wear a tracking device, per royal protocol? Surely it would alert us to her location. Surely it would tell us if she were dead."

I realize then that the King already knows. So does Burke. They know she's not dead. But they don't know where she's gone.

Alone on his dais, King Cibrán is silent for so long, that I wonder what's going to happen. No one else dares to speak. The torchlight leaps and sparks. Next to me, I can hear Kyril breathing, and my leg is falling asleep, cramped beneath me in the narrow canoe.

When the King finally responds, he says only one thing. "She's here."

Kyril flinches, his first reaction of any kind since the Assembly began. The canoe wobbles and sloshes beneath us, and a few reeds slip forward, partially blocking our view.

"Here?" Lady Lynch gasps. "Here in Wisconsin?"

"Elena has not left this city. The trail has been clouded by magic, but she's here, she's alive, and I will find her." King Cibrán sweeps his gaze around the Assembly, causing several Regents to inch backward.

Ruskin rocks on his feet, and a nervous hand clutches the front of his cape. I wonder if he has any idea that Elena drank his vial of *A. archangelica*.

Still clutching his cape, he makes a deep, trembling obeisance. "Your Majesty, what can we do to assist you in the search for your royal daughter? As Acting Dean of The Isthmus, I assure you that my staff—indeed, the entire faculty—are at your disposal."

"Indeed," Lady Lynch says, abruptly standing up. She wobbles precariously on the picnic bench until Ruskin holds out his arm to steady her. "Your Majesty, you know my royal cousin King Nestor has pledged all possible support. He will aid us in finding your daughter, bringing to justice that horrible half-witch whose terrible act of sabotage caused The Isthmus to be exposed—and destroyed."

With a start, I realize Lady Lynch is talking about me. Then I realize something else: Kyril—who by all accounts is obsessed with managing risk—took a huge gamble, letting me into his duck blind. If we're caught, we both could end up in prison. Or dead. Or magicked into ducks.

Kyril inches aside the reeds partially obscuring our view, but with an almost inaudible swish, they fall, landing on the prow of the canoe. Standing behind the Regents, a tall woman in gray turns and looks back. It's Inez Quissel, Distinguished Professor of Wand-craft. Her eyes searching the gloom, she reaches instinctively for her absent wand, then remembers the ban on magic and lowers her hand. Kyril and I freeze, neither of us able to breathe until Quissel returns her attention to Lady Lynch, who hasn't finished destroying my reputation.

"We have every reason to believe Anya Winter is still alive,"

Lynch says. "After sabotaging The Isthmus, Winter attempted to assassinate Dean LaMarche, while he lay helpless and wounded in a mundane hospital. The hospital staff described her exactly. We also know that Princess Elena was last seen heading to the dungeons where Winter was held." As Lady Lynch continues to condemn me, Simon Burke throws up his hands.

"How was this monster allowed to escape?" he bursts out. "What happened to our security? What is wrong with Aradottir?"

"The real question," Lady Lynch smoothly puts in, "is what was wrong with LaMarche? He couldn't protect our students, and he allowed a traitorous hedge witch to infiltrate the faculty of The Isthmus. Sad, but perhaps fitting, that he paid such a terrible price for his poor judgment. His magic is now gone, his mind broken beyond repair."

Next to me, Kyril is completely still. He seems to be waiting for something, as if he knows the Assembly has reached a crossroads of some kind, a momentous decision in store.

Ruskin straightens his shoulders and addresses the King. "Your Majesty, I promise to do better. As Acting Dean, I will make this right. When we establish a new campus, I assure you the students will be protected exclusively by state-of-the-art Eastern security."

"Where?" inquires the King, sending a chill through the Assembly. The mosquito netting shielding the royal dais wavers and trembles, as if completely terrified. "Where on this green earth can three hundred students be protected from harm?"

"Fortress Burke," announces Simon Burke, causing Kyril to gasp aloud. "Your Majesty, I offer my castle—and my protection— to the students of The Isthmus. With your permission, I will bring them all safely to my fortress in Scotland."

CHAPTER SEVENTEEN

W e're going to the Isle of Arran." Kyril takes another bite of pizza, having already eaten two slices. He's sitting cross-legged on one of the lumpy mattresses in his hotel room. Outside, a siren wails. An air-conditioner pumps stale, tepid air. Apparently, this is how people live in the mundane world if they want to pay for everything with cash.

"To Arran?" I protest, squeezing water out of my wet hair. "You do realize that I'm a wanted criminal? And that Scotland is dangerous for hedge witches? And that Princess Elena is here in Wisconsin?"

Exhausted from nerves and hunger and lack of sleep, I've been in a foul mood ever since I attempted to wash the sludge of Lake Mendota off my feet and discovered leeches attached to my ankles. Eight of them.

"Elena won't be in Wisconsin forever," Kyril says, taking a swig of bottled tea. "If the tracking signal on her body is muted, then it means she's been imprisoned somehow. Whoever has her contained will attempt to move her as soon as they can."

Imprisoned? Is that what Ruskin had in mind for me?

I wonder if I should tell Kyril about Ruskin's potion, about the way Elena's afterimage continued to shimmer, long after she faded into the ether. I wonder if I should tell him about Burke, who must have known the storm was coming when he followed Elena to the dungeons. But not even perfect cheekbones make a man trustworthy.

I pace back and forth in front of the cinderblock wall, and then decide I have to trust him, at least a little bit. "I don't know this for sure, but I think Lord Burke may have helped sabotage the castle."

Kyril's eyes reveal nothing. "That is highly problematic, if you're correct, since the students will now be staying at Fortress Burke. I wish I'd known this before."

I take this in, feeling a bit defensive. Kyril hasn't reproached me, and yet I sense somehow that I've let him down.

I decide to tell the truth and be done with it. "Elena was trying to escape Burke and she drank a potion that Ruskin gave me. It was supposed to be *A. archangelica*, but she never returned from the ether."

"Is that so?" Kyril raises an eyebrow. "You really *are* at the center of this storm."

If this is a jibe, I choose to ignore it. "How do you know Elena's been imprisoned?"

Kyril's expression turns bleak, and he picks an invisible speck of lint from the sleeve of his silver hoodie. "I'm familiar with the tracking devices used by royal families."

"Is it possible her tracking device was tampered with, or removed?"

"The standard royal tracker is a tiny daemon, sustained by the beating of the subject's heart. As far as I know, it can't be removed without killing them both."

Kyril shudders, almost imperceptibly, and I shudder as well. Poor Elena has probably had that daemon latched onto her since she was a baby. How horrible to be a princess, under constant surveillance for your entire life.

"Nasty form of technology." Kyril offers me a slice of pizza, his wrist speckled with mosquito bites.

"A parasitic daemon is not a technology."

"You think just because it's magic, it's not a technology?"

"I hate technology, by which I mean mundane computers and electronics. As far as I'm concerned, technology is the enemy. We witches live in a constant state of fear because of mundanes and their stupid, poisonous phones and their digital this and their nanotech that. I spent half my childhood wearing sweaty hats lined with tinfoil because my dad didn't trust wool and lace to do the job."

My pizza, I notice, is ludicrously topped with bits of macaroni and cheese. This is Kyril's fault.

I glare. "But maybe I shouldn't say 'we,' since you're obviously not one of us. What kind of a wizard are you? What kind of a wizard wears a high-tech, RFID-blocking, anti-drone jacket?"

He crooks a smile. "I'm just like you, Anya."

"Just like me? Don't flatter yourself."

"But I am. We both create sequential patterns to wield power. You use strands of fiber, and I use strings of numbers running through fiber. Is that so different?"

"It's completely different, and you are nothing like me. Which is all the more reason for me *not* to go to Arran with you. Not to mention that most of Scotland is in turmoil over the hedge witch uprising."

Kyril abruptly stiffens, and his hands clench into fists.

"It's not an uprising," he says, his voice harsh. "It's a resistance. Scotland is East of the Scandinavian Keel, and the people there have a right to live free of Cibrán's aggression. Queen Marguerite went to Edinburgh on a diplomatic mission to arbitrate the peace process and she never returned—*that's* why the country's in turmoil, and that's why the truce between East and West is breaking down."

"The point is that we can't do anything about it."

Kyril closes the lid on the pizza box. "Only because you don't want to."

"What is that supposed to mean?"

"Look," he says, suddenly out of patience. "Do you want to find the princess, or don't you? Do you want to find out what happened to Arcanos Hall, or don't you?"

"Elena's my student, and The Isthmus is my home. Of course I want to find out."

"Then come to Scotland with me. Regardless of whether your suspicions about Burke are correct, we both know we'll find our answers at Fortress Burke. Whoever sent that golem with the data scourge is either a part of the university system, or its active enemy, so it stands to reason that wherever the professors and students go, the saboteur will follow. And by saboteur, I don't mean you."

I don't want to admit it, but he may be right. If Ruskin's potion has put Elena into some kind of prison, then it makes sense to follow Ruskin to the new campus. And if Burke was behind the data storm, then it makes sense to go to Fortress Burke.

"But how would we even get there?"

That's a key question. You can't take a flying carpet all the way across the Atlantic. (I mean, you could, but it would take nearly a month.) And airplanes are too dangerous to risk, so any witch who wants to travel East has to either go by ship or use one of the clockwork portals built in the Age of Arcanos. But the portals in the East are closely monitored, mainly to prevent hedge witches from escaping their indentured servitude and fleeing to the West.

"I've got a plan," Kyril says, setting aside his tea and reaching for his duffel bag.

"You do realize the portals are being watched?"

He doesn't respond. I watch him pack his bag, and I realize I don't actually know anything about him. He says he wants to manage risk, to recover Arcanos Hall, but why? What exactly is he, and who is he working for? He has an agenda—not to mention secrets—of his own, but I can't be sure that his interests and mine are even partially aligned.

I scan the prison-like walls of the hotel room, and I realize I took a huge risk coming here after the Assembly, even getting into Kyril's truck with him. What was I thinking?

"Does your plan involve flying?" I finally ask, guessing he'll want to stay in the mundane world. "Because I am *not* getting on an airplane."

"We have to, Anya. The only other choice is the fairy ring in the old orchard."

"Fairy ring? Please tell me you're joking. You know people *die* in fairy rings, or get sent to the wrong place. They're dangerous, primal forms of magic."

"Of course they are," Kyril says, finishing his tea. "They're hooked up to the ley lines. That's why we're going to fly instead."

Ley lines are dangerous forces, poorly understood and best to be left alone. Because if there's one thing you should know about magic, it's to be very, very careful with things you don't understand. Perhaps this knowledge once belonged to the Arcanos wizards, but their secrets have been forgotten. The shields surrounding our castles were built before our time, and the goblins who crafted our portals have gone forever underground.

"I can protect you," Kyril says, interrupting my melancholy thoughts about the Age of Arcanos. "And I can buy you a plane ticket. I have all kinds of frequent flyer miles."

"Frequent? You do this frequently?"

When I try to imagine a dangerous journey on a treacherous airplane in the company of mundane strangers, my mind recoils. That would be like hitchhiking on the freeway, getting into a flaming car driven by a madman, and heading off a cliff into a toxic waste dump.

"It's not safe for witches to fly in airplanes. Or use computers. Or do any of the things that you apparently love to do."

"Anya, look at me. No, really. Look at me."

Reluctantly, I meet his gaze.

"Do I look like my mind has been broken? Do I look like I'm without any powers? Apart from data storms, most mundane technology isn't toxic at all; it's just a form of interference."

"It's not safe," I protest. "What makes you think it ever could be? And who are you anyway? Why won't you come clean with me?"

He just shakes his head. He won't tell me anything of substance because he doesn't trust me any more than I trust him. So we're at an impasse.

"I'm sorry, Kyril. I'm not going to Scotland with you on an airplane. That's my final answer." Now that I've said it, I feel an inexplicable sense of loss.

"Fine. I'll go alone."

"Go right ahead."

He slides his computer and his phone into a metallic mesh sack—obviously a Faraday bag—and tucks the bag into his satchel. Then he holds out a stack of twenty-dollar bills, crisp and new and completely unlike the grimy wad of bills my father exchanged for my silver. "I'm driving to O'Hare. Here's some money, to help you stay hidden."

I fold my arms across my chest, insulted. "I don't want your money."

"Anya. Come on."

"If you're going to leave, just go."

Kyril takes a breath and says nothing, then he tugs open the metal door and jumps into his truck. I watch him through the keyhole until there's nothing left to see.

And that is how I ended up alone in a seedy hotel on the outskirts of Madison, eating macaroni-topped pizza and feeling sorry for myself. The macaroni wasn't even very good.

～

I wake before dawn to the sound of wolves. Sounds like there are two of them, most likely hunting in the marshy wetland across the freeway. Instinctively adjusting my shawl, I peer through a gap in the heavy drapes. An empty parking lot stretches out beneath the streetlights.

After being awake for over forty hours, I desperately needed sleep. I'm still exhausted, but at least my brain is functioning again. I struggle to remember what day it is, and belatedly decide it's Thursday.

Now what? A quick inspection of my room reveals peeling concrete walls, a pizza box, and clothes drying on the towel rack. I cram a stale piece of pizza into my mouth. In the cold light of day, I know I have to get to the Isle of Arran. Burke and Ruskin are there, possibly even Princess Elena, who drank a potion intended for me. Elena needs me. But even more than all that, Dean LaMarche asked for my help.

Find out, he said. Find out who's tearing this university apart.

If I'd had any faith in humanity, I would have gone to the airport with Kyril. But my parents didn't raise me to place myself in someone else's power.

Digging into my bag, I retrieve my invisibility cape. I'll get to Scotland on my own.

CHAPTER EIGHTEEN

Despite my history of telling lies, I'm a big fan of honesty, so I'll be the first to admit when I don't have a plan. But I do have an invisibility cape, and that's better than nothing.

With the portal at Arcanos Hall gone, the students will have to get to Fortress Burke through Portal Point. The only other portals nearby are mail portals, unsuited for living things. (I mean, you could send someone through a mail portal, but they might not be alive when they arrive on the other side.)

I'm guessing some of the students won't go to Fortress Burke—their parents will want them sent home instead. That could create disorder at the Point, possibly allowing me to slip into the portal undetected, so I just need to get close to the students.

Unseen, I head back to Madame Olann's yarn shop. It's one of those late September days when the air is cool and humid in the mornings, hot and muggy in the afternoons. My boots are a bit damp, and they're probably going to give me blisters, but at least they don't squeak. There's a hazy particulate floating through the air that reminds me of pollen. I don't know what it is, but it smells like magic, like some kind of potion gone airborne. No time to worry about that now.

When I arrive at The Narrow Gauge, there's a sign on the door: "Closed for Inventory. Grand Reopening October 31st."

Taping the sign to the door is my student, Bertha Bratsch.

I'd expected to see some of my other students—Fob and his cronies, maybe some of the weavers in my flying carpet class. But I hadn't expected Bertha.

She looks like a wreck. Her eyes are swollen, and her full chest heaves up and down, as if she's been running hard. Red splotches stain her freckled cheeks, accentuated by the creamy lace of her white bison shawl. She tugs open the door. Concealed by my invisibility cloak, I silently follow her inside.

The mundane floor of the yarn shop smells wooly and comforting, as usual. But it's completely disorganized: windows shuttered, tables and chairs pushed back against the walls. Bertha heads for the back room and climbs up through the trap door next to the four-harness looms. I follow her up the ladder, and when I get to The Narrower Gauge on the second floor, I realize my students have already gone. So has Madame Olann's mysterious loom.

In their place is a haggard woman with chalky skin, curled up under a blanket by the fire. Her hair is stringy, her face prematurely lined. Her fingernails are thick and gray. There's something almost uncanny about her, something that isn't quite right.

Bertha slips into the club chair across from the sofa and removes a tea cozy from the teapot. "Your tea's ready. Gotta have some tea."

"So tired," the woman sighs, her papery eyelids fluttering.

Bertha fills a flowered cup, splashing a bit into the saucer. "It's Earl Grey, ma. Your favorite. Doesn't it smell good?"

Bertha's mother lifts her drooping head and sniffs the air, her gaze shifting past Bertha to the wood floor beneath my feet. "Smells like fish."

"It's oil of bergamot," Bertha says, her voice strained. "Smells like oranges. Not like fish."

The woman abruptly sits upright, throwing off her blanket and exposing a gaunt, wasted figure. Nostrils flaring, she points a bony finger at my invisible boots. "Stranger, you've brought the lake with you."

Eyes wide, Bertha spins around, faster than I would have imagined possible, and flings the entire pot of tea into my chest.

You've probably never been scorched by hot tea while completely invisible. I can tell you that it's not much different from being scorched by hot tea while completely visible, except that you're screaming and flailing about unseen, until your cape falls off and your assailant recognizes you.

"Miss Winter!" Bertha gasps. "What are you doing here?

"Ice," I sputter, fanning at my burning chest. "I need ice."

Bertha races up the steps to the attic kitchen, leaving me alone with her mother, whose eyes are cold steel, hungry and searching.

"Have a seat," she says with a guttural rasp, tapping the leather sofa cushion with her thickened nails.

"Um, thanks, but if it's all the same to you . . ." My scorched skin flashes with a sudden chill, as I belatedly realize I'm talking to a werewolf. *Oh, shit.*

I gape at her, and her lips curl back, revealing sharp, pointed teeth.

Bertha comes down the stairs with the ice. "Oh, for goodness sake, ma. Stop growling at Miss Winter! She's my professor."

Moments later, with a bright blue ice pack pressed against my chest, I'm nervously introducing myself to Hulda Bratsch. Having spent my childhood caught between two worlds, I'm aware that prejudice is a terrible thing. Fear of people who are different is a poison, and I don't want to be poisoned. But werewolves are incredibly dangerous—especially to their loved ones—and they kill without thinking, without even knowing what they've done.

"Anya Winter," Hulda repeats my name slowly, as if storing it in a great treasure house. Her cold eyes never leave my face. "You're a long way from home."

What does that mean?

"Please, drink some tea." Bertha returns once more, setting down a tray with Madame Olann's best tea service. "We've got another pot of Earl Grey."

Bertha's face is still swollen, her cheeks puffy and red, and belatedly it occurs to me that I've interrupted something.

"Bertha, are you alright?" I don't bother to ask why she isn't with the other students, since that's now abundantly clear. She's taking care of a werewolf.

Bertha and her mother exchange a weary glance, and she pours me a cup of tea.

"I'll just be glad if we can get home to the Apostle Islands."

"The Apostle Islands?" Twenty-two sparsely populated islands near the shores of Lake Superior, they're a haven for trolls and other magical beings. "But aren't you going to Fortress Burke to finish the school year?"

She drops two lumps of sugar into her cup. "Not going."

"But what about your scholarship?"

"Not going."

"You should go," her mother says, in a voice that would have been firm if she were anything other than a spent, sickly werewolf.

"You say that because you don't remember! You don't remember last night in the wetlands, how you nearly killed that man. But *I* remember. We have to go home. There's no place for us here," Bertha concludes bitterly, pouring herself the dregs of the tea.

"There's no place for me here." Hulda's voice is a soft growl. "But you aren't me. You aren't like me. You have your own life."

Ignoring her, Bertha shoves a large biscuit into her mouth.

I press the icepack against my chest, suddenly grateful for all the lonely years I spent in a converted missile silo. Everyone thinks their own dysfunctional childhood is the worst. But then they see a broader world.

"Have you talked to Monsita Olann?" I ask, mainly to steer the subject away from Bertha and Hulda's painful silence. "If you have, you probably know I'm a wanted criminal."

"We heard something about that," Bertha says, her voice casually neutral. "Not that we believe it."

"You don't?"

Her pale eyebrows arch upward. "Kidnapping the princess? Forcing the Regents to destroy the university? Attempting to assassinate the dean? You don't have it in you."

"Thanks . . . I guess."

Hulda taps a long gray nail against the side of her teacup, and it rings like a dinner bell. Her wolfish eyes don't blink. "What exactly are you doing here, Anya Winter? If you're trying to clear your name, you should know you'll never succeed. Reputations can't be repaired. The magical world is too small for that. Once you've been marked as an enemy, you'll be hated and feared forever."

Bertha gazes glumly into her teacup, as if seeing the charnel house that was her childhood, and I realize that if there's anyone in this world I can trust to keep a secret, it's a werewolf and her only child.

"I'm not trying to repair my reputation. I'm trying to make things right. Princess Elena hasn't been kidnapped by strangers. Arcanos Hall hasn't been destroyed. But they're gone, and I have to find them both."

Hulda doesn't even blink, but Bertha's eyes widen. "How can I help?"

"I need to get to Scotland. I was thinking I could slip into the portal with you, if you're going to Portal Point."

She and her mother exchange worried frowns. "Then you don't know?"

"Don't know what?"

"Madame Olann took the last portage out this morning. She waited until dawn so she could warn us. King Cibrán thinks Elena is still in Madison. His men have taken over the city. They've closed Portal Point, locked down the entire isthmus."

Realization dawns. "The pollen in the air outside—"

Bertha nods. "It's a marking potion. No one who's touched by magic can get out."

My first reaction is selfish dismay, but then I see Hulda's face and my blood runs cold. This is so much worse than I thought.

"You're trapped here, aren't you? Surrounded by all these people. There's still one more night with a full moon, and you don't have a safe place to transform."

Hulda pulls back dry lips and reveals a sharp set of canines. "This shop won't contain me, not at night, not with the smell of human flesh permeating the city. No ordinary building can. We can't get back to the wetlands outside the city, and there's no other place we can go. I think we may have reached the end of the road."

She exhales with a hollow stare. "Did you see the great spinning wheel on the first floor? It has a spindle of pure silver."

"Suicide is not a plan, ma!" Bertha cries out. "You can't think like that."

Hulda turns a cold eye on her daughter. "We knew this day would come. It's time for you to live your own life. And I will die before I let myself kill another human being."

"Wait," I say, frantically scrambling to come up with a plan that doesn't involve the werewolf's suicide. "There's got to be another way. There's always hope."

Hulda regards me wearily. "Hope's a little hard to come by when you've had the life I've had."

"But there are options we haven't considered—there must be!"

My first thought is the steam tunnels under the university. But I can't guarantee they'll be secure or accessible anymore— the King's guards could be searching there as we speak. Then I remember Kyril's words at the hotel.

"What about a fairy ring? I heard there's a ring somewhere close, near an orchard."

Bertha frowns, puzzled. "You mean the Old Orchard by Portal Point?"

Hulda lets out a harsh whistle. "So the legends are true. There's a fairy ring on the isthmus. It's a slim chance, but it's a chance nonetheless."

⌒〜⌒

Once you step inside a fairy ring, you can't get out. Not while there's a full moon. You're entirely subject to the wild magic inside the ring. In general, that's a very bad thing. But if you're a werewolf, then it might just be a good thing.

Provided that the fairy ring in the Old Orchard is still intact, then Hulda may have a safe place to transform. I don't know whether that same ring can also transport me to the Isle of Arran, but I figure we'll take things one at a time. Right now, I've got a werewolf to manage.

Madame Olann took her best yarns with her to Scotland, along with her floor loom, which must have taken a massive effort to move. But she left a lot behind, including a beautiful invisibility cape that suits Bertha to a tee. So Bertha and I are soon hurrying unseen down the Lakeshore Path, heading for the Old Orchard, which is right near the base of Portal Point. We've both been coated with the strange magical pollen that's blowing over the city, but so has every other witch remaining in Madison. I'm guessing that most of King Cibrán's security team is patrolling the perimeters of the isthmus, so as long as we don't approach the boundary, perhaps we can remain undetected.

"What will Cibrán's men do if they find you?" Bertha whispers.

"If I'm lucky, they'll kill me." I shudder, and the air around me ripples. If Cibrán has brought Eastern magic with him, then he's probably also brought Eastern justice.

Bertha is silent, undoubtedly thinking about her mother. East of the Scandinavian Keel, werewolves are killed on sight.

Hulda is sleeping away the morning in Madame Olann's garret, and something tells me I'm never going to get another chance to talk to Bertha about her future.

I wait for a spandex-clad team of bicyclists to speed past, and then I take my chance. "Your mom's right, you know. Your life is your own. Once you get her safely back to the Apostle Islands, you really should go to Fortress Burke with the rest of the students."

"And leave her behind?" I can't see her face, but she sounds angry and defensive.

"Yes," I say, as coldly as I can. "Leave her behind."

It's funny how we encourage people to do things we'd never do ourselves. I think about what it must have cost my dad to send me away to a magical boarding school, just months after losing my mom. I didn't want to go, but I was twelve and he gave me no choice. He was alone after that, completely alone, and the only consolation he had was that he'd given me the best possible chance to live my own life. He raised me to go where he could not.

There's a crew team rowing on Lake Mendota, and I slow my pace to watch their boat sweep by. Eight women pull their oars in perfect time, while their coxswain chants directions, her small body hunched in the stern as she glides into the sun. They can't see where they're going, but she's guiding them. She's guiding them to a place they can't see.

"Bertha, listen to me. You're so talented, you could be certified in anything—you could even learn to use a wand. A hedge witch with a college degree! Don't you want that?"

Bertha makes a snort of disgust. "I'm guessing the rumors about you are true, that you really do have a mundane father. That would explain why you don't understand what it's like for me here, why you don't even understand your own position on campus. Did it ever occur to you that maybe the university isn't all that it's cracked up to be?"

I bark out a bitter laugh. I don't need Bertha to tell me that The Isthmus is backstabbing and corrupt. "You sound like Madame Olann. She's always saying the university exists only to perpetuate the status quo."

"You know she's right."

I sigh, unwilling to argue. If I want to convince Bertha to stay in school, I'll have to try a different approach.

We're now on the very edge of the isthmus, just where it meets the narrow peninsula forming Portal Point. I look around, aware that Cibrán's security forces should be nearby. Sure enough, a flare of blue light is just visible between the UW-Hospital and Eagle Heights. That must be the boundary on our left, a quarter mile away. On our right, only two hundred yards away, is another blue flare, this one blocking access to the Point.

There's only one way we can go—into a tall stand of stinging nettles, straight ahead. So we plunge into the weeds, heading for the Old Orchard.

The presence of nettles makes me confident that there really is a fairy ring in the orchard up ahead. For centuries, the stalks of woodland nettles have been retted and spun into enchanted fiber, then knitted or woven into magical textiles. It's said that the only successful resurrection shroud in the history of magic was woven with nettles harvested from a graveyard.

"Do you know the story of the princess whose brothers were turned into swans?" I whisper, holding my arms above my head to keep my cape from snagging. Nettles can pierce through dense clothing, and they sting like you wouldn't believe.

"She used knitting magic, didn't she?"

"Right. She couldn't speak to anyone for seven years, and she had to spin nettles into yarn and then knit a coat for each of her

166

brothers. She saved them."

Bertha pushes past me, leaving a wake in the nettles. "But only after the priests tried to burn her at the stake for witchcraft. How is this a *happy* story?"

"I'm just saying it's a good thing the princess knew how to knit."

Bertha's voice drops, barely carrying over the wind in the trees. "It wasn't knitting that saved the princess and her brothers. It was silence and perseverance. And I know all about that. My mother was turned into a werewolf when I was five. Stop trying to convince me to go back to school."

I'm about to respond when the dense thicket of nettles gives way to a clearing. Instinct kicking in, I clamp down hard on Bertha's invisible shoulder just before she steps in the clearing.

She tumbles backwards, yelping in surprise. "What's wrong?"

"It's the fairy ring," I hiss, pulling her to her feet. "You almost stepped inside."

CHAPTER NINETEEN

At the most basic level, a fairy ring is a perfect circle of enchanted mushrooms. The ring in the Old Orchard is a large, perfect circle of very imperfect mushrooms, most of them wilted and black, or with their heads knocked off. In the center of the ring is another perfect circle, about eight feet in diameter, this one made up of tender green shoots surrounding an overgrown plum tree. I wasn't expecting to see that inner circle.

I throw off my cape, and Bertha follows suit.

"So what do we do?" She hovers on the edge of the ring, her worn slippers almost touching a decaying mushroom. "How do we know whether it works?"

I crouch down and examine the mushroom barrier, trying to remember my mom's stories. "We need to get inside and see what's going on with that inner circle. Circle the fairy ring nine times, counter-clockwise. Never circle the ring a tenth time. Then step inside. As long as the sun is up, we can still get out again."

"What happens if we circle a tenth time?"

"I don't think we want to find out."

I orbit the fairy ring with care, and Bertha paces behind me.

Nervously joining hands, we step inside the ring after the ninth circle, and a gust of wind hits us right in the face. Bertha turns her head, the ends of her shawl flapping, her eyes narrowed into slits. Then, just as suddenly as it came, the wind is gone.

"What was that?" she gasps.

"Raw, primal magic," I say, wiping sweat from my forehead. This fairy ring is definitely operational. "Better get used to it."

Fairy rings create a perfect seal surrounding wild, uncontrolled forces of magic. Imagine a jar of food forgotten in the cupboard, filled to the brim with something dangerously expired. Now open the lid.

The ring of leafy tree shoots is just a few feet away, a perfect circle surrounding the dying plum tree. I inch closer, wondering what to make of the tiny little shoots, and then I realize what they're for. They radiate out from the old plum as if connected by spokes of a wheel.

"An earth loom," I marvel. "Someone grew an earth loom inside this fairy ring."

"What's an earth loom?"

Inching my way around the earth loom, I visualize the invisible warp threads leading from the shoots to the old tree. "If you want to know, you'll have to take my course on woven textiles."

Bertha rolls her eyes. "Nice try, professor. What does it do?"

"Controls chaos."

Let me be clear: an earth loom is not a foolproof way to control the chaotic magic of a fairy ring. An earth loom is more like a ship made from the sea itself. It can't protect you from the surging waves, but it can buffer and direct your journey.

During a full moon, the forces inside a fairy ring could take you anywhere, at any time. But a fairy ring that's equipped with an earth loom is a different matter. The earth loom might not take you where you want to go, but it will take you where you *need* to go. If you're a werewolf, that could be your salvation.

"We'll need fresh nettles to weave into the loom," I tell Bertha. "Lots of them. When the moon rises, they'll help buffer the forces in the ring. The fairy ring will contain your mother after she transforms, but hopefully the earth loom will keep her from being sent away at random—it might even transport her home."

Bertha produces a small dagger, her face grim. "To help my mom, I'll cut down every nettle in this forest."

"They can't be wilted," I caution, remembering my mother's herb-lore. "They have to be alive, still tied to the earth. We'll have to pull them up by their roots." Realizing what this means, I lean forward and tear the bottom hem from my skirt. Woodland nettles can sting you through your clothes, and the only way to uproot them is to wear gloves, or to wrap your hands in strips of fabric.

"Let's go," Bertha calls from the mushroom border. "We don't have much time."

Soon, we're carrying armfuls of uprooted nettles back to the fairy ring, then carefully weaving them into a circular web between the young suckers and the old plum.

Did I mention that nettles sting? Yes, I did.

I flex my linen-wrapped fingers. "Thank the Elders that Madame Olann's house is filled with herbs. We're going to need a strong poultice when we get back."

"We've got to hurry," Bertha says, with an eye on the light fading from the leaves. "My mother—she's desperate. If she thinks she doesn't have a way out . . ."

"I know, Bertha."

"There's no cure for people like my mom, and there isn't anybody who wants to invest resources in finding a cure, because nobody thinks it will happen to their family." She goes on braiding nettle stalks, her face set. "When I got the scholarship to come here, it took me all summer to set up a safe zone in the wetlands so I could care for her when there's a full moon. I wanted to study potion-making, to *see* if I could help people like my mom, and I thought coming here was worth the risk."

"You could be a really great chemist."

She sniffs. "That's not going to happen. No one's going to take a hedge witch like me under their wing. I'll never obtain any elite skills. I might not even earn a wand. The Regents had to give me the scholarship based on my test scores—King Nestor's education edict insisted on that. But they don't want me here. I don't belong at Arcanos Hall."

"You belong here," I insist, folding the weft of nettles into the web. "Don't ever let anyone tell you that you don't. Just because other people are prejudiced, doesn't mean that you don't belong. When I came to The Isthmus, Ruskin was the only professor who would even talk to me, but that doesn't mean I don't belong."

"You never went to college, did you? I heard you got hired even though you don't have any certifications or a wand."

Bertha's tone isn't accusatory, but I find myself on the defensive anyhow. "Dean LaMarche gave me the job. He said we needed a textile curriculum, and that I was the best candidate."

Bertha lowers her voice, even though we're alone. "Want to know what I heard? Some of the students wanted to get out of taking your classes because you were just a hedge witch, but they couldn't. The dean forbade it."

I nod, mentally thanking the dean. "That's because the magical bylaws of the university contain an unbreakable charter, that there must always be a professor of textiles, that each student must always take at least one class."

Textiles are an ancient form of magic, not to be forgotten. Whenever I'm tempted to feel like a second-class citizen, I remind myself that the Arcanos wizards who founded the university believed in the value of textiles. They believed in people like me.

"I wonder what would have happened if they'd broken the charter," Bertha muses, handing me the last plait of nettles. "Magical charters are pretty intense. Don't they work the same way as a curse?"

I fold the nettles into the loom. "They do. When old Zemlinsky died, Dean LaMarche had to find someone right away. And since no one in the aristocracy studies textiles anymore, they had to hire a hedge witch."

This explains so much, like the way Inez Quissel and the other professors pretended I didn't exist every time I entered the faculty lunchroom. They refused to treat me as an equal. A rabbit hole of memory beckons—Ruskin's web of lies, Quissel's disdainful remarks about my training—but there's no time for that now. The sky is turning red.

I step back from the earth loom. "Our loom is ready, and there's a full moon rising."

CHAPTER TWENTY

Have you ever flipped to the last page of a scary book, just to reassure yourself that everything is going to be all right? If you have, then you probably don't want to know what the next few hours involved. Seeing a woman go through the agony of transforming into a werewolf is nothing you want to witness firsthand. There's a whole lot of anguish, pleading, and dread. It's really much better to skip ahead.

A huge gray wolf is snarling and pacing inside the fairy ring, flinging itself against the barrier of mushrooms, only to be repelled by the forces holding the ring intact. Breathless and appalled, Bertha and I watch from outside the circle.

I'm pretty sure I'm going to be permanently traumatized by having witnessed this transformation just once. But Hulda's daughter has had to face this her whole life.

I struggle to find the right words. "Bertha, I'm so sorry."

She glares at the gaunt, four-legged beast inside the ring. "Tell you one thing. I know for sure I'm going to find a cure."

This is probably the last thing I expected her to say. But there it is in her eyes: the kind of determination that fuels discovery, the kind of drive that can change the world.

I feel suddenly lighter, as if I've kicked off a heavy pair of boots. Bertha's situation is certainly terrible, but there may yet be an unburdened future for her and her mother, free of the deadly curse. They could be happy someday.

The werewolf bares its terrible fangs and circles the earth loom, clawing suspiciously at the braided web of nettles.

"Do you think she'll go into the loom?" It's not clear how much of Hulda's personality has carried over into her werewolf side. She's just a beast now, with deadly claws and a molting gray coat.

Bertha shakes her head. "She won't remember we talked about it. If she enters the loom at all, it will be by accident."

"Maybe that's for the best. With the loom buffering the ring, we know she'll be safe here tonight. But if she steps inside, we don't know for sure where it will take her."

"Are you saying it might not work?"

"Bertha, this is the first earth loom I've ever made. I know the principles, but—"

Before I can finish, the werewolf abruptly tips back her massive head and emits a bloodcurdling howl. Bertha covers her ears with her hands and darts a glance back at the nettle fields. We're less than a quarter mile from the boundary of the isthmus, less than a quarter mile from King Cibrán's guards.

"I hope they didn't hear that," I say as a flash of azure light soars over the trees.

"They heard it." Bertha's face hardens. She reaches into her tote and withdraws her invisibility cape. "They're coming for the wolf."

"These capes aren't going to do us any good. We're both coated with that magical pollen. They'll spot her inside the ring, and then they'll find us as well."

"They'll kill her in the morning," Bertha growls. Her eyes narrow, and for the first time, I see something wolf-like in her expression. "I'm not going to let that happen."

"Bertha—you're not going in there!"

"Damn right I am. She'll catch the scent of my blood, and she'll follow me into the loom. Didn't you say the earth loom takes everyone where they need to go? If it works the way you say it does—and it had damn well better work—then it will take me to the Apostle Islands. There are trees everywhere, trees she can't climb." She throws the cape over her shoulders, and pulls up the hood.

"You're risking your life!" I cry, but she's already gone.

Once you enter a fairy ring, you can't get out again. Not when there's a full moon. I told you that before, but it meant something different then. Now I'm watching in horror as the werewolf goes mad with bloodlust—eyes gleaming red with hunger. She leaps across the fairy ring, teeth snapping together as she catches Bertha's cape in her jaws. Visible once more, Bertha has jumped into the branches of the old plum tree. She hangs for a moment, gazing down into the web of nettles.

"Follow me," she calls to her mother. "Follow me home." And then she falls into the darkness of the loom, and the wolf lunges after her with a crash.

They're gone at once, and the earth loom lies empty and broken.

I don't know where the ring has taken them and I don't know whether to be relieved or horrified, but I don't exactly have time to decide, since I'm still in a tight spot. Voices are shouting in the darkness of the woods—soldiers approaching.

A whooshing flare soars above the trees, and then blue lights rain down on me like glittering fragments of brilliant blue topaz.

"There it is!" On the edge of the nettle field, flecked with blue light, a man raises a crossbow, and my heart completely stops.

Once I step into that fairy ring, I won't be getting out. And if the earth loom is broken, then I'll be subject to the wild forces of magic inside the ring. Under a full moon, those forces could take me anywhere. But it sure beats an arrow to the chest.

I hurl myself over the threshold, and the fairy wind hits me so hard, I almost lose hold of my satchel. Staggering closer to the woven braids of nettles, I can see the loom has broken where Bertha and the werewolf plunged through. A faint afterimage flickers—a wolf pacing on a shoreline, a young woman hanging from the branch of an old pine. They're okay.

Bertha Bratsch, you are a total badass. And you're right: you don't need a diploma to change the world.

Outside the fairy ring, an arrow soars from a crossbow, hitting the ring barrier and snapping into fragments that spark and flash and ricochet through the trees.

"You there!" yells the shooter, a tall man in Carpathian armor. "Hands up!"

But I couldn't raise my hands even if I tried. A gust of wind blows the broken nettles apart, and the mushrooms glow white beneath the yellow moon. It's midnight, and the ring is spinning with wild magic. I'm falling and there is no ground.

I can't feel my hands or my feet, but the empty pit in my belly tells me I'm traveling fast, caught in the spiraling web of the fairy ring. I've crossed the boundary and entered another plane. I've lost my hold, at risk of spiraling forever.

Frantic, I try to remember my hedge lore. I'm no good at spoken spells, no good at all, but still I call out the words of the Hearthstone, the most powerful homing spell I know. The wind tears the words from my throat.

For a moment, a crumbling ruin appears before me: a decaying stone amphitheater, long shadows stretching over broken marble pillars. I glimpse a turquoise sea, and the tall masts of a wooden schooner. Whatever this place is, it isn't home. Then the vision is gone, and I'm landing hard in a marshy bog. I'm soaking wet, and it's pouring rain.

CHAPTER TWENTY-ONE

I've never set foot outside the Midwest, but I can tell right away I must be near an ocean. Waves crash on rocks close by. A hint of sunrise peeks through the rain. The air is fresh and biting, scented with brine.

I roll to my side, snagging my head on something rough, only to discover it's a soggy, bedraggled sheep gnawing on my hair. She stares at me, placidly chewing.

"Hello," I say out loud. She looks like an enchanted Shetland ewe, which means I might be somewhere in magical Scotland. I reach out to touch the smooth white blaze on her face, but she snorts and ambles off, black and white rump disappearing into the rain.

I pull myself upright, heels sinking into a bog. The waves are coming from the east, but from the west as well. So I must be on some kind of peninsula.

Taking stock, I decide I'm most definitely alive—which is excellent—and still in possession of my satchel. My head is killing me, but at least I haven't been eaten or infected by a werewolf. Retrieving my invisibility cape, which thankfully appears undamaged, I drape it over my body. Then I check the rest of my gear:

a few skeins of handspun yarn, the Hollerith cards and my passport, my dad's grimy wad of twenty-dollar bills. Plus a pair of silver epaulets and a notebook in Old Norse—both taken from Elena's dead visitor, neither of any value so far.

I head for the shoreline, and with each laborious step, a wet shoe makes a loud squelching gulp. The mist clears and my steps grow steady as the bog gives way to stone.

In front of me lies a broad platform of clay-colored rock, with smooth ripples spreading out like a hardened wave of orange lava. There's a mundane woman walking across the rippled surface, her spindly legs knocking around in an oversized pair of green rubber boots. She gives me a hard stare before continuing on her way.

I don't spend a lot of time thinking about my appearance, but I glance at the nettles tangled in my wet linen skirts, and I realize I probably look like a feral child. Belatedly, I remember I'm also a wanted criminal.

Then I freeze in place, too shocked even to breathe. That woman could see me.

As a matter of instinct, I raise my hand to adjust my invisibility cape, but it's perfectly intact. Why isn't my cape working?

I wonder if my Hearthstone Spell actually worked, or if the fairy ring and the broken earth loom brought me here of their own accord. Whatever the ring did, its wild magic obviously compromised my invisibility cape in the process.

I pull off the cape and tug at its cabled pattern, hoping to see the stitches glisten with power. But they're lifeless coils of ordinary yarn. A quick inspection reveals that my skeins of handspun and my mother's precious shawl have also been stripped of magic. Not even my woven bracelet is intact. Which means I'm stuck on an island in a foreign country with no armor, no invisibility cape, and no functional yarn. Stupid fairy ring.

Stripped of magic or not, my mother's shawl is still my greatest treasure. As I'm gently slipping it back into my satchel, I discover a greasy clump of crimped gray wool clinging to the eyelet lace. A parting gift from the Shetland sheep.

To make a new shawl, I'll definitely need to collect some more wool. A trail curves along the edge of the peninsula, and I follow it, spotting a few more tufts of fleece clinging to brambly thorns of wild gorse. I pull a tuft free, then grab another.

I'm about to pocket a handful of enchanted wool when I realize the fairy ring could have destroyed more than just my magical artifacts. It also could have destroyed my ability to perform magic.

Terror crashes over me. I remember Dean LaMarche's sad resignation at the loss of his powers: "They're as good as gone."

But I would be lost without my magic. I wouldn't be myself anymore.

Frantic, I roll a greasy clump of Shetland fleece between my hands, alternately tugging and twisting at the draft until it forms a few inches of yarn. Then I hold it taut between my fingers and try to breathe some of my life energy into the yarn. But I'm shaking so hard, I can't hold my hands steady.

Drawing a ragged breath, I focus my energies and try again. When you spin yarn, you're essentially storing energy in fiber, and when you spin magic yarn, you're storing magical energy in fiber. To my relief, the yarn abruptly flares with a tiny burst of power, forming an energized single.

My powers aren't gone. I can still create spells.

There are a number of things in this world that are unambiguously bad, and one of them is being caught molesting someone else's sheep.

Certain breeds of primitive landrace sheep—Shetlands included—have fleece that simply breaks when it gets too long. So they're susceptible to rooing, which is just a fancy name for tugging the fleece off their bodies instead of shearing it.

Fifteen minutes later, I'm frolicking on the hillside with a flock of Shetland ewes, gathering up loose tufts of their fleece, when a shepherd appears on the windswept moor.

Bundled in rain gear and leaning on a staff, he's a man in his fifties, weather-beaten face set in a permanent scowl. "Just what are you doing? Are you wanting me to set my dogs on you?" Right on cue, a pair of vicious brown dogs comes bounding over the ridge.

"What?"

"Don't think I canna see what you're doing!" He points his staff at the mound of stolen fleece spilling from my satchel. "You don't belong here. And yer stealing my fleece."

Too exhausted from magical travel and ordinary sleep deprivation to tell even one more lie, I hold up my mother's drop spindle, which is made from maple and embellished with runes. "I'm sorry, I'm not a thief. I didn't mean to steal. It's just . . . I need some fiber to make yarn. Please. I have money—I can pay you."

Something changes then, and the man looks me up and down, eventually producing a distorted grimace of a smile. "Why, you've been riding the hedge, have you? Came in through the Fairy Glen?"

I can only gape at him. He's a hedge witch.

He points his staff at my chest and utters a word of power, and at once invisible bonds pin my arms to my side. "Whoever you are, you'll be coming with me."

CHAPTER TWENTY-TWO

W hat do you want?" I stumble up the hillside, arms trapped at my side, while the man digs through my satchel. He pauses over my mother's shawl, his eyes narrowing at the fine lace pattern.

"I'll be asking the questions," he snarls. "You aren't the first spy we've had in these parts. Where'd you get this lace? And what're you doing in Lochranza?"

"Lochranza?"

He gestures with his staff as we crest the ridge, indicating the village in the harbor below. "You're in Lochranza, the tip of Arran. Don't play the innocent with me."

The village of Lochranza is anchored by the ruins of a castle. Empty and desolate, the crumbling, roofless structure stands on a promontory overlooking a serene harbor.

Nudged down the hill by my captor's dogs, I can't stop looking at the castle. The ruin is clearly mundane—probably just an old royal hunting lodge—but that's not the important thing. The important thing is the location. The castle stands on a long, narrow peninsula, one shaped like a beckoning finger. Just like Portal Point.

There's power there, hidden in the ruins. Maybe that's where Lord Burke's castle lies. Maybe that's where the students and professors have gone—to Fortress Burke, the replacement for Arcanos Hall.

"I'm not going to ask you again," the man says. "Where did you get this shawl?"

"My mother made it for me."

"Twisted horseshoes? Running through eyelet lace? Like hell, she did."

He marches me over to a copse of trees, which glimmer faintly, suggesting the presence of a cloaking spell. We cross a threshold of some sort, and immediately, an old farmhouse comes into view. A low fence made of stone surrounds it. Yards of wire netting stretch out above the stone fence, protecting the colorful gardens from the sheep, who have followed us—bleating incessantly—down the hill.

"Get inside," he snaps, as the gate swings open of its own accord.

A woman appears in the doorway. Her shoulders are stooped and rounded, her graying hair pulled into a bun. "Who's that, John?"

"A spy. Found her snoopin' round the cliffs above the Fairy Glen."

She sniffs. "Always thinking everyone's a spy."

"I'm not a spy," I protest as I'm hustled into the cottage. Inside, two cracked leather chairs and a spinning wheel form a crescent around a neatly swept hearth. A battered steamer chest hugs the wall beneath the narrow window.

"I'm telling you she's a spy. Came in through the fairy ring up in the glen."

The woman laughs merrily. "So we know she's either very stupid or very brave."

"Stole my fleece, she did." John holds up the satchel, which overflows with contraband roving. "Saw her with my own eyes, stripping it right off the sheep's back."

"Your fleece?" Recklessly, I decide to throw caution to the wind. "Aren't all the sheep on this island property of Lord Burke?"

There's a sudden, total silence. The woman covers her mouth with a work-worn hand. Then John rushes forward and shoves me into one of the leather chairs. "I'm a free man! You hear me? A property owner! And these sheep are my own, free and clear."

"Does Burke know that? Does he know you're living here?"

"I knew it! You're working for the bastard."

"Never!" I cry, trying to stand, but the chair holds me magically in place. "He's the one who put Rocco in jail."

John tosses my mother's shawl to the woman. "Look at this, Patsy. The little spy had it in her bag."

Patsy takes a deep breath. Then she unfolds the lace slowly and carefully, as if unwrapping a wedding gift.

"Well, then," she says, with the air of someone who's seen a puzzle come together.

At this point, I'm completely beside myself. "My mother made that for me. You have to give it back."

Instead of replying, the woman slips my shawl into the old steamer trunk. "What else has she got in her pack, John?"

His face grim, John reaches into the satchel and pulls out the pencil-scrawled notebook I'd taken from the dead man in Elena's wardrobe. "She has Liam's book."

Aghast, Patsy lets the lid fall on the trunk. She rushes forward and grabs the book, brandishing it like a weapon. "You killed him! You killed my cousin!"

"What? Who? No!" I try to get away, but I'm trapped in the chair. "I didn't kill anyone."

"His epaulets." John holds up the silver ornaments I'd taken from the dead man's coat. "She took them as well. When she killed him."

"The man who was wearing that coat was already dead," I protest. "He died on the roof of Arcanos Hall, struck by lightning. All I did was knit him a shroud."

"Arcanos Hall?" Patsy takes a step back. "In the West? How

can that be?"

John exhales, walks over to the window. His voice is quiet, almost resigned. "Liam was exchanging letters with a witch from the West. He told his friends about her . . . said she was working for the cause."

My mouth drops open. Princess Elena was working for the cause?

He turns on me, gripping the silver epaulets. "You! You're the one who lured the poor lad to his death. We found him at Machrie Moor—where you were paid handsomely to betray him, weren't you?"

I try to hold up my hands, but they're pinned to my side. "No one paid me to betray anyone. I don't even know what a Machrie Moor is. Whoever killed your cousin took his coat and went to The Isthmus in his stead."

"He was a big guy," I add, not knowing if it will make a difference. "His coat didn't fit."

They stare at me, as if this detail were somehow too particular, too specific, to be untrue. For a moment, I imagine they're relenting. Perhaps they believe me.

"They didn't find his coat at the moor," Patsy murmurs, her tone cautious. "And this witch—look at her eyes, John."

He cuts her off. "We'll see what Nico has to say."

"Who's Nico?" I ask.

"Nico's the one who's going to lead us all to freedom. But there'll be no freedom for the likes of you. And if you're lying . . . "

Turning his back on me, John heads out the door.

Trapped in a battered leather chair, desperate with exhaustion, I am not about to be offered up to some clan chief who might be willing to kill me. I need to get out of here.

However. The magic holding me in this chair is stronger than anything I've got, and without charms or yarn for spells, I'm stuck here. Unless I can get Patsy on my side.

She's washing dishes at the chipped enamel sink, pretending to ignore me. But her posture is expectant, watchful.

"Why did you take my shawl?"

No answer.

"My mother made that shawl, from yarn she spun herself." I don't know if I'm getting through to her, but one of the things I know about the truth is that it's more powerful, more potent than any lie. And I know Patsy wants the truth.

"She was dying. I was twelve, and my mother was dying. There was something in her lungs, from when she worked in the ether mines. She'd been working underground, trying to pay off her indenture. But she was sick, she needed medicine, and there were always more debts. Her whole life was debt, and she could never get ahead."

Standing at the washbasin, Patsy has stopped moving.

"She told me how she got free. She spun a web portal and found her way out. And the shawl—she made that shawl for me. Her name was Laurel. But you already know that."

Patsy finally turns, her face streaked with tears. "What do you want?"

"Just give me my shawl and let me go. It's more than anyone ever did for my mom."

CHAPTER TWENTY-THREE

I'm not the sort of person who dwells on the past. It doesn't do any good. Our history wells up behind us like a reservoir, treacherous and deep. All those years my mom barely survived, my dad's empty kitchen, my own disappointed search for love—if I open those floodgates, I'll be drowned. It's better to keep moving.

But as I hurry away from Patsy's house, I can't shake the feeling that I'm leaving a story behind. Patsy knew my mom. She could tell me stories about the past, maybe even a story that could make a difference. But there's no time for that. There's only what I owe to Dean LaMarche, to Elena. I've got work to do, and I can't risk being caught here when John and his friend Nico come back.

Below me, the village of Lochranza is hemmed in on all sides by mountains and steep hills. A single road hugs the narrow bay, edged with whitewashed cottages and a small church. Not far from the church, a skinny promontory leads to the ruined castle.

I have no idea if the ruined castle is also the site of Fortress Burke, but I have a strong hunch there's magic on that peninsula, which means it's the best possible place for me to start looking.

I shoot a glance behind me. Patsy and John's house has already disappeared, cloaked in the spell keeping them hidden from the world. I wish I could do the same, but until I can make another invisibility cape, I'm stuck with being visible and exposed. So I stroll down the hill, heading for Lochranza.

The town is gloriously green and completely overrun by enchanted sheep. They're everywhere—in the gardens, on the deserted golf course, rubbing their shaggy coats against the automobiles. Above the cloud of woolly bodies and whitewashed cottages, above the lush grass and the black slate roofs, a forest stretches up to a range of craggy mountains, reminding me that the peaks themselves could be a source of magical power.

The narrow road is festooned with a single telephone line, which has an oddly reassuring effect on me. There can't be a large number of dangerous electromagnetic fields in a town with a narrow road and only one phone line. This island has probably never seen a data storm. If the rest of Arran were like this, I could actually roam around like a country witch, free as a bird, without a hat or a shawl.

I make my way to the promontory, where a group of tourists have parked their bicycles on the shingle beach. I'm about to follow them to the castle, when I see John emerging from the ruin. Leaning on his staff, he's turning his head to speak to someone still inside.

I can't risk being caught again, not after seeing the worry in Patsy's eyes as she let me go. John's probably found his friend Nico, the one who's going to interrogate me—he's probably about to bring Nico home.

Spinning around, I sprint back to the road, heading for the little church I passed on the road. It isn't currently a church, however. There's a little sign stapled to the wire netting above the fence: Castleview Bed and Breakfast. After spending my night with a werewolf and a fairy ring, I could use both a meal and a bed. I'll get some rest, and when the sun goes down, I'll find Burke's invisible castle.

I'm sure all kinds of sonnets have been written in praise of sleep, so I won't bother to describe how blissful it was to exchange a few of my dad's grimy, hard-earned dollars for a room of my own, one with a small bed and a slanted ceiling and an oak door with a strong lock. There's even a heated towel bar for drying my damp clothes.

It's nearly dark when I awake, and the rumbling in my belly immediately reminds me of the tin of chocolate biscuits I saw in the breakfast room. I get dressed and stick my head into the narrow hallway. The rose-shaped stained glass window at the end of the hall is glowing like a giant plate of gemstones. Chocolate biscuits await me. Maybe even some tea as well. But floating down the hallway is a voice I know all too well.

"Do you mean you've actually seen fairies?"

I inch closer and peer into the breakfast room. Sure enough, sitting at the table and noshing on the chocolate biscuits I'd earmarked for myself, is Kyril.

(It continues to be unfortunate, how handsome he is.)

"Fairies, aye!" says his companion, a burly man with a stack of tourist books. "My mother had the gift of sight, same as me. But you'll see none of the Fey here on Arran. *This* island is full of ghosts."

I retreat into the hallway and lean against the wall, completely disgusted. The last thing I want right now is to deal with Kyril.

My only way out of Castleview is the staircase in the breakfast room, unless I want to jump out my second story window onto the flagstone terrace. But Kyril shows no sign of wanting to leave. Instead, he's urging the man with the gift of sight to tell him all about ghosts.

"Here in the north of Arran, the most restless spirit is a man name of John McLean," the man says. "No one in Lochranza wanted to bury the poor sailor, because they feared the plague. So he was left to rest in unconsecrated ground, and he won't stay put.

If you don't place a stone next to McLean's marker as you pass, he'll haunt yer steps."

I doubt very much that any ghosts will lead us to Castle Burke. But Kyril seems to think this is useful information.

"Where does McLean haunt people?" he asks, sounding ridiculously eager to be haunted. "Next to his gravestone?"

"No, my boy. At Machrie Moor. Near the standing stones."

This comment attracts my attention. John mentioned Machrie Moor—he said Patsy's cousin Liam was found dead there. There must be a portal at this moor, and where there's a portal, there's a source of power. Maybe that's where Lord Burke has his castle. Maybe that's where Aradottir has sent my students.

Of course, I still don't know how Elena is connected to this place. Why was she writing letters to Patsy's cousin? Was she working to liberate the hedge witches?

Elena doesn't strike me as a revolutionary, but that's at least more plausible than her claim that she was randomly rendezvousing with some guy she met through a personals ad, especially when she told me herself that she was in love with someone else. If her evil father were trying to force her into a marriage she didn't want, is it really so improbable that she would undermine his tyranny by joining the resistance?

I slip back into my room, eager for night to fall. I simply have to wait until Kyril is gone, and while I'm waiting, I can get some work done.

My invisibility cloak is completely unsalvageable. So is my shawl, and it would take all night just to spin enough yarn to replace it. So it's futile even to begin. But spinning and knitting are apotropaic acts: repetitive rituals imbued with the power to avert misfortune. I've lived through many black days where the simple act of working with wool has helped me ward off evil, and right now, I need all the help I can get.

Seated cross-legged with my mother's spindle dangling over

the edge of the bed, I draw a clump of roving into a thin draft, spinning the greasy fleece into yarn. I've managed to spin only a few dozen yards when someone knocks on the heavy oak door.

"Anya, it's Kyril. Open the door."

I let my spindle fall. How did he know I was here?

"I know you're in there. Heard you paid with a soggy stash of U.S. currency. Open the door."

With a sigh, I shove the yarn aside and unlock the door. "Well, well. What a surprise."

He breezes in, all cheekbones and manly swagger. "I know, right? Fancy meeting you here." He's dressed in his metallic Faraday hoodie and is carrying a paper box that smells absolutely delicious.

"What do you want?" I growl, ignoring the rumbling in my empty belly.

He plops down on my bed, drops the paper box on the rickety nightstand. "Thought you'd be glad to see me. Thought we were going to work together."

"Maybe I don't particularly trust you," I say, with a glance into the hall. The burly tour guide is still droning away about ghosts in the breakfast room, so I shut the door and lock it tight.

Kyril cocks an eyebrow. "What's not to trust? I offered you my frequent flyer miles. What more could you want?"

"Frequent flyer miles? See, that's the problem right there. You wanted to take me to an airport, where I could have been caught or lost my magic or both! You really know how to show a witch a good time."

"Well, anyway. I see you made it to Arran on your own." He says this so dismissively I want to strangle him.

If only he knew what I went through to get here. Only Bertha and Hulda do, but they've both gone to the Apostle Islands, probably for good. I feel a sudden pang of longing that I can't explain. I wish I had someone to share things with. I wish I didn't feel so utterly alone.

"I brought you some fish and chips from the pub." Kyril reaches into his drone-resistant windbreaker and produces a neon-bright bottle of orange soda. "You can wash it down with an Irn Bru."

"Well, I am hungry," I allow, and the next thing I know, I'm crouched on the edge of the bed stuffing my face with fried cod and vinegary fries.

He leans back against the iron bedframe, watching me eat. "You're usually such a fanatic. Why aren't you wearing your shawl?"

I swallow a gulp of Irn Bru, which is disgustingly sweet. "Fairy ring stripped away its magic."

He whistles. "So you did take the fairy ring. No one can say you're not brave."

"You missed the part about the fairy ring stripping all the power from my shawl. I need to find some new gear. I don't want to lose all my magic."

"Have you ever considered that maybe you've already lost some of your magic? Or that you never had much in the first place?"

I glare at him, indignant, and seize my spindle full of yarn. "I have *not* lost my magic. Do you see this yarn? It's an energized single, twisty as a serpent, infused with raw power, spun by Yours Truly."

Kyril frowns a little. "So you can spin magic yarn. Kirsten Aradottir told me about you. Everything you do—knitting, weaving—*that's* all a form of engineering, and I mean that as a compliment, by the way. You don't have any certifications. You can't use a wand."

I decide right then and there that I will hate him forever. "That doesn't mean I've lost all my magic! It's bad enough living in this world as a second-class citizen: I don't need you suggesting I'm not even a proper witch."

He holds up his hands, abruptly conciliatory. "I'm sorry. I didn't mean to be so insensitive. What I meant to say is that you're not one of them. You're one of us."

"What do you mean, 'one of us'?"

"Look, the universities want to teach everybody that there's only one valid kind of magic—primarily wand craft and charms—but we know that's not true: there are many kinds of magic in the world."

"Well, you're right about that," I concede, tossing my spindle aside. "Think about all the forms of hedge craft practiced outside the Empire."

"Of course. We don't even know a fraction of what's out there. So why are the university folk so confident, so absolutely certain that the magic they wield is the only kind that counts?"

"Because it keeps them at the top of the social hierarchy?"

"Exactly." He retrieves the fallen spindle and gives it a tentative spin, but the yarn breaks at once and the spindle lands on the bed.

I sniff in disdain. "You would fail my basic textiles course. You would fail utterly."

He cracks a smile. "True, but I'm good at other things."

"Like what? You've got an arsenal of charms, but I'll bet you didn't make them."

"No," he says easily. "I didn't make them. But I do make other things."

"With your computer?"

He pauses, thinking. "One time I was telling Kirsten Aradottir about my computer magic, and she told me the Icelandic word for computer is *tölva*."

"*Tölva?*"

"It means 'number witch'. Sometimes I think that's what I am: a sorcerer who manipulates numbers into magical codes."

"Well," I say, stuffing another fried potato into my mouth. "'Number witch' definitely sounds better than 'strange wizard-engineering hybrid'."

He laughs. "Definitely."

After that, I finish my dinner in silence, and he watches, not saying anything until I crumple the greasy wrappers and throw my satchel over my shoulder.

"Where are you going?" he asks.

"Know anything about a place called Machrie Moor?"

He rubs his chin. "Famous historical site, midway down the island. Group of Neolithic standing stones. Contains an intact portal built in the Age of Arcanos."

"Well, that's where I'm headed." I'm still annoyed with him, but I'm smart enough to acknowledge that I shouldn't be doing this alone. "If you've got a map and a torch, I'll let you come along."

"I've got a flashlight, a GPS, and a satellite phone."

I can't help but roll my eyes. "Of course you do."

We reach Machrie Moor just before midnight. Isolated and peaceful, hidden between a river and a mountain range, it's a circle of jagged limestone pillars, each one almost 20 feet high. A few yards away stands another stone circle, this one made from low granite boulders.

"Beautiful." Kyril traces the beam of his flashlight up the length of the tallest pillar. "This place is like Stonehenge, only better."

"Probably much better," I whisper, gazing reverently upward. These monoliths have been standing here for a thousand years. "So many tourists visit Stonehenge, it's almost impossible to access its power anymore."

Kyril switches off his flashlight, and for a moment I can't see anything. Then my eyes adjust to the starlight and the gibbous moon. The stones glow crimson in the gloom, and the air around us crackles with power.

Kyril's fingers graze the surface of the nearest standing stone. "There's a portal here, but it's tightly controlled. Probably to keep hedge witches from leaving the island."

"A man died here," I say, before I can think better of it. "A hedge witch."

"Died here?" He draws closer, and a breeze chills the damp moor.

"His name was Liam." Reluctantly, I give Kyril an edited version of the events at John and Patsy's house. No need for him to know about the possible connection to Elena—or my mother.

"This whole island's on edge," Kyril muses, his face in shadow. "Burke's hammer is coming down hard. Cibrán wants Burke to help him control the islands, but I think Burke is more ambitious than that. One thing's for sure: he'll have a fight on his hands. The hedge folk have had their fill of exploitation."

"Apparently, there's a leader named Nico that John went to meet—"

Before I can finish, a shadow passes over the moon, and the ancient stones begin to vibrate. A blue light glows at the intersection between the stones.

"The portal's opening!" Kyril backs away.

"Hide!" I duck behind a nearby granite boulder, just as a man materializes in the portal, bathed in blue light. He throws back his hood, and I barely manage to suppress a shriek of surprise.

It's Professor James Ruskin, my bastard ex-boyfriend and the so-called Acting Dean of Arcanos Hall. His eyes are dark hollows, his shoulders stooped under his cloak. He looks like he's aged a decade. He stumbles from the portal, clutching a wizard's hat. A heavy object bumps around at the bottom of the hat, just above the pointy tip.

With a nervous glance around, Ruskin heads inland, his steps silent and swift. I count to ten, and then I follow his trail, aware that Kyril is right behind me. We climb into the hills, leaving the grassy moor for a sharply sloping rock field.

A dense cloud slips in front of the moon, and I slow down, hardly able to see where I'm going. Afraid I'll make too much noise scrabbling over the rocks, I pause on the hillside, pebbles giving way under my feet. Then I realize I've lost sight of Ruskin.

Kyril appears at my elbow, his features barely visible. "Where is he?"

"We've lost him," I gasp, my lungs burning with cold air.

"Just wait," he whispers back, and so I wait.

It's absolutely silent on the hill above the moor. I can hear the ocean, more than a mile away, the rhythmic sound of distant waves crashing hard and pulling back. I can hear Kyril breathing, soft and low. Then the clouds part, and moonlight glints on the slate roof of a crumbling stone farmhouse. That must be Ruskin's destination.

"There," Kyril says. "He's in there."

We crawl up to the house and crouch beneath an open window. Kyril sinks to the ground, pressing his back against the lichen-encrusted stone, and I follow suit. The air is scented with cold peat and damp earth and something else—something that doesn't quite belong. I inhale, trying to place the clean, peppery scent. It smells almost like juniper.

Then voices emerge from the interior.

"Please," Ruskin says, his voice frantic. "You need to be patient."

"Patient?" a woman snarls. "Are you insane? You need to get me out of here!"

Unmistakably, it's Princess Elena.

I inch up to the crumbling open window and peer in, expecting to see the princess inside the cottage. But instead, an apparition awaits me.

A ghostly image of Elena flickers on the uneven wall, projected by some kind of magic lantern resting on the table. She's seated on a stone ledge, glaring angrily at a herd of enormous white rabbits. If looks could kill, those rabbits in the projection would be dead, and Elena would have an entire wardrobe made of their fur.

Meanwhile, Ruskin is waving his wand over the magic lantern, which rests on the wizard's hat. The lantern looks like one of those snow globes that mundane folk display during the holidays. I can just glimpse the turrets of a miniature castle inside the globe.

With a shudder, I remember Ruskin's vial of *Angelica arch-angelica*. Was this what Ruskin intended for me? A tiny, portable prison?

Projected on the pockmarked plaster wall, Elena is burning up with rage. One of the fuzzy rabbits hops onto her lap, and she shoves it out of her way. "For the love of all that's holy, get me out of here! There's nothing to eat here but tepid water and lichens. And I told you: I'm allergic to angora!"

Ruskin gives his wand a futile flourish. "Believe me, princess. I'm trying! Something's wrong with my formulations. I can't get any of the rabbits out of the hat."

"I don't want the rabbits out of the hat! I want myself out of the hat! Why can't you free me?"

Kyril inches up beside me, peering through the window at the ethereal display of bunnies and royalty. "What the hell? That's Elena," he breathes, sliding back down.

There's no time for me to wonder how Kyril knows the princess, because at that moment, Ruskin sees me.

"Anya!" he gasps, the color draining from his face. "What are you doing here?"

"You!" I rush around the side of the cottage and duck into the low doorway, hoping Kyril will have the sense to stay out of sight. "What have you done to Elena?"

"Anya?" Elena's ghostly projection jumps to its feet. "Is that you? I'm trapped in this castle with eleven hundred bunnies. You've got to save me! Ah-choo!"

I would be very glad to save Elena, whatever that might involve, but my timing couldn't be worse. Outside the cottage, a man's voice breaks through the darkness.

"You there! In the doorway. Turn around, and put your hands up!"

I freeze in my tracks. Out of the corner of my eye, I spot a group of soldiers in the moonlight, led by Lord Burke.

CHAPTER TWENTY-FOUR

Have I mentioned that my ex-boyfriend is a worthless invertebrate?

Seeing me with my hands up, Ruskin hastily shoves the snow globe into the wizard's hat. Instantly, the ghostly vision of Princess Elena and her horde of rabbits disappears.

"Stand back," he commands, which strikes me as oddly ludicrous, since I'm still in the doorway with my hands up. Behind me, the thudding boots of soldiers closing in.

"What are you doing?"

"Destroying evidence." Ruskin raises a trembling wand and casts a basic incendiary spell. A hot, metallic smell fills the air.

"But she'll die!" I can't even deal with this man's cowardice. Forgetting the soldiers, I rush into the cabin and snatch the smoldering wizard's hat, scorching my fingers.

He recoils. "You can't do that! They'll find us with the princess! They'll kill us both."

"They won't," I say, pitching the hat with all its contents out the open window. If Kyril has a single trustworthy bone in that lanky body of his, he will take the hat and get his ass (and

Elena's) out of sight.

Within seconds, the dilapidated cabin is filled with soldiers, Ruskin is cowering, and I'm being tightly gripped by thick gloves, blinking in the glare of luminescent torches.

"What have we here?" Lord Burke strolls in, towering over his men. He's dressed in a hooded green shooting jacket, his untidy beard curling over an ornate gold clasp.

I tell myself not to panic, but terror prickles my entire body with tiny bumps. We can't let Burke know about Elena. And since he knows I suspect him of sabotaging Arcanos Hall, he's going to want me dead, first chance he can get.

Burke languidly sniffs the air. "Consorting with a terrorist, are we? Burning something magical? I expected better of you, Ruskin."

Ruskin's face blanches pale as porridge. White-knuckled, he brandishes his wand. "Confess, you wretched witch! What have you done with the princess?"

What a backstabbing, rat-faced weasel. I'd love to tell Burke everything that Ruskin has done, but I can't if I want to protect Kyril and Elena. Ruskin doesn't deserve saving, but it looks like I'll have to save him anyway. I'm not sure how else I'll free Elena—or get out of this bind.

I clear my throat, hoping Kyril has had time to disappear with the hat. "Professor Ruskin, I already told you: I don't know anything. I don't care what you do to me. I can't confess to something I don't know."

This was apparently the right thing to say. Ruskin sags with relief as Burke's lips twist into a cruel smile.

"Now, now," he says, throwing a friendly arm over Ruskin's drooping shoulder. "We have standards here. We're not barbarians. We can't be engaging in torture. Not yet."

On second thought, that wasn't exactly the response I was hoping for.

Burke takes a single menacing step closer, and the soldier

gripping my arms flinches. Then Burke leans in, his voice silky, his coarse beard scraping my cheek. "Tell me something, Miss Winter. Are the hedge witches planning to storm my castle? You think you can destroy me the way you sabotaged The Isthmus? Is that what this is all about?"

My eyes narrow. "I'm not the one who unleashed the golem at Arcanos Hall."

Burke's face darkens, and Ruskin starts in surprise. "Lord Burke, I'm sure Anya—"

"This is out of your hands, Ruskin." Burke signals his men, and abruptly a canvas bag covers my head, enveloping me in darkness. "Take her to the dungeons."

You know how the dungeons at The Isthmus weren't all that bad? Well, Burke's family seat is not Arcanos Hall. The dungeon in Fortress Burke is impressively squalid, replete with live rats, dripping water, and cold, damp stone. Worst of all, it's directly beside the kitchen storerooms and smells like mildew, tallow candles, and pickled herring. I'm pretty sure I'm going to be sick.

The back wall of my cell appears to be solid granite, which means we must be in the mountains. Seems about right, since I distinctly recall stumbling uphill in handcuffs with a canvas sack over my head. It's icy cold, and I'm thirsty. Not thirsty enough to lap at the fetid water dripping down the side of my cell, however.

Adding even more to my ordeal: the rats. Big ugly gray ones with hairless tails and long, overgrown, hideous and discolored teeth. It's the teeth that scare me the most. There's no point in trying to sleep, since the thought of waking up to gnawing teeth would turn anyone into an insomniac.

After spending the rest of the night in these horrid conditions—handcuffed, beset by rats, and deprived of my satchel with all my worldly goods—I'm graced with a visitor.

"Oh, Anya. My poor, dear Anya." Wrapped in a long wool tartan and clutching a luminescent torch, Ruskin peers through the rusty bars. "If only you had drunk that potion yourself."

"Really? That's your takeaway from this? You think *I* should have been the one trapped in your stupid crystal ball?"

Ruskin bristles. "Well you have to admit it's very inconvenient for us both that Princess Elena is trapped in there instead. With my lab destroyed, I can't easily get her out, and by the time I have the resources to do so, King Cibrán will have tracked her here to Scotland. And if he finds out what I've done, I'll be arrested and sentenced right alongside you. And all because you weren't willing to accept my protection."

"Protection? Is that what you call your voyeuristic little prison?"

Improbably, Ruskin's eyes fill with fat, sloppy tears. "How can you be so ungrateful? Was there ever any place for you at the university? Of course not! But I—I was going to save you. I was going to give you a home, Anya. All those magical bunnies supplying yarn, your own luxurious palace to decorate as you wish, the opportunity for romantic—"

"Enough!" I cry. "Don't make me puke. I'm sick already from all the pickled herring. It smells like a vinegar factory down here."

His nose twitches. "Herring? I hadn't noticed. But then, I haven't got a great sense of smell." He lifts his chin, his expression ludicrously noble. "The unhappy side effect of decades of dedicated potion making. One has to make sacrifices for one's art, you know."

The rhetorical impact of this speech is undermined somewhat by the appearance of a small brown rat from beneath the folds of his tartan. It's marginally less hideous than the other rats, particularly since I can't see its teeth. Nose twitching, it inches toward my cell.

Oblivious to the vermin under his tartan, Ruskin is still carrying on about the price he's paid for his art. "And when I think about the sacrifices I've made for love . . ."

I turn away in disgust, nearly tripping over the rat. "Oh, give me a break."

But a break cannot be had, because at that moment the outer doors open with an excruciating screech, revealing Lord Burke and a shifty-looking pair of thugs.

"Morning, Ruskin." Burke descends the stairs, his scarlet cape billowing behind him. "Time's up, Miss Winter."

"What do you mean? Time's up for what? You think I'm enjoying myself down here?"

He signals his men, and one of them unlocks the cell.

"Time for your day of reckoning." With an evil smile, Burke slips a glass beaded chain with a heavy clockwork medallion over my head. "You've committed a Class One offense."

"Class One?" To his credit, Ruskin looks genuinely stricken.

"Conspiracy to expose the magical community and undermine its system of law."

I try to protest, but my thirst suddenly increases, my tongue turning to cotton in my mouth. The medallion weighs heavy on my neck, so heavy there seems no point in fighting its weight. Some kind of powerful charm. I know I should try to do something, but I feel strangely weary, the whole world suddenly hopeless.

The thugs hustle me up the slippery staircase to the main hall, Burke and Ruskin following right behind. Fortress Burke is a nineteenth century Scottish castle, a sprawling old pile decorated with dark wooden panels, bold tartan rugs, and lots of taxidermy. Everywhere I look, dead animals stare with gaping mouths and glassy eyes, as if to say, "Don't expect to get out of here alive."

We enter a narrow drawing room that looks like a vampire bordello: intricate parquet floors, blood red wallpaper and a fantastical fireplace. By fantastical, I mean there's a marble frieze above the mantel, which appears to depict an epic Roman orgy. Standing near the warm fire, prudishly averting her gaze from the *bas-relief* tangle of writhing marble bodies, is Lady Lynch.

Seeing me in handcuffs, she stiffens. "The traitor! You've found her!"

I open my mouth to defend myself, and not a word comes out. Behind me, Burke chuckles darkly. "Cat got your tongue?"

"Urmph," I manage to say, sounding exactly like Rocco.

"Fret not, my lady," Ruskin soothes Lady Lynch. "Soon this nightmare will be over."

"Send for the senior faculty," snarls Burke, shoving one of his thugs toward the door. "Let's get this hearing underway."

"Hearing?" Lady Lynch asks, looking pleased, while Ruskin develops a sudden interest in his perfectly manicured nails.

That's when it hits me: I'm going to be charged with a Class One offense, the most serious of magical crimes, for which the approved punishments are horrific indeed. I once heard a story about a traitorous wizard who lived out his days on a chain gang near Saskatoon, transformed into a Malamute, pulling a dog sled for the postal service.

My shoulders slump, the clockwork medallion physically weighing me down. I want desperately to scream, but it's too hard. The medallion is more than just a silencing charm: there's something futile and defeatist mixed in there as well. Burke has not only made sure I can't defend myself, he's also arranged that I won't have the energy to try.

He turns his attention to a gilded mirror above the mahogany sofa table, adjusting the gold clasp on his scarlet velvet cape. His expression: complete confidence. He knows he'll soon have me out of the way. And Ruskin will be no help—he looks like he'd rather be anywhere than here. So much for his passionate desire to protect me.

I really ought to be panicking right now, but thanks to Burke's medallion, the panic feels distant and muted. No point in trying to escape.

I gaze up at the marble frieze above the fireplace, then quickly realize its orgiastic revels are really too eye-popping to contemplate. Left of the fire, however, hangs a large oil painting of Lord Burke. The portrait appears somewhat faded, the canvas fraying a bit near the gold frame. But Burke is wearing the exact same expression of fatuous self-satisfaction he's displaying now. I can't bear to look at his smug face, so I focus on the details—the impressive signet ring on his pinky, the ornate clasp securing The Order of the Red Star to his chest.

For some reason, the brushwork on the portrait reminds me of the dean's painting at Arcanos Hall—the invisible woman in the red leather gown. If only I knew who that unseen woman was, or what she meant to Dean LaMarche. If only I could find out what happened to Arcanos Hall. But the entire castle is gone, and there's no chance of ever finding it again.

The double doors abruptly fan open, revealing the senior faculty of The Isthmus, Professor Inez Quissel leading the way. Behind them, I glimpse my former students crowding the balcony above the main hall. Fob and his cronies—Fryar and Milosz—look positively gleeful.

"It's true!" crows Fob. "There she is! Lock her up and throw away the key!"

I ought to be distraught, but all I can think is that Fob's iridescent coiffure is ridiculous. I mean: he looks like a blue-haired rooster.

What on earth has Burke's medallion done to me?

"How disappointing." Inez Quissel produces a sneer so elegant and contemptuous, she briefly morphs into a younger version of Lady Lynch. I'm thinking they must have attended the same finishing school, with advanced course work in Withering Disdain and Patrician Contempt. "And how worrisome for supporters of the university. We cannot allow the alumni to lose faith in The Isthmus, not when voices are already calling for the university to be disbanded."

She turns to Ruskin. "As Acting Dean, it's incumbent upon you to make a powerful statement."

"Powerful," Ruskin mutters abjectly. "Yes. Statement."

Burke draws the doors shut, provoking howls of disappointment from the students in the main hall. "There's really no need to waste time with extradition to the West. We have a quorum of Regents and senior faculty. Pursuant to University Code 152, we will handle Miss Winter's offenses internally before handing her over to local authorities." He looks around meaningfully. "If all are agreed, of course."

A chorus of agreement fills the room.

I take in the cold, unsympathetic faces of my former colleagues, and I realize Ruskin was right about one thing, at least. There was never a place for me at the university. I'd thought The Isthmus could be the home I always wanted. But a home consists of people, and there's a giant moat of power and privilege around these elite scholars—a moat that I could never bridge. I didn't see the gulf before. I thought it was just their fine clothes or their advanced training that set them apart. But the truth is clear now: their loyalties are only to their own kind.

"I propose that Miss Anya Winter be remitted to the custody of King Cibrán for sentencing. A unanimous vote is required," Burke continues. "All in favor, say 'Aye.'"

My eyes dart about the room, as they open their mouths in unison to say, "Aye." Ruskin opens his mouth, his eyes locked on mine, but no words come out.

"All opposed, say 'Nay.'" Burke strokes his beard triumphantly, while Ruskin presses his lips together and huddles under his tartan cloak. Worthless coward.

I'm about to give myself up for lost, when the oak doors swing open with a heavy boom, and a raspy voice says, "Nay."

It's Madame Olann. She shuffles in, her bony frame as hunched as a grasshopper's, the embroidered fabric of her kerchief glittering like a confetti-strewn cake.

Burke closes the doors behind her, his face clouded.

"You!" Lady Lynch glowers at the old witch with unconcealed rage, and suddenly there's a very real possibility of a catfight between two eminent witches. "Who gave you the right to vote?"

"Dean LaMarche." Madame Olann complacently unrolls a scroll with a distinctive cursive and a large wax seal. "It was one of his last acts as dean, may the Elders send him healing."

"Ruskin," snaps Lady Lynch, jabbing him with her elbow. "You are now Acting Dean. Rescind this woman's voting privileges at once. She's only a replacement, after all, for an adjunct hedge witch! And we have a traitorous criminal to deal with."

"Um." Ruskin appears to be frozen.

"Do you want a prolonged trial, with public exposure of our difficulties, and more scandal for the college? Have you considered how these affairs could affect the faculty?"

"Exactly," Professor Quissel chimes in, turning to the other professors for confirmation. "What good will it do for us to have tenure if the entire university is shut down?"

There's a chorus of angry voices, and it occurs to me that my former colleagues don't want justice as much as they want security. The rest of the world could burn, as long as they had their ivory tower, shored up and protected. Normally, this would be an upsetting revelation. But the entire conversation seems hallucinatory and absurd. My nose tingles, and I fight the urge to sneeze.

"This entire affair has interrupted me in the middle of some very important business," Madame Olann says, flicking a meaningful glance at me as she strolls up to the fireplace. "Still, I think we ought to wait until Kirsten Aradottir gets here."

This provokes an outraged reaction from Lord Burke. "Are you serious? Aradottir?"

"I am at your service," a voice calls out. Everyone turns, gaping at Captain Aradottir, who stands at attention beside the doors, having managed to enter the room without being seen or heard. She's dressed for Council business—her long black hair tightly braided, the heavy crimson folds of her Regent cloak grazing her boot cuffs. Her two pale guards—the beetle and the stick—flank her on each side.

Lord Burke exhales loudly, eyes fixed on the Ice Captain. But Madame Olann hasn't even bothered to turn around. Instead, she extends her wrinkled hands, warming them over the fire. Her gaze drifts over to the fraying canvas of Burke's portrait.

"It's going to be interesting," she says, "seeing it all unravel."

CHAPTER TWENTY-FIVE

"Captain Aradottir, what an absolute pleasure." His voice flat, Lord Burke stiffens as Aradottir strolls to the center of the drawing room. "When did you get here?"

"Never mind that." Aradottir casually unfurls a scroll. "By royal decree of King Nestor of the West, I'm taking this prisoner into custody."

"We're dealing with this matter ourselves." Burke spits out the word "matter" as if there's a foul taste in his mouth. That's all I am: a foul matter to be dealt with.

"No, you are not," Aradottir says, impassive as always. "May I gently remind you that the faculty of The Isthmus are not authorized to handle charges relating to the Kingdom of the West's national security?"

"But we're on Arran. Which is King Cibrán's territory, and under my jurisdiction."

"Arran is disputed territory, which is why King *Nestor's* prisoner will be safely confined on these premises as we await an international tribunal. With your permission, of course."

The two of them stare each other down, before Burke finally

snaps. "Back to the dungeons, then."

At this, Ruskin huddles under his tartan and Lady Lynch returns to gloating. But Madame Olann brings her hands together in front of her dress, fingers grazing past each other as if she were twiddling her thumbs. I know that gesture: she's tying knots.

Why is she tying knots? And what did she mean when she said that things would unravel? These are the only thoughts piercing the toxic fog in my brain as Aradottir and Burke herd me out of the room, past the peanut gallery of jeering former students, and back down the stairs to the dungeons.

The entrance to the dungeons slams shut behind us, and Aradottir clears her throat.

"Should we place a ward on the door?"

"Good idea," Burke says conversationally. "We don't want any company right now."

I make a choking sound, almost too terrified to breathe. Either Burke is planning to torture me in private, or he's got something even worse in mind. At any rate, he'll have plenty of privacy for his interrogation: these dungeons are empty except for the rats.

I hardly know if Aradottir's presence is a good thing, or yet another disaster for me, especially since she's never presented herself as an ally. After all, she was just merciless enough to have laid a string of explosives around Arcanos Hall. To protect the secrecy of The Isthmus, she was going to blow it up completely.

Something close to anguish hits me then, and I remember how much I loved Arcanos Hall. Memories rush by with irresistible force: the stacks of precious books in the library; the narrow spiraling stairs leading down from the mail portal; the way my embroidered skirts would drag behind me on the worn stone steps; the wooly smell of yarn and roving in my tiny room; the baskets of undyed fleece stacked beside my spinning wheel.

There's no denying I was a second-class citizen at Arcanos Hall—an outcast among the faculty, a subject of derision for the students. But I loved it there, and I wanted to stay. For the first time in my life, I had a real place in the magical world, a place where I could learn and grow, where I hoped I could belong.

Still handcuffed, I stumble past the narrow corridor leading to the kitchen storerooms, and the acrid scent of pickled herring and burnt tallow hits me like a physical blow, obliterating all my memories of wool and warmth and home. I'm homeless and imprisoned, completely without allies, and surrounded by rodents, both literally and metaphorically. The truth hurts.

I lose my footing on the slippery stairs, grasping frantically with my cuffed hands for the iron rail. Burke grips my arm and drags me backwards down the last few steps. But behind us, Aradottir pauses beside the kitchen corridor and produces a worn scrimshaw wand. With an almost imperceptible gesture, she casts a spell into the darkness. Her wand disappears so quickly, I'm not even sure it really happened.

We reach my cell, and the small brown rat scurries to hide under the rotting wooden bench. Aradottir drops her knapsack beside the metal bars as Burke shoves me inside.

"Let's make her comfortable." Aradottir opens a folded leather pouch and selects a delicate skeleton key, removing my handcuffs in an instant.

I massage my aching arms and try once more to grasp at Burke's medallion. But I can't close my fingers around it. Like a greasy bottle, it slips from my grasp.

"Still can't talk?" Burke sneers. He closes my cell door as Aradottir exits and locks it tight. Then he leans up against the bars, gripping the beaded chain holding the medallion, a sinister smile on his face. "See that bright red bead? The shiny new one? That's your voice, little witch."

I back away, keenly aware that only Aradottir's presence is keeping me from being tortured or murdered right at this very moment. Burke still wants to find Elena. But he can't afford for anyone to know he was in the dungeons of Arcanos Hall during the evacuation. He can't afford for anyone to know he was prepared for that data storm, because he was the one who released it.

This is why I've been silenced. He can't risk interrogating me in public.

A hollow boom echoes through the entire dungeon, as if something heavy has been slammed against a metal door. The bars of my cell reverberate like a perverse musical instrument, and bits of debris flake down from the stone ceiling.

Aradottir's posture changes at once, her eyes fixed on the darkened corridor leading to the kitchens. A hint of a smile flits across her face, replaced by stony resolution.

Burke reaches for his battle wand. "What the hell was that?"

There's another boom—and this time it's clearly coming from the kitchen corridor where Aradottir had cast her spell.

She brings out her scrimshaw wand. "Could be an attack. We must secure the area."

Burke scowls. "But the prisoner—"

She cuts him off. "She'll be safely locked up until we return. To the kitchens!"

Burke charges up the staircase, cursing. Silent as a cat, Aradottir glides up the stone steps behind him. Both disappear into the darkness.

Several minutes pass, bringing nothing but silence. Aradottir and Burke don't return. I sink onto the rotted bench, but apparently, the rats view this as an invitation. The small brown one scuttles up the side of the bench, its hideous hairless tail twitching as it encroaches on my territory.

I jump to my feet, and with a single well-aimed kick, I send the rat scrambling. Most of the time, rats will stay at least seven feet away from a human being. I've heard it said that whenever they get closer than seven feet, it means they know they have the numbers to overpower you. With a shudder, I wonder how many rats are in these dungeons, how bold they will become. Better to not find out. Better to keep moving instead.

I pace for a few minutes, before noticing Aradottir's knapsack, still leaning against the bars of my cell, forgotten. She's left it behind. I hesitate, wondering if Burke and Aradottir will return. But there's no sign of them. Fingers trembling, I stretch my arm through the bars to open the flap. Inside, a cloudy crystal ball and a battered wizard's hat.

With a shock, I realize it's Elena's snow globe. Which means that either Kyril trusted Aradottir to have it, or that Kyril is now dead. (This thought gives me a sharp, unanticipated pang.) Perhaps Elena would know something. If only I could reach her . . .

The globe is too large to bring through the rusty bars into my cell. Sinking to my knees in front of the cell door, I search for a way to illuminate the globe. But the glass remains cloudy, like a huge, milky pearl.

How to open the globe? Ruskin claimed he couldn't get Elena free, not without the correct potions. But there must be a way to communicate with her, even without opening the globe.

I close my eyes and try to focus. What did Ruskin say when we found him with Elena in the cabin? *I'm trying to get the bunnies out of the hat.* The hat must be the key.

A quick inspection shows the dark indigo fabric has a blistery effect, like dense seersucker. Some of warp threads are pulled taut; others are loose and puckered. I look for the exception—there's always an exception—and then I spot it: a deliberate flaw. It's a thin red warp thread, puckering where it ought to lie flat.

I give the red thread a tug, and almost immediately, the cloudy dullness of the globe gives way to brightness and transparency. Ruskin's tiny castle comes into view.

Like a rainbow cast by a prism, a riot of colors coalesces in the darkness, projected against the damp prison wall. And then I see Elena. Propped up against a bookshelf stuffed with ancient books, she's clumsily spinning angora into yarn. Her technique is frankly terrible. Under her traveling cloak, she's wearing a taffeta kaftan embroidered with gold. The horde of angora rabbits surrounds her, looking like a fuzzy pack of oversized pompoms.

I try to speak, but no sound comes out. Elena huddles over her makeshift spindle, her face streaked with tears, and I feel awful, ugly and voyeuristic. She doesn't know I'm here.

Not knowing what else to do, I clap my hands. Dropping the spindle, Elena looks up. "Anya?"

I hold up my hands, pointing at my throat, but then a voice sounds in the darkness.

"Elena, is that really you?" Kirsten Aradottir is suddenly standing outside my cell.

"Urmph?" I manage to blurt, shocked at the Ice Captain's sudden reappearance. I should have known she'd lured Burke away for a reason. She never would have left the globe behind, except on purpose. She wanted me to open it.

Elena is equally shocked. "Kirsten! What are you doing here?" she cries, and I realize with surprise that she and Aradottir know each other.

"What are *you* doing here? And what have you done?" Aradottir paces outside my cell.

"What have *I* done?" A line forms between Elena's finely arched brows, and her image flickers. "I haven't done anything. I'm trapped here in this castle!"

Aradottir's face clouds with emotion. "When I saw you last, you were standing before a furnace, outlined by flames. For a moment I thought you were a fire goddess, returning in glory to the earth. I'd never seen anything so beautiful. But I was wrong, wasn't I? You killed a man, and you were only there to conceal your crime."

If Aradottir saw us in the furnace room disposing of the corpse, she should have turned us in. She's an Ice Captain, after all. So why didn't she?

I think back to my conversation with Elena in the Arcanos dungeons. And then it becomes ridiculously clear: Aradottir didn't turn Elena in because she loves her.

"I didn't kill that man," Elena whispers, her ghostly features shimmering against the damp stone. "I didn't want anything bad to happen to anyone. I just . . . I just wanted to get free, to do something that mattered for once. But he wasn't who he said he was."

"How can I believe this? How can I believe anything you say?" Aradottir's expression is hard to read, but she seems to be poised between anger and hope. "For months, I've been tracking the bandits who kidnapped Queen Marguerite. How could I have known the trail would lead me to you? You conspired with those bandits, you helped them sabotage the Drini shields, and then you disposed of the man who could incriminate you. You did this. You, of all people!"

"That's not true! I had nothing to do with the missing queen. I had nothing to do with Arcanos Hall."

Aradottir wavers, her eyes full of anguish. "Elena, you have broken my heart."

Elena throws up her hands, pleadingly. "Don't you see? I was trying to run away. I was trying to join the resistance. Kirsten, you must believe me."

I don't know much about love, not as much as I hope to learn. But I do know that relationships don't allow you to unravel your mistakes. If you make a critical error in matters of the heart, you can't just strip everything back to the moment where you went wrong. If you cut too deep, if you cause a loved one pain, there will always be a scar, and you will have to live with what you've done.

Aradottir stands immobile, an acrobat on a tightrope, as if she's aware that she and Elena have reached a critical moment, where everything they have is at stake.

Her voice softens. "I do believe you. I've been an Ice Captain for so long, I've forgotten what it means to trust. Still, I believe you. But now, what can we do? We're both compromised, and you're in this prison. How can we get you safely back home?"

"Please," Elena whispers. "I don't want to go back. I don't want to marry Lord Burke."

At this, Aradottir's face creases, as if she's suffered a physical blow. It's hard to know what she would have said next, because an echoing boom abruptly reverberates through the entire dungeon, coming from the top of the stairs. Someone is coming.

Elena's eyes widen, and Aradottir puts a finger to her lips.

Horrifyingly, it's Lord Burke. "Captain!" he shouts. "Get up here now! King Cibrán is at the gate."

At the sound of his voice, Elena recoils. She and Aradottir stare at each other, and time inches forward like a glacier.

Then Aradottir finally speaks. "Be safe, my love."

She tips the snow globe into the hat, disrupting its spell, and Elena's response is cut off, replaced by the sound of dripping water. Still staring at the damp wall where Elena's image had been, she takes a deep breath, as if waking from a dream. Then she's gliding up the stone steps, gone like a frozen gust of wind.

The dungeon is silent and dark, and once again, I'm alone with the rats.

Exhaustion takes over, and the weight of the medallion—which I've been trying to ignore—becomes more than I can handle. I curl up on the rotted bench, hopeless and dejected. I think about poor Elena, trapped for days inside Ruskin's globe, lonely and scared and wracked with tears. I give myself permission to weep—I even try to cry—but nothing comes out. And then, because I've been awake all night, because I'm half-broken by stress, because the numbing effect of the medallion cannot be denied, and because jetlag is very real, I collapse into a heavy sleep.

I wake to find the small brown rat on my chest, its tiny claws hooked onto the bronze clockwork medallion. It's probably a good thing I can't scream, since I would have blown out my own eardrums if I'd had the ability to do so.

I freeze, too terrified to move. I consider rolling off the bench or grabbing the rat, but I'm aware that Burke's medallion and exhaustion have combined to slow my reflexes, and I'm also aware that the rat is only a foot away from the delicate tissue of my eyeballs.

The rat lifts its head, revealing ghastly front teeth—impossibly long and horribly yellow. Then it returns its attention to the clockwork medallion. My flesh is crawling like a garden full of slugs, but I force myself to remain still, hoping against hope that this rat is some kind of flea-infested ally.

Have you ever been underwater for too long, desperately swimming upward, not sure you'll make it before your lungs explode? And then you break the surface, and for the next several moments, your entire body is completely given over to the act of gulping fresh air? That's the only comparison I can find for what happens next, as the clockwork medallion suddenly breaks apart, restoring my voice and my strength of purpose. I can breathe, I can speak, and my will is my own.

"Oh thank the Elders," I manage to say, tearing the heavy beaded chain away from my throat as the shiny red bead falls away in fragments. Then—irrationally—I start to scream, batting the rat away from its precarious perch on my chest.

I run to door of the cell and shake the corroded metal bars. "Captain Aradottir!" I cry, and scream some more. I don't know why I'm calling her. Maybe because I can't believe she would ever turn Elena over to Lord Burke. Maybe because she's the only one likely to hear me.

"You've really got to stop screaming like that," a voice says.

My heart literally stops beating, and I slowly turn, disbelieving.

Seated on my prison bench, dressed in rat-colored khakis and a silver jacket, is Kyril.

"You!" I gasp, instinctively covering my chest with my arms. "The rat!"

He smiles, revealing a perfect set of teeth.

I've spent a lot of time in the company of elite wizards, people with powers far greater than my own. I've seen Regents and professors wielding charms that cost more than I could earn in a year. But only now, staring at Kyril, do I realize that I've been terribly naïve. The wizards at The Isthmus may seem elite compared to exploited hedge witches or other magical beings. But they aren't the true elite. There's a level of power and wealth implied by Kyril's transformation that goes beyond anything I've ever seen.

Out of the blue, I'm reminded of my childhood self, how I envied little Sylvia Reynolds because she had five pairs of shoes, not knowing until years later that there were people in the world whose shoes numbered in the hundreds.

"I've come to rescue you," Kyril says, with an infuriating air.

I turn my back. "As if I'd let you."

"You're counting on Ruskin, then?"

I whirl around. "What about him?"

"I understand that you and the professor—"

"He's my ex," I snap, inexplicably on the defensive. "What? Am I not allowed to have an ex-boyfriend?"

"You have an interesting history, Anya Winter."

"Not any more interesting than yours. How do you know Aradottir? Why did you give her that globe? Why didn't you want Burke to see you? And where did you get all those high-end charms?"

"Charms?"

"You've obviously replenished your supply. How else could you have turned yourself into a rat?"

He raises an eyebrow, patting the pocket of his jacket. "I have a few tricks up my sleeve."

"Like a reversible transformation charm." I shake my head, disgusted. "That must have taken a whole coven of hedge witches a whole month to produce. And you just used it up, the way you used the people who made it."

Kyril regards me calmly. "Nanotech cloaking devices are incredibly effective. You know there are other ways to gain power in this world, besides taking it from other people." Standing up, he pockets Burke's medallion and slowly grinds the chain beneath his boot heel, crushing the remaining beads.

"I don't even know what that means." I watch the glass beads on the chain crumble into dust, and it seems to me I can hear a chorus of voices crying out in relief. Perhaps each of those beads held the voice of someone Burke had wronged. Perhaps, at this very moment, they've each regained the ability to speak.

"You don't know?" Kyril asks. "All your life, you've made your own magic. You've never had the money for charms or a custom-made wand. You've never had the training to wield them. Is it really such a surprise that there are others who build their own spells, the same way that you do?"

We're interrupted by the groan of a heavy metal door. At the top of the stairs, a figure appears at the entrance to the dungeons, framed against the light. A luminescent torch sputters and grows in strength, shining azure as the door closes. Someone is coming down the stairs.

"Damn!" Kyril shoves his hands in his coat pockets, long lashes pressed together, then doubles over as if someone has punched him in the gut. His face contorts, a vein throbbing in his forehead. Then his entire body seems to deliquesce, melting and diminishing like a spent candle, leaving only a trembling brown rat.

I nearly fall over, belatedly aware that I've been holding my breath. I cannot believe Kyril simply did that, without even a wand to focus his power. After what I've just seen, the person coming down the stairs is almost beside the point. But I turn to face him anyway. It's Ruskin, huddled in his garish tartan robe, his face pale.

"Oh, Anya," he says, as if he's steeling himself for something truly terrible. He raises a trembling wand.

"What do you want?"

He starts, realizing I've regained my voice. There's a brief, obvious glitch, followed by a quick recalculation. Then he lowers his wand. "My dear girl, you've got to help me."

"Help *you*? Please tell me you're kidding."

"King Cibrán is here. He tracked me through the portal. He's come for his daughter."

CHAPTER TWENTY-SIX

King Cibrán's not my problem," I storm. "You're the one who kidnapped the princess. She's probably in a state of utter torment right now, thanks to you."

Ruskin waves a graceful hand, dismissing Elena's purported anguish. "A spoiled girl like her? Frankly, she could benefit from a few limits on her freedom."

"Oh sure, why don't you tell the king that?"

"Absolutely not!" His posture shifts subtly, and I realize I'm about to be conned. "Now listen very carefully, Anya. Here's what happened. As a service to the magical community, I have long been developing my Alice in Wonderland potion, considering it a valuable resource for protecting our way of life. We all know that Captain Aradottir left you in the dungeons of Arcanos Hall in punishment for your treachery, but I was determined that you should receive a fair trial. I'm committed to the rule of law, you see."

I roll my eyes. "Of course you are."

"Unfortunately, when I attempted to use the potion to transport you to a secure containment facility, it was mistakenly consumed by the princess instead."

"Of course it was."

"Never would I attempt to kidnap the only daughter of His Imperial Majesty."

"Of course not!"

"So you see, all you have to do is support my explanation . . . "

At this, the small brown rat perched on my prison bench begins chirping loudly. I turn and hiss at him.

" . . . because if you don't, he'll have me executed," Ruskin concludes, "and then the princess will never be free."

I take in the smug features of the man I'd once adored, and all I want to do is tear out my hair. Well, tear out his hair, actually. How could I have been so stupid? How could I have failed to see what a self-serving snake he was?

Granted, the accumulated effects of Ruskin's glamour potions may have played a role in increasing his attractiveness, but glamour doesn't take away your free will. So I must have been either terribly lonely, or completely insane. Probably the former, if I want to be honest, which—to be honest—I really don't.

Ruskin's expression grows impossibly earnest and soulful, no doubt aided by a boost of charisma compound. "You must help me find the globe, and you must help the king understand that I will need time to reverse the potion. The ingredients can only be harvested on the Lofoten Islands, where—"

"What about me?"

"You?"

"Are you going to help me prove I didn't destroy Arcanos Hall? Are you going to make sure I get justice?"

Ruskin doesn't miss a beat. "Of *course*! Anya, how could you doubt me?"

I feel a tugging on the left side of my dress, and I look down to see the brown rat hanging by his claws from the hemline. The rat—I refuse to call him Kyril—frantically chirps at me. His teeth are ghastly, like miniature tusks.

"Not now, you stupid rat!"

Ruskin peers through the bars, sees the rat, and delicately recoils. "Oh, Anya. Reduced to these awful conditions. How horribly degrading. I'm so sorry."

"You know what? I'm not sorry! I'd rather be stuck in a cage with vermin for the rest of my life than lift a single finger to help you. In fact, as soon as King Cibrán arrives I'm going to tell him the truth: that you kidnapped the princess on purpose. That you and Lord Burke conspired together to destroy the university from within."

His eyes grow round. "You can't! You wouldn't! That's not even true."

"I'm going to tell everyone about the data storm that sickened Dean LaMarche and compromised our entire campus, how Lord Burke knew it was coming because he and his cohorts unleashed it themselves, and how you aided and abetted—"

"No! No!" Ruskin stumbles away, covering his ears and his perfect sideburns with his hands. "I didn't know Burke was behind the attack! I didn't aid or abet him! Why would I do such a thing?"

"If I'm going to spend the rest of my life in prison, then I'm going to make damn sure that you do, too!" I catch my breath and realize I'm gripping the iron bars of my cell so hard that my hands have started to ache. I'm angry, and what's more, I've been angry for a long time. Where did all this anger come from?

I must have been sleepwalking for months. Blindly going about my business, working with people who'd spent their whole lives exploiting people like me, grateful just to have a place at the table and a roof over my head. But I wasn't just blind: I was willfully ignorant. I refused to see how unfair the entire system always was.

"Why should I take the fall for you? Why is your story more credible than mine? Why is your *work* more valuable than mine?"

The rat unleashes a volley of chirping and resumes tugging at my skirts, so I scoop it off the floor and give it a shake. "Shut up!"

The rat bares its ugly teeth, thrashing its tail and practically threatening to bite me, and then—so suddenly that I can't even adjust in real time—the rat turns into a dark-haired man of a hundred and seventy pounds, and I collapse under the weight of him in my arms, landing hard on my tailbone.

"Ow!" I yell.

"Ow!" Kyril howls.

"What sorcery is this?" Ruskin's jaw drops, which is hardly surprising, since he'd last seen me in a cage with a rat, and now there's a full-sized man in the cell disentangling his limbs from my own.

"Sorry, but we really don't have time to mess around," Kyril says, clambering to his feet. He produces a clockwork scarab and expertly slides it into the lock. "Burke wants you dead, Cibrán wants your boyfriend dead, and the two of you are standing here bickering."

"He's not my boyfriend." I pull myself gingerly to my feet, my bruised tailbone slowing the process considerably. "And I was not bickering."

"Whatever." Kyril pulls open the door. "Come on."

I cannot believe he just did that. "You had a scarab all this time? Why didn't you just use it before?"

Ruskin, meanwhile, has begun to gape at Kyril even more, if such a thing were possible. "Are you . . . ? Could it be? Oh, yes! Yes, you are!"

Kyril practically jabs his finger up Ruskin's nose. "You don't know me. You've never seen me before. I was never here. Do you understand?"

"But—"

"Another word from you and you'll get no help from me."

Ruskin swallows audibly, and I can't tell if he's thrilled or terrified. "Yes, sir."

Sir?

"To the kitchens," Kyril says, not looking at me. "We've got to get out of here."

So what was that all about? Ruskin seems to know who Kyril is, which explains why Kyril is always wearing camouflage and seems so eager not to be seen. Is he some kind of wanted criminal? Wizard celebrity? There's no time to ask, since I'm on my hands and knees following Kyril through a minefield of pickled herring barrels. We're in the narrow corridor branching off from the dungeon staircase. In front of us, another locked door.

Ruskin pants and grunts like he's halfway through a triathlon. "Sir, if I might ask—"

"No, you may not." Kyril is gripping a chunky silver ring, barely visible in the gloom. I glimpse a flash of crystal. I'm guessing it's some kind of charm. Or, perhaps, another one of Kyril's technology devices.

We crouch behind the rime-crusted barrels, eyes watering from the stench of vinegar. How much pickled herring do these Scottish wizards eat, anyway? Then the main door to the dungeons creaks open and we hear a voice that's all too familiar.

"You need to find Ruskin," Lord Burke rasps, his bulky form crowding through the half-open door. "I don't care how many years you go back. If he's crossed the king, then we're done."

Beside me, I can feel Ruskin flinch.

"I'll do what I can," Burke's companion says through the doorway, and I realize it's Lady Lynch. "But you must remember your promise. When all of this is over, my nephew will succeed Nestor as king."

"Understood, my lady. Understood." There's a pause, and then a flash of light. "And now, I've got some loose ends to tie up."

It's my turn to flinch, as I realize I'm the loose end that needs tying. That flash of light was a wand charged for battle. Burke has come to interrogate and kill me.

The door creaks shut and Burke heads down the corridor toward the dungeon stairs. It's only a matter of moments before he'll see the cell door open, and me gone. There's no time to lose—we've got to get out of here.

Fortunately, Kyril has come to the same conclusion, because the moment Burke rounds the corner, Kyril is on his feet and tugging open the door. "Quick, now!"

I rush into the bustling kitchen followed by Ruskin, only to find that there's no Kyril with us. A pastry chef in a white hat sees me, shrieks aloud, and drops a platter of profiteroles. A trio of kitchen helpers stands open-mouthed and gaping. Then I feel a hand gripping my arm. It's Kyril. The jerk has made himself invisible.

Which is actually ridiculous, because why would you go to the trouble of making yourself invisible if you're practically shackled to two people who aren't? I mean, how is this helping us? Kyril must *really* not want to be recognized.

His grip tightens, steering me past industrial ovens and long rows of copper pots and into a vast receiving room filled with wooden crates, shipping containers, and parcels. At the end of the room, marked by a distinctive bronze anchor, stands a large delivery portal, currently being unloaded.

"We're getting out of here," Kyril says, dragging me straight toward the pallid hedge witch unloading the mail portal, who, upon seeing Ruskin and me, fumbles a bushel of apples.

"But we can't travel in a mail portal!" The one at The Isthmus was so unstable, it frequently pulverized our leafy greens.

"That's right," Ruskin sputters. "They're not even safe for livestock."

"You want to take your chances with Cibrán?" Kyril yanks invisibly on my arm. At first, I don't understand what he means, and then, through the stone mullioned windows, I see it: a company of Cibrán's soldiers massing on the green.

"Take Ruskin's arm," Kyril commands, "and hold onto me."

"Why should I go anywhere with you?"

"I can protect you. I will protect you."

"But I don't believe you. I don't trust you." My heart is racing so hard I can barely breathe.

"I do," Ruskin blurts in Kyril's direction, and to my surprise, he seizes my arm. "I trust you."

A commotion arises in the kitchens, doors slamming, pottery breaking, Lord Burke's voice bellowing in rage. "Where is she?"

And then, before I even know what's happening, we're rushing into the mail portal, screaming at the kitchen worker to get the hell out of our way, the tall gothic arches are closing around us like a trap, and my entire body feels like it's plummeting off a cliff in total darkness; I'm pretty sure I'm going to throw up, but before the bile has even finished rising in my throat, we're staggering out into the sun, Burke's fortress nowhere in sight.

Beside me, Ruskin is howling and hopping on one leg, having stumbled into a wheelbarrow and banged up his knee.

I blink, taking in my surroundings. The breeze is briny and cold. We've portaged to the outskirts of a small mine, no doubt a gemstone facility producing charms. Buckets and wheelbarrows gleam in a watery shade of pure blue, shielded from mundane eyes by simple water glamour. We're on the lower edge of a sloping mountain, forests rising above us, the slate-roofed village of Lochranza stretched out below.

"So now what are we going to do?" Kyril asks, suddenly visible again. He pockets the dull white crystal and rolls his neck with an audible crack.

I cast about for a moment, and come up with something resembling a plan. "We've got to find Nico."

"Nico?" Kyril looks completely baffled.

"John said he's the one who's going to lead the hedge folk to freedom. Whoever he is, he's no friend of Burke's. Which means we need him on our side."

"Okay," Kyril says slowly, stretching out his vowels. "And how do you propose we find him?"

"The castle in the harbor. That's where John went to meet him."

"I hate to say it, but going to the castle in the harbor is a really good idea."

"You hate to say it? Really?"

"To the castle, then." Kyril takes off in a dead sprint down the overgrown rocky trail.

"Wait! Where are we going?" Ruskin hobbles clumsily after him, waving his arms like an idiot. I sigh, and break into a run. I liked Kyril better when he was a rat.

CHAPTER TWENTY-SEVEN

The last place I saw the old shepherd was at the ruined castle on the promontory, which makes it a good spot to start looking for his mysterious friend Nico. We approach carefully, trying to blend in with the tourists—an act made easier by the fact that Ruskin is wrapped in his garish tartan and is now sporting a matching cap.

Following at a respectable distance behind a mundane couple, we trudge across the narrow tongue of land to Lochranza Castle, a moldering stone pile with a tiny door and even tinier window positioned directly above the door. I recognize the tiny window—ideal for dumping hot coals on intruders—as a murder hole, a common feature in castles built in the Age of Arcanos.

"Was this ever a magic castle?" I ask Kyril. "Because I've been getting a very distinctive impression. Like it was made by wizards or something."

He squints up at the castle. "There's definitely something here. Ley lines, for sure, like the ones we found at The Isthmus. The *Gothica* has only one note about Lochranza, saying the Elders 'took advantage of the location,' whatever that means."

"So you're familiar with the *Almanach de Gothica*?" Ruskin

asks in his most pleasing manner, practically fawning. Just like him to suck up to whoever's likely to butter his bread. He clearly thinks Kyril is some kind of a big shot, worth ingratiating himself with, at least until he decides to betray us. Which, being Ruskin, he undoubtedly will.

"I had a copy at home," Kyril says with a shrug, and I recall that the *Almanach de Gothica* purports to describe all the noble families and strongholds of the Empire, both East and West. Supposedly, grand dames and doyennes like Lady Lynch spend their days of leisure paging through the *Gothica* looking for peers to marry their aristocratic daughters. I can't imagine Kyril reading it. Given the amount of time he spends hunched over a laptop, he isn't the sort of person I'd expect to have anything in common with the likes of Lady Lynch. Who is this guy anyway?

We pass a group of school children hanging out on the shingle beach, all of them messily devouring ice cream drumsticks.

Ruskin shudders with disdain and huddles under his tartan. "Eating Cornettos, in this freezing weather. It's nearly October. Kids these days."

The last phrase stops Kyril in his tracks, and no wonder. I cannot believe I ever dated someone who would talk about "kids these days" without irony. In fact, if I weren't so busy trying not to get killed, I would probably want to kill Ruskin, then myself.

"Do you know how to make ice cream?" Kyril sounds curious rather than scornful.

Ruskin bristles. "Of course. I'm a potion master! What kind of a question is that?"

Kyril smiles approvingly. "Good. We need someone like you on the team."

This whole exchange puts me over the edge. These men are bonding over frozen custard, while there's a psychotic Scottish lord and a deranged Carpathian royal less than five miles away who both want us dead.

"Ice cream? Seriously, Kyril? That's your idea of a useful skill? You want someone who can make you dessert? No wonder you spend half your time disguised as a rat. And you did a rat-like thing! Why did you give the snow globe to Aradottir? She left me to rot in jail, and now she has Elena, and who knows what's going to happen next!"

Kyril gazes calmly into the middle distance, watching a group of tourists pose in front of the castle. "Kirstin Aradottir's a woman of principle. She wouldn't lift a finger to get you out of jail. Not if she thinks you belong there. But she'll do anything to free Elena from captivity."

"Apparently, you missed the part where she snarled at Elena for throwing a dead man into a furnace. Or maybe you were too busy being a rat."

"I didn't miss anything. I saw the way those two were looking at each other. They've been in love for years, ever since they met at the diplomatic summit in Prague. But Cibrán would never allow them to be together, and an Ice Captain can't afford to be involved with an Eastern royal anyway. So it's been a long, hard road for them both."

This makes me feel a lot less worried about Elena's situation, and it's almost enough to make me approve of Aradottir, despite the fact that she left me in a dungeon to rot.

Kyril picks up his pace as the tourists file into the castle. "As soon as these guys leave, let's get inside."

We draw close to the castle, and I reach out to touch the cool, mossy stone. My skin prickles. "Something's here."

Kyril and Ruskin exchange a glance, and I know they've sensed it as well. A key advantage to being on a remote island like Arran is that the limited interference from technology makes it possible to really *feel* the presence of magic.

Ruskin drags his boot toe through the gravel, making a tiny trench. He scrunches up his face. "Do we know what we're going to say to this Nico if we find him?"

"No idea," Kyril says unconcernedly.

"I see." Ruskin processes this. "Will I be called upon to make ice cream at some point?"

Kyril laughs. "Probably not, since I prefer sorbet. I just like to know whether people can make things."

"Well, I studied chemistry with Madame Lepotsky," Ruskin says with a touch of pride, "the last great potion master trained by the Elders. Which is why I source all my own organic ingredients, and process everything myself. I'm not one of these modern wizards who can't even identify a plant."

"How did you develop your Alice in Wonderland formula?" Kyril flexes his fingers. "And the snow globe with the miniature castle—did you invent that as well?"

Ruskin hesitates, either embarrassed or evasive, but before there's time for him to answer, the tourists file rather noisily out of the castle, giving us a chance to slip inside.

The interior of the castle is almost indistinguishable from the exterior. Crumbly twelfth-century stonework, less crumbly fifteenth century stonework, modern metal railings, explanatory placards. There's not much to see, which explains why the tourists didn't linger.

"There's definitely magic here." I make a beeline for a low door-way. Crepuscular gloom lies beyond the door, half-concealing a room with damp, mossy shaded walls. "But I don't see anything."

Kyril peers cautiously into the semidarkness. "A concealment barrier," he whispers. "There's something in this room, something that wasn't here before."

This surprises me. "You've been here before?"

"Allow me," Ruskin says grandly, producing his wand. He mutters an incantation, rhythmically twitching his wand like a conductor at the symphony. Almost at once, the hidden room comes into view, dimly lit by mage light. Inside is a magnificent loom. It's profoundly familiar, and yet so wrong, I feel a sudden unease.

"A loom?" Ruskin is puzzled, and possibly disappointed.

"Well, that's interesting." Kyril steps up to the loom, raising his hand as if holding up an apple. Light pours through the gaps between his fingers, illuminating the tapestry stretched across the loom, and then I know where I've seen it before.

"I know that loom! It belongs to Madame Olann." I hurry forward, and sure enough: there are the telltale runic markings above the breast beam. She must have brought it with her when she left The Narrow Gauge.

I survey the tapestry depicted on the loom, a circular stone well with flowers scattered on a green lawn, and then my unease makes a sharp right-hand turn and goes straight down a hellish road into the uncanny. "But this can't be the same loom. There's no way."

Overcome by a weird sense of dread, I back away from the frame.

"Whoa, there." Ruskin says. "No need to be upset. So it isn't her loom after all."

"It is! But it isn't. And it can't be. This is the same loom. See those markings—a magical script. Same as Madame Olann's. But it's not the same weaving. Before, there was a woman in the tapestry. She had flowers in her hair."

Kyril draws a sudden breath. "Flowers?"

"How can the woman be gone? This is the same loom. There—woven into the fabric—that's the same well. It would take the better part of a year to make a tapestry like this one. So how could a woven image just disappear?"

Kyril leans over the tapestry, his fingers tracing the woven flower petals scattered across the foreground. "What if the tapestry is like a motion picture? You know how in a film, every frame is still, but the projected image seems to move as it passes through the light? What if this is the opposite? What if this tapestry looks like a static object, but it's actually moving?"

"That's a great idea," Ruskin says, more fawningly than ever.

"No, it's a ridiculous idea," I say, unaccountably irritated by the suggestion. "If it were possible to weave a tapestry that actually moves, I would know it."

Kyril raises an eyebrow. "Right. Because you know everything there is to know about textile arts. Except that you don't know how the exact same loom could have a weaving on it in which a woman has disappeared."

"Okay, so I know *almost* everything there is to know about textile arts."

"It's not so far-fetched," he muses. "Remember those stories about a tapestry that could bring a unicorn to life?"

"Impossible. A myth."

"Not impossible. What if the unicorn was already alive, just somewhere else?"

"A weaving that's a portal," Ruskin says, with admiration.

"Yes!" Kyril is emphatic. "A door to another realm."

It makes sense, I acknowledge privately, remembering the earth loom I fashioned to guide the fairy ring through space and time. Not to mention the Fibonacci web portal I knitted with my mother's last ball of angora yarn. But the magic in Madame Olann's tapestry must be orders of magnitude beyond any of that.

"Tell me about this woman," Kyril says. "What did she look like? You say she had flowers in her hair? What kind of flowers?"

"Daisies, I think." I try to calm myself, wondering why the altered weaving has me—and Kyril—so rattled. "She was leaning over the well, so I couldn't see her face."

"Marguerites," he murmurs distractedly. He traces his finger once more over the scattered petals in the tapestry's foreground.

Before I can ask him about it, the entire room is flooded with blinding cobalt blue light. Kyril dives behind the loom and disappears at once. His reflexes absolutely beggar belief.

"Put yer hands up! Both of you!" It's my former captor John, accompanied by his wife Patsy and a trio of rebel wizards. He strides forward, blasting us with mage light.

232

Ruskin staggers under the piercing blue rays, protecting his face with uplifted arms. "Who the hell are you?"

"I'll ask the questions," John snaps. "Whatter ya doing here?"

Patsy hangs back, holding a crudely fashioned wand, with an eye on the open castle door. "John, please. We must hurry."

"We're looking for Nico," I blurt out, jerking my chin toward Ruskin. "We have information about Lord Burke. Don't we, professor?"

The mage light dims to a bearable level, and the old man fixes a beady eye on Ruskin. "Information?"

"Um, Burke is definitely planning something." Ruskin's obviously trying to ingratiate himself without revealing anything that might get him in trouble should the tide turn.

I shoot him a dirty look. "Burke is trying to destabilize the West. He started by sabotaging The Isthmus. He wants people to believe they need security more than they need freedom. He's trying to start a war."

"And how do you know this?" John approaches me menacingly.

"John, please," Patsy repeats. "We need to find Nico."

"As it happens, I'm already here." We turn in unison, as if executing a perfectly choreographed dance, to see Kyril emerge from behind the loom.

"Nico!" John's weathered face cracks with pleasure. "When ye didn't return, we feared the worst."

"What? You're Nico? The leader of the uprising?" Not only can Kyril turn into a rat, he's also some kind of revolutionary hero. This really is more than I can stand.

"Afraid so," Kyril says, brushing past me and greeting the rebels. "What's this about soldiers? I thought Cibrán's men were at Fortress Burke."

John shakes his head. "Now they've joined with Burke's men and are heading down the mountain. They've taken a professor— Madame Olann—into custody. They're claiming Princess Elena's been kidnapped."

"She's not the only one who's been kidnapped," Kyril says darkly, with a glance back at the loom. "I've sent for reinforcements," he tells John, "But we'll need to buy some time. Round up everyone you can find."

"We're to make our stand here?" Patsy asks, gazing up at the crumbling granite walls.

"No better place," Kyril says. "No better time."

She presses her lips into a line, and with a grim nod to her allies, they depart.

With a pang, I watch them go. She and John have been keeping Kyril's secret, but they have other secrets as well. How did Patsy recognize the pattern on my mother's shawl? What connection do they have to me?

"What do you mean, there's no better place or time?" Ruskin demands from the courtyard entrance, becoming hysterical. "Look outside!"

We all hurry over to the doorway. In the woods above the village, we glimpse flashes of metal and the telltale haze associated with cloaking magic.

Ruskin wrings his hands. "Cibrán's brought his troops; Burke is probably with them. They're on their way to the village, soon we'll be outnumbered!"

Kyril draws me aside. "Look, I realize I should have come clean about—"

"Never mind," I say. "So now you're a famous revolutionary. And a rat. Whatever. I hope your reinforcements are good, because otherwise, we're all going to die here."

"Exactly!" Ruskin howls. "We're all going to die!"

"And for the record, I just want to say that in the future— assuming we don't die here—I'm going to do things differently. I'm not going to listen to either of you."

"The tapestry," Kyril acts as if he hasn't heard us. He practically pushes me over to the loom. "How do you make it work?"

"What do you mean, how do I make it work?"

"You said this tapestry had a woman sitting next to the well. A woman with flowers in her hair. So it's a magic tapestry. How do you activate the magic?"

"There's an army approaching, and you need to know this now?"

"Yes, now!"

I scan the loom, and then notice something I should have seen before: the tapestry is drooping in the center, no longer taut. Perhaps Madame Olann was about to remove it from the loom but didn't have time to finish. She said she was working on something important. I remember her odd gesture in Burke's castle: she was tying knots.

"It needs to be tied off."

"Tied off?"

"Right. Magic textiles don't work—not properly, at least—until they're bound off. Madame Olann didn't get a chance to bind this off. So we need to cut it from the loom and tie the warp threads into a series of knots."

"Right. So we'll cut it off. Have you got a knife?"

"A knife? I've been in a dungeon, Kyril. How on earth would I have a knife?"

"A knife," Kyril snaps, turning to Ruskin. "Bring me a blade."

Ruskin produces an enameled switchblade, managing to look terrified and disdainful at the same time. "This is hardly the best use of our time. We should head for the woods, before the soldiers find out we're here."

"If you leave, you're on your own. We're staying right here," Kyril says, with an air of command. "And we're not leaving until this tapestry is complete."

When you're making a flying carpet or a woven tapestry, binding off is actually the fastest and easiest part. Woven fabric doesn't unravel into chaos the way knitting does—so to stabilize the selvedge, you simply have to make sure your warp threads are evenly knotted with magic knots.

I quickly cut the tapestry from the loom, lay it on the ground, and begin knotting the warp into tassels. The woven daisy petals stir and rustle on the fabric, as if buffeted by an invisible wind. But when I tie off the last knot, something unexpected happens.

With a rustling sound that soon becomes a roar, the tapestry morphs and changes, its two-dimensional flowers taking shape and becoming real. Then a woman in white rises up from within the tapestry, as if the fabric has provided her with corporeal form. Streamers of wool trail behind her. What was once a weaving is a now a human being.

The woman's hair is raven dark, with a silver streak at her temple. Her clothing is simple—a linen dress, a large hand-knit shawl draped loosely over her shoulders. Holding her shawl together is a diamond brooch in the shape of a daisy.

I stare, disbelieving. I've opened a door. A door to another realm.

Across from me, Kyril is frozen. There was something about the weaving that troubled him, something about the flowers. And now I realize where I've seen this woman before. Her face is one of the most famous in our world.

"You . . . you were in the weaving," I stammer, as the woman stares blankly at me. "You had flowers in your hair."

His expression remote, Kyril takes a step closer, then another.

Ruskin is dumbfounded, then awestruck. "It's King Nestor's wife, Queen Marguerite." He rushes forward and falls—practically plummets—to his knees. "Your Majesty! My queen! I am your humble servant."

She starts in surprise, and mechanically extends a jeweled hand for Ruskin to kiss, just as Kyril comes into her view. Her eyes widen. "Kyril? Is that you?"

Kyril shuffles forward, his shoulders hunched, his voice small. "Mom," he says. "I thought you were dead."

CHAPTER TWENTY-EIGHT

In an instant, the ruined courtyard becomes the cloyingly sentimental site of a happy reunion. Kyril is hugging the weeping queen, Ruskin is fawning harder than ever, and I absolutely cannot wrap my head around any of this.

"You're a prince? Are you kidding me?"

Kyril extracts himself from his mother's embrace. "Prince Dominic of the West. Kyril to my family and friends."

"But Prince Dominic is ugly. I've seen pictures of him. And pictures don't lie!"

He tugs at the drawstrings on his silver hoodie. "With the right photo-disruption technology, pictures certainly do lie. They can tell any kind of story you like."

My resentment bubbles, like acid in a cauldron. "In that case, I want two balls of yarn. I haven't forgotten! You still owe me!"

I don't know why this information makes me so angry. I mean, it's great that the missing queen has been found alive, and it's great that Kyril has his mom back, and it's great that the mysterious Nico hasn't turned out to be yet another person who wants to kill us all, but I feel hurt, and I feel deceived and left out, and there's no real reason for my fury, but I'm feeling it anyway.

"Mother, this is Anya Winter," Kyril says, with sudden formality, brushing away what may have been a tear of his own. "And James Ruskin. They've been helping me. My friends, this is Queen Marguerite of the West."

Queen Marguerite nods in my direction, her damp eyes crinkling, then favors Ruskin with an absolutely dazzling smile. Ruskin goes into paroxysms of prostration.

"Such an honor," he hyperventilates midway through a deep bow, "your humble servant, to be sure." Loathsome lickspittle.

"You were inside that tapestry," I marvel. "How did you get there?"

She closes her eyes with infinite weariness. "I was trapped in Faerie, locked in the void. I glimpsed the world only in fragments, with no way to communicate. Not until Monsita Olann wove the tapestry, and you bound off the magic to get me out."

A vein pulses in Kyril's throat, and his fists clench. "I will make those monsters pay."

She reaches out to touch his arm, and her lips curve into a smile: half tenderness, half cruelty. "You'll do no such thing. *I* will make them pay."

Kyril manages to smile in response, and for the first time, they look like mother and son. It's a happy moment, but it's not meant to last.

A clap of thunder abruptly draws us to the castle door. Outside, a magic storm has erupted, scattering the tourists and sending the sheep bleating for the hills. In the woods above the village, I glimpse battle standards and a flash of steel.

"They're heading our way," Ruskin wails, wringing his hands. "It's too late to flee."

A lone figure strides swiftly down the narrow peninsula leading to the castle, wind whipping her coat and hair as the storm picks up. It's Kirsten Aradottir.

I head out into the wind to meet her, salt spray biting at my cheeks.

"I see you've escaped. And found a place to take a stand," she says in her clipped, precise way, surveying me with a frown.

"Kyril set me free."

"Did he now?" Her eyebrows arch very slightly.

After a pause, she reaches into her satchel, producing the wizard's hat. "Is he inside?"

"Yes. And there's more—" I'm about to tell her about the queen, but she cuts me off.

"I'm sorry to say we'll soon have company. King Cibrán has taken Monsita Olann into custody. He's traced Elena to me." She shoves the hat into my arms. "I'll set wards around the ruins. Get inside."

I return to the castle door, but an appalling sight stops me in my tracks. Cibrán and Burke have entered the village, side by side. They're approaching the base of the promontory, followed by menacing thugs. Joining them is Inez Quissel, who's strutting like a puffed-up rooster. With Ruskin fled, she's probably declared herself Acting Dean.

The mundane villagers hurry away, obviously responding to some kind of aversion spell as well as the storm. Meanwhile, Cibrán's soldiers are massing in groups on the road, congregating near the boats, blocking the base of the peninsula. Everywhere I look, more soldiers. They'll soon have us surrounded.

My heart racing, I back through the doorway and join Kyril and the others inside.

"We know you have what is mine," Cibrán bellows through a magic amplifier, his toad-like voice suffused with rage. "Hand her over, Ice Captain. Your treachery will not go unpunished."

"Turn yourself in!" rasps Lord Burke, his voice amplified even louder.

At the sound of Burke's voice, the queen stiffens. "That voice!"

I shudder. "Lord Burke."

"He's the one who used blood magic to banish me to the nothingness of Faerie. So many months I spent in isolation . . . " She crowds next to me at the doorway, but Kyril stops her.

"Please, don't let them see you."

"Not you, either," I add, with a meaningful look at Kyril. "We can't risk either of you being recognized."

With everyone's attention focused on keeping Kyril and his mother out of sight, no one is prepared for what happens next, which is that Ruskin rushes through the narrow door and runs clumsily away from the castle.

"Hallo! Hallo there! Lord Burke! King Cibrán! Did you see my signal? They've been holding me captive!" Traitorous bastard. I cannot say I'm surprised.

Rounding the side of the castle, Aradottir spots him and breaks into a sprint. Ruskin tries to make his way to the end of the peninsula, but she seizes him by the scruff of the neck, spinning him around in a great flapping swirl of flailing limbs and tartan wool.

"We're not letting you go, Ruskin. We need you to free Elena." She drags him back to the castle and shoves him through the entrance.

"May the Elders be my witness, I had nothing to do with this! It's all a big mistake!" Ruskin manages to yell, before Kyril yanks him through the doorway and shoves him up against the castle wall.

"I thought you were my humble servant." The queen observes quietly, her face half-concealed as she covers her hair with the loose folds of her lace shawl.

I snort. "Humble, my ass."

"Why didn't Aradottir just hand over the princess?" Ruskin frets. "Why did she have to lead them here to us?"

Kyril glares at him. "Maybe she doesn't want Elena to be forced into a marriage she doesn't want."

"Elena? Cibrán's daughter? She's here?" Queen Marguerite is all questions, so I quickly update her about Elena's imprisonment in the snow globe.

"Burke hopes to rule someday," I add, as Aradottir hurries in. "So he's financing Cibrán's army, for a price. Cibrán is bankrupt, and Elena is basically his only asset."

Aradottir stiffens, not seeing the queen. "Elena is not an asset, she's a human being. We must find a way to free her."

"So you've had a change of heart?"

"My heart is none of your concern," Aradottir replies icily. With a swift wave of her scrimshaw wand, she casts a final ward on the castle door. "We need to form a plan. There's no easy way off this island, and the portal at Machrie Moor is surrounded."

"We could try to make it to the fairy ring," I suggest. "That's how I got to Arran."

Kyril shakes his head. "No. My mother is still affected by her imprisonment in Faerie. She can't travel by fairy ring. We must stay here, and wait for reinforcements."

"Your mother?" Aradottir starts in confusion, recognition dawning as she sees the queen. Her shoulders straighten, and her mouth forms a circle, then clamps shut.

"You needn't worry about me," Queen Marguerite murmurs. "I can stay behind."

Kyril won't hear of that. "To be murdered or sent back to Faerie? Never!"

"They've got us trapped out here on this peninsula." Ruskin is very close to blubbering. "And thanks to all of you, I'm going to die."

"It's not a disadvantage to occupy this narrow spit of land," Aradottir says. "There's only one approach for us to defend."

She turns to address the Queen, gravely bowing her head. "And we have more resources than I had thought. Welcome back, Your Majesty. We've been searching for you. I am Kirsten Aradottir of the West Fjords, Captain of the Arctic Cordillera, and Regent of Arcanos Hall. I am at your service."

The queen just nods, but it seems as though she's conveying

a wealth of information with that simple gesture: acceptance, approval, and most of all, an assignment of command. I stare at them, the army outside half-forgotten.

Aradottir takes a deep breath, the queen's enigmatic message received. "Despite being outnumbered, I would say we possess more than a few tactical advantages."

Ruskin tugs at his once-perfect hair, apparently on the verge of a nervous breakdown. "You're making it sound like we're at war."

Aradottir doesn't blink. "As of this moment, we *are* at war."

CHAPTER TWENTY-NINE

Having decided we're at war, Aradottir doesn't waste any time. "Burke will wait until the village is clear. So we'll start by contacting Elena. Ruskin, get that globe open now."

"Only if you promise to release me." Ruskin folds his arms across his chest.

She glares. "You've committed an act of treason. I don't negotiate with traitors."

"Never mind," I say, throwing Ruskin a dirty look. "I can open the globe."

I place the wizard's hat on the ground and extract the shimmering globe. I can't imagine being imprisoned in a miniature castle—Elena must be terrified. But I'm realizing now that her entire life has been spent in captivity.

If you're anything like me, perhaps there was a time when you entertained dreams of being a princess. But the dream becomes considerably less appealing when you realize what the life of a princess is really like. Wearing six pounds of diamonds on your head will give you a massive tension headache. Being under constant surveillance will give you chronic anxiety. And worst of all, even if your father isn't a toad-faced Carpathian dictator, there's little chance that you can marry whomever you happen to love. You're an asset, a pawn, something to be leveraged and bartered off.

Still want to be a princess? I sure don't.

When I finally get the snow globe to reveal its contents, I find Elena surrounded by darkness. Gone are the bookshelves and the dusty marble benches. The horde of white angora bunnies is likewise nowhere to be found. Instead, Elena is seated alone on a stone floor, ash and dirt streaking her fine taffeta kaftan. Her chain mail cap is askew, its pointed cat ears drooping. Her makeshift spindle, with its lumpy angora yarn, lies discarded nearby. In front of her is a dusty metal structure that I immediately recognize as an unused furnace.

"Elena," I whisper, trying not to startle her. On Aradottir's advice, I've retreated into the darkened room, where Elena's image flickers on the wall above the empty loom.

She turns, her face glum. "Oh, Anya." She waves a weary arm at the projected image of the furnace. "Recognize that?"

"It's a furnace."

"It's *the* furnace. The one I used to burn what was left of that soldier."

This confuses me, but I let it go. "Are you okay?"

"I'm still here, aren't I? Stuck in this rabbit-infested prison. Maybe I deserve it."

"Deserve it? What are you talking about?"

"Kirsten said I was compromised. But I was trying to change my life, trying to make a difference. And that guy on the roof was trying to blackmail me. He threatened to tell my father I was going to run away. He said if I didn't do what he wanted—" She breaks off, too overcome to speak.

"Elena, we know you aren't a criminal. That guy on the roof wasn't the resistance fighter who sent you those letters. He wasn't a rebel at all. He was working for Lord Burke, and he helped kidnap

Queen Marguerite. He killed Liam so he could take his place, and he sabotaged the Drini shields."

"Working for Burke?" In a flash, her tears are gone, replaced by a steely core. Her voice grows taut with vitriol. "So that guy wasn't just trying to blackmail me. He was also helping to destroy Arcanos Hall. And he was a murderer!"

"Exactly. Besides, you didn't kill him yourself."

"That's right. I didn't kill him. He was struck by lightning. Is that the Divine Hand of Retribution or what? Does Kirsten know about this?"

"I do now," Aradottir says, as she steps into the room.

"Kirsten!"

"I'm sorry I didn't believe in you, Elena. I never should have doubted you for an instant. I let you down, in more ways than one, and everything that went wrong between us is my fault."

Elena presses her knuckles against her upper lip, her eyes bright. "That's not true. It's not your fault I got into trouble."

Aradottir sadly shakes her head. "Don't let me off the hook. I should have trusted you, and I didn't. I owe you so many apologies I don't even know where to begin. But right now we need your help."

"You need *my* help?" Elena asks in wonder, and it occurs to me that this is probably a new experience for the princess, being asked to help.

"Tell me about the furnace. Why do you think it's the same as Arcanos Hall?"

That's actually a good question. It's just like Aradottir to get to the heart of the matter.

"I've been exploring," Elena says, waving her arm at the flickering stone wall, "and this whole place is exactly the same as Arcanos Hall. It's completely empty—except for the books in the library— but the structure is the same. That stuffy little room by the stairs where Anya had her office—it's the same. The statues, the steam tunnels, the dungeons, the carved hinges here on the gate. It's all the same as Arcanos Hall."

I struggle to understand what this means. "So maybe the miniature castle inside the globe is modeled on Arcanos Hall."

Aradottir frowns, her gaze fixed on Elena's image, which flickers faintly above the loom. "What if it isn't a miniature castle? What if it's a full-sized castle, and you're the same size you've always been?"

Elena scrambles to her feet. "You mean I haven't been shrunk to the size of a pea?"

Aradottir doesn't exactly smile, but her face moves. "No. I don't think you have."

"Then Ruskin's crystal globe wouldn't be a prison; it would be like a spy glass instead."

"Exactly."

Elena and Aradottir both look almost giddy, and I swear if they weren't separated by whatever dimensional distortions the globe has created, they would probably be hugging right now. Time for me to take my leave. Especially since I've just figured something out.

I return to the central courtyard, in search of Ruskin, that treacherous, taxidermied fraud. The sky above is black with Cibrán's magical storm, and Ruskin is still on his knees before Queen Marguerite, begging her indulgence.

"You must understand, Your Majesty. I was just so frightened, you see?"

"Frightened?" the queen draws herself up, imperious and august. The silver streak at her temple gleams like a bared blade. "You're afraid of a small company of soldiers and a pair of mountebanks who steal their magic from the poor? Let me tell you what you should be afraid of. Nightfall."

"Nightfall?" Ruskin quivers.

"Nightfall. Because when the sun goes down, Lord Burke and his minions will find out exactly what these months in the chaos of Faerie have done to me. It will take a long time for the power of

Faerie to leave my body, and even longer for my anger to subside. This conflict will be ugly indeed, and if you fail to support me now, you will not live to regret your choice."

"Whoa," Kyril says, gaping at his terrifying mother. "I asked dad to ready his troops, but I don't think we're going to need them."

Queen Marguerite shakes her head. "There will be no need for soldiers, my son. If anyone is going to be violent, it will be me."

"Can we please avoid fighting?" Ruskin begs, wringing his manicured hands. "At least until I'm safely away?"

Aradottir rejoins us, her face solemn. "There are different kinds of war, open and covert. We will try to contain and deescalate this crisis, but it's not realistic to imagine that we can completely avoid conflict. Monsita Olann is in custody. The students are being used as pawns. People could get hurt."

"People have already been hurt," says the queen. She fixes her gaze on Ruskin. "And the traitors will pay a price."

Ruskin blanches white as cauliflower. It's clear he's underestimated the queen, underestimated Kyril, underestimated everything except his own cleverness.

And I have a few words for this clever man. "Ruskin. Give me the potions."

"What?"

"I know you have them. You can lie to the king, and you can lie to the queen, and you can lie to Burke, but you can't lie to me. I *know* you. You always have a backup plan."

"But my potions were all destroyed," Ruskin says. "They were destroyed with Arcanos Hall."

"What's this about?" Kyril asks.

"There's no way this conniver would have allowed his potions to be destroyed. If he knew the castle was in danger, he would have taken them with him."

I fix my attention on Ruskin. "You didn't make that snow globe yourself, did you? You found it in the cellars of Arcanos Hall, just like you found the recipe for the potion you used on Elena. It's ancient magic, devised by the Elders."

Kyril grabs Ruskin by his embroidered lapels, dragging him to his feet. "You're double-crossing us! I knew it. Tell us the truth, you miserable scum!"

"Well, I did find the globe in the dungeons," Ruskin blubbers, "but that doesn't mean—"

"You're holding out on us. You wouldn't have given me that vial when I was in jail if you didn't have the antidote with you. You *do* have the potions to get Elena out, and you have more potions to get inside. The only question is: why haven't you used them already?"

I pause, trying to figure this out, and then realization dawns. "Because you want to save them for yourself, don't you? As a last resort, if it all goes to hell. What better way to escape the consequences of your actions than to choose your own prison?"

Ruskin wrings his hands. "You don't understand what I've had to go through, how many titrations of *A. archangelica* I've created, how many rabbits I've had to stuff into that goddamned hat. This is my life's work, don't you see? Recovering the great legacy of the Elders. And you could have been a part of it, if you'd just been willing to—"

"Silence!" It's said that a lady should never raise her voice, but Queen Marguerite has earned the right to disregard any petty rules of protocol. "Give me those potions now."

Ruskin hesitates, then unwraps his tartan cape and produces a small amber flask, shielded with finely woven copper mesh.

"I'm sorry, your Majesty," he says, uncapping a bottle of potion. The juniper scent of *A. archangelica* floods the courtyard. Before anyone can react, he tips back his head and takes a swig of *A. archangelica*.

"No!" Kyril shouts, as he and I both lunge for the bottle. Next thing we know, we're colliding with Ruskin in a juniper-scented spray of spilt potion and shimmering light, and the world is moving in a half-speed blur, while the queen's eyes open wide with shock, then fade from our sight.

CHAPTER THIRTY

When I was a little girl, my parents took me to visit an old quarry on a rainy day. I don't remember much about it— just blocks of limestone and the sharp scent of petrichor. Strange that this memory should come back to me as we plummet through the darkness and the void: I see and feel nothing, but it's there in my nostrils—the acrid stirring of dust as raindrops hit parched earth and stone.

Then the memory is gone and we're collapsed in a heap on a grand staircase. A broken chandelier swings above our heads, and a friendly marble face comes into view. Comfortingly familiar, it's a statue of Michael the Wise.

"My leg!" Ruskin thrashes about in his wooly tartan. "Get off me!"

"Oof!" Kyril grunts, climbing on top of Ruskin, pinning him to the floor. "Where the hell are we?"

I look around. "This might be Arcanos Hall."

"Impossible," Ruskin says. "The castle was destroyed. Now let me go."

"It was not destroyed. Now give me the antidote."

"Well, I haven't got one." Struggling, he gestures at the shards of amber glass on the floor. "That potion *was* the antidote. And now there's nothing left! You've trapped us here! Idiots!"

"Anya? Is that you?" Dirty and bedraggled, Elena approaches, flanked by a few dozen snow-white angora bunnies.

"Elena." Forgetting about Ruskin and the potion, I throw my arms around her.

"Thank the Elders, it is you." She hugs me so hard my ribs hurt. "I've been so worried. And something happened to my connection with Kirsten—is she okay? Are you prisoners? What's Ruskin doing here?"

"We've come to rescue you," Kyril says with predictable flair, which isn't exactly true, but I decide to let him get away with it because he recently had his knee in Ruskin's chest. "Don't worry about the captain. She's preparing for battle, alongside my mother."

Elena's eyebrows scrunch together. "Kyril? What are you doing here? Did you say your mother—?"

"Long story, Elena. Let's get out of here."

"But there's no way out."

"That's what you think," Ruskin interrupts with a sneer. He flings his tartan over his shoulder and strides up to the massive oak doors at the front of the entrance hall. They're studded with so many metal bolts that they resemble the skin of a giant ostrich.

"That's not going to work," Elena tells him.

"What's not going to work?" Ruskin heaves open the door, and I rush forward to see what's outside.

Beyond the castle stretches a narrow land bridge scattered with marble blocks and broken pillars, which lie in a jumble, bleached by the sun. On either side of the land bridge, a wine-dark sea. We're on an isthmus, under a dull sky promising rain.

In the distance, I can see the ruins of a stone amphitheater built into a hill, and with a rush of inexplicable longing, I realize it's the same place I'd glimpsed as I hurtled through the broken fairy ring, desperate to find my way home. What is this place? Is it even real?

"Don't bother trying to get out," Elena repeats, but Ruskin isn't listening. He shoulders his way through the door, extends his foot over the threshold, and immediately goes flying backwards in a great flash of cobalt light, which knocks him on his rump and sweeps Elena and me to the floor.

"Ouch!" Elena shoves Ruskin away. "Get off me!"

"That is one massive energy field," Kyril says, pulling me to my feet and extending a hand to Elena. "Are the windows all the same?"

Elena nods. "The same. Some kind of shield. There's no getting out."

Ruskin dusts himself off and makes a great show of smoothing his hair, looking for all the world like a cat that's busy preening, pretending it hasn't just slipped off its perch. "Well, then. I guess we'll just have to stay here until I can recreate the formula. It's probably for the best. Much safer than being in Lochranza right now."

Kyril wrinkles his nose. "For the best? Are you kidding? We're missing our chance to liberate Scotland, to send Cibrán's soldiers back East."

"Cibrán's soldiers?" Elena's face turns pale, then hard. "We need to find our way back and face them."

"But what if we lose?" I ask. "Your father will try to make you go back to your old life."

"That's not going to happen. I'm a free woman, and I'm going to fight. People have the right to shape their own futures. Just because your old life is all you've ever known, doesn't mean you can't walk away and start again.'"

We all look at each other, and Kyril whistles. "Whoa. You are definitely not the same princess I went to summer camp with."

"I'm just trying to find my real self," Elena says, her eyes flashing. "And my real self is a fighter. For so long I was afraid to speak up or fight back, afraid my father would hurt the people I cared about. But I'm done with being afraid."

"Well, all this talk of fighting is completely beside the point," Ruskin says with a disdainful scowl. "Since we're stuck here and will continue to be stuck for the foreseeable future. Unless I can find some ingredients to work with."

"There are no ingredients," Elena replies. "And there's nothing to eat, unless you like tepid water and lichens."

"We're not stuck," I say with sudden conviction. "Maybe we're here for a reason."

Ruskin rolls his eyes. "We're not here for any reason, except to stay out of harm's way."

"Shut up, Ruskin. This castle's on an isthmus, isn't it? So what if this is *The* Isthmus? Another version of Arcanos Hall."

"I'm not following you," Kyril says. "It's like ancient Mesopotamia out there, and in case you've forgotten, Arcanos Hall is in Wisconsin."

"I am aware of that. In case you've forgotten, I grew up in Wisconsin." I turn to Elena. "Didn't you say the structure of this building is the same as Arcanos Hall?"

"It is," Elena says, gesturing to the marble statues lining the balcony. "Look at this courtyard. It's exactly the same."

"Then it must have a room that controls the Drini shields, just like in Arcanos Hall. We've got to go underground. I think I have an idea."

"How is that giant knitting machine going to help us?" Kyril asks. "We couldn't do anything with the shields last time, besides making the castle completely disappear."

"If we could make it disappear, then maybe we can make it reappear. At the very least, we can find a way to get out of this building."

Followed by fuzzy white rabbits, Elena leads us across the main hall to the tiny spiraling staircase that leads to the dungeons and from there to the steam tunnels.

On the dungeon level, right next to the steam tunnel entrance, there's a door that corresponds with my old room. It appears to

253

be the same door, only missing a few hundred years of scratches. The wood is different, but the hinges and the shape of the keystone arch are the same. Elena is right: somehow, this *is* Arcanos Hall.

I'm tempted to open the door and look inside, to see my old room in a different incarnation, but something holds me back, some kind of irrational fear. Kyril has already opened the heavy doors to the steam tunnels, and Elena is leading the way down the narrow spiraling stairs. So I follow, leaving untold mysteries behind.

Soon we're in the steam tunnels, standing before an elaborately detailed bronze gate. Bathed in a soft golden haze are the two giant gleaming needles that maintain the Drini shield. They're standing still, surrounded by tangled threads of shimmering gold light. There isn't an attached contraption with the burned-out punch card machine, but otherwise, it's just like the device Kyril and I tried to repair only a few days before.

"What are those streaks of light?" Elena asks.

"The ley lines," I say, fumbling with the latch on the gate and finding it open. "Primal sources of power drawn from the earth. Same as the ones that run beneath Arcanos Hall. They form the shield that protects this castle and keeps it from being seen."

"This is eerie." Kyril gazes up at the knife-sharp carvings on the arched ceiling. "And I'm beginning to think that time travel is real. This place is exactly like Arcanos Hall."

"Whatever this place is, being here is a very bad idea," says Ruskin. "Let's go upstairs, where things are considerably less creepy."

I swing open the gate and step into the shield room, and Kyril follows. The threads of golden light waver as I step into them, but nothing seems out of the ordinary, and no force field knocks me down.

"It seems safe enough," I begin, when one of the angora bunnies joins me in the light, immediately turning a dull shade of gray.

"Wait a minute!" Kyril recoils. "That bunny—what happened to it?"

Elena stares and takes a step forward. "It's just an ordinary rabbit, a cottontail."

I hold up my hands, forestalling her. "Don't step into the light. Ruskin, did you do something to these rabbits before you sent them here?"

"Um, I may have turned them into angoras."

"It looks like they've lost all their magical modifications." Elena takes a breath, her eyes huge. "Something in that light erases any changes made by magic."

The look on Ruskin's face is hard to describe, but it closely resembles nausea. "This is your brilliant idea? Getting involved in some kind of energy field that strips away magical enhancements? Why did we have to come here? We're going to be trapped in this castle for eternity!"

Elena gives him a dirty look. "Enough, Ruskin."

"It's Professor Ruskin, and don't you forget it."

"I don't have to listen to you. I'm not a student anymore. And I'm *not* going to be a princess anymore." Elena pushes her way past him and into the light.

Ruskin is aghast. "What are you doing?"

"Renouncing my royal title. Getting rid of my magical modifications." A wave of golden light strikes her face, the ley lines casting an odd shadow before fading away.

Her eyes widen, and her soot-smudged fingers trace over a faintly hawkish bump on her nose, a bump that wasn't there before.

She catches my eye. "Different face?"

"Different attitude," I say, but I can't stop staring. With her original nose back, she looks more human, less like a perfectly crafted porcelain doll.

She strokes the bridge of her nose. "It's so strange. I feel the same, except for one thing."

"Your nose?"

"Not my nose. When I saw what happened to the rabbit, I was

afraid. But then I decided I wanted to be done with all the magic acting upon me. Done with the new nose I never asked for, done with the surveillance daemon embedded next to my heart. The same daemon my father has used to track my movements for my whole life, following me everywhere I go. I can't feel it anymore. It's gone, and I'm all by myself again."

"Well, I like the new Elena."

She ducks her head, smiling. "Just trying to get back to my real self."

"Getting back to your real self sounds good," Kyril muses, edging his way around the light. "Maybe I should join you. What do I have to lose? Besides a few upgrades, of course."

"Are you kidding?" Ruskin scoffs, appalled. "Upgrades are *everything*, and I'm not giving up any of mine. I'm staying out here, where I can rebuild my antidote." He backs away from the gate, adjusting his impeccable coiffure. The angora bunnies crowd around him, snowy orbs of fuzzy white perfection. It's just like Ruskin to put appearances first, and there's really no telling how many years his upgrades have taken off his age.

"Good luck with that," I say. "But Kyril, are you sure you want to get any closer? You might lose your ability to turn into a rat."

"For your information, that's not a magical enhancement." Kyril grins. "That's a combination of nanotechnology and hard-earned skill."

I catch myself grinning in return. Unfortunately, Ruskin chooses this exact moment to spring into action, slamming the gate behind Kyril.

"Ha!" He crows, locking the gate with a flowery wave of his wand. "Looks like you three are stuck inside, without any magic, while I'm free to go where I please."

"Free?" Elena groans in disbelief. "Oh, sure. Like the way I've been free ever since you trapped me here."

"No, not free like that. Free like this!" Ruskin reaches into his coat, producing a large amber vial. "As soon as it's safe to get out, I'll just take this antidote and be on my way."

Kyril clenches his fists. "Unbelievable. You said there was no potion left."

"Sure I did," Ruskin scoffs, "and you're a fool to believe what other people tell you."

"But what about us?" I ask, incredulous. "You're just going to leave us here? Why not share the antidote? Surely there's more than enough to go around."

"Sorry, Anya. I can't risk losing control of the potion. I've got to look out for myself. I'm sure you understand." Ruskin slips the potion under his tartan cloak and straightens his collar.

"What I understand is that you're a liar. You said you loved me. Just two days ago! Did you ever love me? Did you ever love anyone?"

Just for a moment, he wavers, his haunted expression revealing something I've never seen before: anguish and torment, a flash of unbounded despair. Then it's gone, replaced with a charming smile.

"Did I say I loved you?" he scoffs. "I meant I loved pulling the wool over your eyes. You made it so easy."

CHAPTER THIRTY-ONE

Y ou despicable worm!" I grip the bars of the locked gate, shouting curses at Ruskin's departing form, but it doesn't do any good. I've been conned again.

"Are we screwed?" Elena asks. "I think we may be screwed."

I struggle with the latch on the gate. "Kyril, can you turn into a rat and get through?"

He reaches into his silver hoodie and pulls out a computer tablet. "No, I cannot. I've got a blue screen of death."

That sounds very bad. "Do you have any of those lock-picking scarabs? Any remaining charms?"

He responds with a small shake of his head.

"Then we're definitely screwed." With acute embarrassment, I realize my eyes are stinging.

"It's okay, Anya," he says quietly, tucking away his tablet and leaning back against the gate. "We all thought Ruskin was telling the truth. He said there was no potion left. He fooled us, too. But you had an idea, right? And we can still go forward with your idea. We can still get out of here."

I cover my face with my hands, unable to speak. You know

what's the worst part of realizing you can't trust others? Losing faith in yourself. Faced with the humiliation of being conned, you begin to doubt your own judgment. And then you doubt everything.

"I'm such an idiot," I finally manage. "My dad taught me always to watch my back, but I didn't listen. Why do I always have to be so trusting?"

"You're not an idiot," Kyril says, still surprisingly calm. "And if the only thing your dad ever taught you was to watch your back, which I suspect isn't true, then he did you a disservice. My folks taught me to manage risk, but they also taught me to seek out people who can get things done. That's why I'm here. Because I believe in what you and Elena can do."

I wipe my face with the back of my hand. "You do?"

"When we landed in this forsaken old pile, henceforth to be known as Ruskin's Folly, I had only three choices: to fend for myself, to side with Ruskin, or to put my trust in the two of you."

"Good choice," says Elena.

"Well," I sniff. "You could still join Ruskin. He might change his mind about helping Lady Lynch's nephew become king."

Elena is aghast. "That idiot Fob? King of the West? Are you joking?"

"Fob is Lady Lynch's nephew?" Now it's my turn to be aghast. "But he's a moron! And why should Fob become the next king? Kyril, aren't you Nestor's heir?"

Kyril shrugs, indifferent. "I would be, but I'm the product of a morganatic marriage."

"A what?"

"Morganatic. I'm undocumented on the distaff side, because my mother's not in the *Almanach de Gothica*. In fact, she was born outside the Empire. Many people claim that disqualifies me from inheriting the throne, since she might actually be a hedge witch— or even worse, a mundane."

"You have got to be kidding me. That is so messed up."

Elena groans. "It's not like aristocrats with purely magical backgrounds have any special powers. They just think they do."

"They have money and privilege," I tell her. "That's what they really have."

"Yeah, well." Kyril opens his hands. "I don't really want to be king anyway, though I'm sure I'd make a better king than Fob."

"If you become king, you'll have no life," Elena says with a small shake of her head. "Not only will you take power that belongs to the people, you'll also risk giving up your true self. Believe me, I've thought about it."

It's clear she's thinking about her relationship with Kirsten Aradottir. I try to imagine what Elena's royal life was like—her coercive father insisting she marry Burke, just to further his political agenda and pay his debts. It must have been hell.

"I've thought about it too," Kyril muses. "The thing is: the people are always more powerful than the crown. So the only way to rule successfully is to remember that, and to try to be one of the people." He takes a step toward the ley lines.

"Stay away from the light!" I gasp. "You might lose all your magic."

"I don't have much magic. Not what *you'd* call magic. But I do have a daemonic royal tracking device I'm most eager to get rid of."

He approaches the still needles of the Drini, and the golden threads of the ley lines scatter patterns of light across the angles of his face. A streak of silver cuts through his dark hair, bold as a lightning strike.

I hold my breath, unable to take my eyes off Kyril. I've been afraid to trust him ever since we met, and I have all kinds of reasons not to trust anyone, but here he is, throwing his lot in with the people. "How do you feel?" I finally ask.

He looks curiously at his hands. "How do *you* feel?"

"I feel the same." I extend my hands in front of me, turning them over to see the faded scorch marks on my wrists.

"I feel different," Kyril says. "There's something that was always there, running in the background, just on the edge of my conscious mind, and I can't feel it anymore. It's gone, and I'm on my own."

"Yes," Elena says, abruptly elated. "We're on our own."

"Yes," I say, abruptly dejected. "We're definitely on our own." I decide to tug once more at the locked gate, but it doesn't move.

"So?" Kyril says. "We still have each other, and we have knowledge and power and skills. If you can pull yourself together, then we're actually no worse off than we were ten minutes ago. Forget Ruskin. Forget the gate. Let's figure this out."

"But it's hopeless. We're stuck here in this shield room."

Kyril waves his arm, indicating the giant needles of the Drini. "Last time we were here, you made the entire castle disappear. So, I've got an idea. Whatever you did, let's not do that again."

I bristle. "You know something? I could really use a little charity right now."

"Anya, I'm not putting you down. Things disappear. Believe me, it happens. One time, when I was working in the mundane world, I made an entire jewelry store disappear, which was definitely not what the owner had in mind."

I turn, my interest piqued. "You made a jewelry store disappear?"

"That sounds like the opposite of a successful heist," Elena says.

"It was a company that sold gemstones online—a favorite supplier of the royal court, actually. Their payment system was compromised by a virus, so I took the servers offline, and poof!" His fingers flare open, as if he's tossing flower petals. "Their entire web presence disappeared."

He sees me staring, so he adds, "It wasn't really gone. I had just quarantined the servers to keep the virus from spreading."

"But you're talking about websites," Elena protests. "Those are Internet places. They aren't real places in real life."

"Places on the Internet are real. They're just real in a different way."

261

"Wait." I say, remembering my father and his tedious bedtime stories about The World of Technology and Its Many Dangers, specifically his admonition never to put anything important on the Internet. Agitated, I pace back and forth in front of the Drini. "You say you took the servers offline, and while they were offline, the store disappeared. What if . . . what if that's what we just did?"

"But I was talking about an online store."

"Yes, but you said places on the Internet are real. They're just real in a different way. What if this place—this castle—is real in a different way? What if we've taken it offline?"

Kyril chews on this. "Okay. Let's say, for the sake of argument, that you're right. Then what can we do?"

"I don't have a real plan," I admit. "It's just that I keep thinking about Madame Olann. She talked about watching it all unravel. What did she mean by that?"

Elena gazes up at the ley lines and their tangled threads of light. "Does she want us to unravel the spell? Wouldn't that make the entire spell go away?"

"Not if the spell contained a lifeline."

"A lifeline?" Kyril asks.

"A failsafe, a woven line of thread that keeps a spell from unraveling all the way."

"Of course," Elena interrupts, becoming excited. "If you're knitting a spell and the pattern becomes corrupted, you don't have to risk unraveling the whole thing. If you've put in a lifeline, you simply rip it back to the last point where you knew you were right. You can always go back to the place where you last were sure."

"Exactly. When they built this castle, when they built the shields, the Elders were creating an incredibly complex spell, so they must have put in at least one lifeline."

"Oh," says Kyril, his eyes gleaming. "So having a lifeline is like when you're modifying a program and you save an earlier version of the code so you can restore it again if something goes wrong."

"Exactly. Don't you see? The Isthmus is real, but it's not real in the same way we're used to thinking. Maybe it can be restored to the way it was before. That's how we'll get back home."

"If you're right," Elena says, straightening the cat ears on her chainmail beret, "then the Arcanos wizards were programming the Drini like it was a computer."

Kyril nods, thinking. "And all we have to do is reverse-engineer the code—"

I step up to the ley lines. "This location that we've come to contains a corrupted version of the spell. If we strip away the corruption and restart the pattern, then maybe everything will be restored. That's the thing about knitting: it can always be unraveled and redone."

"But what's the pattern?" Kyril asks. "We don't have a card reader—we don't even have your card anymore. How are we going to rebuild the code?"

"The code?"

"The Hollerith card. It was part of a binary code, probably some kind of patch. You need to extrapolate the code from the pattern on the card," Kyril insists. "Then you can unravel back to the lifeline and restore the code."

"If you know so much about machines, why can't you do it?"

"Because whatever code was on that card, I couldn't read it. I mean, I can read Hex and Assembly and I can pick my way though a core dump if I have to, but this was something beyond me." He takes a breath. "But it's not beyond you. You saw the card. You carried it in your hands. You must remember."

"But it was only a fragment," I protest.

"Just try to remember."

I summon up a memory of the punch holes on Rocco's card. It was only a portion of the code, but there was a pattern implied. It had shape and meaning, and it was undeniably familiar. I press my hands against my forehead, trying to recall.

And then I remember, and everything falls into place.

"The edge of a horseshoe," I murmur. Without thinking, I step into the light. "Twisted horseshoes running through eyelet lace. Same as my mother's shawl." One of the first patterns I ever learned. If Kyril and Elena say anything in response, I don't hear it.

I move through the light, and the threads of gold shimmer about me, revealing a mesmerizing tangle of lace. There's no way to read it. Hypnotized, I let the threads swirl around my body, at which point I realize the ley lines can be felt on my skin. I close my eyes and sink into the pattern, and the lace floats around me, tactile and endlessly spiraling. I feel the pattern evolve, following the twisted horseshoes to where the lines converge, and then at last I find the main thread. What follows is destruction.

When you unravel, you uncreate. A pattern that took months to knit can be reduced in moments to a single piece of string. If you don't have a lifeline, you'll end up with nothing. There's a chance you'll never be able to rebuild.

But it's exhilarating to tear it all down.

◠◡◠

"Anya, are you okay?" A cool hand touches my brow. It takes me a moment to realize it's Elena.

"What happened?" I tip back my head, woozy with vertigo, and realize I'm lying on the stone floor. My lips are chapped, and my throat is dry.

"You went so far away," Kyril says. "You didn't hear us shouting at you?"

"We were so scared." Elena looks stricken. "It was like you were in a trance. For hours. We couldn't get you to come back. What were you doing?"

I swallow hard, trying to remember. "There were threads, twisting and intersecting, so many of them, all converging toward a single point. But the convergence never came. I finally caught them in my arms, tried to bind them together, shaping them into—" I break off, shaking my head. "I don't know if it worked."

Kyril tilts his head, indicating the Drini. "The needles are creating a pattern now."

I roll to my side and catch my breath at the beauty of it all. The giant needles are moving slowly, and golden threads of the ley lines have formed a uniform row of horseshoes and eyelet lace, disappearing into the granite wall.

"So they are," I whisper.

"I think it's working," Elena says with satisfaction. "Good thing you know how to knit."

"Yes, a very good thing." Ruskin's voice startles us all. He's resting his elbows on the bars protecting the shield room, a hazy projection looming behind him.

"You!" I try to stand, but the blood rushes to my head and I nearly pass out.

Kyril catches me before I crash against the flagstones. "Ruskin, let us out of here!"

But Elena has rushed forward, her attention focused on the blurry projection behind Ruskin. The projection has a human shape. "Kirsten!"

Ruskin smirks. "I was just telling dear Captain Aradottir how brave and self-sacrificing you were, volunteering to enter this dangerous room in a courageous attempt to fix our shields."

Kyril's face turns red. "We didn't volunteer! You locked us in!"

"Are you locked in?" Ruskin swings open the gate with an elegant and dismissive flick of his wand. "It doesn't seem that way to me."

The hazy projection behind Ruskin comes into stronger focus, revealing Aradottir, whose attention is fixed on Elena. The princess gazes back, an unconscious hand creeping up to touch the bridge of her nose.

"Your Highness," Aradottir says, with unusual formality. "With Queen Marguerite's support, we've managed to deescalate the crisis. King Cibrán has agreed to vacate the Isle of Arran, and Lord Burke has fled."

"Fled?" Elena looks stunned.

Aradottir allows herself a hint of a smile. "He has literally disappeared, along with a famous oil portrait of his ancestor, Simeon Burke. His castle, Fortress Burke, shall be sequestered by the authority of King Nestor. Given the dramatic change in his legal and financial circumstances, it appears Lord Burke will be unable to honor his promise to marry you."

"Good riddance," Elena snaps. "As if he ever had a chance with me!"

Aradottir's smile broadens, practically showing her molars. "Moreover, Professor Ruskin has shared the most wonderful news. He says he's found a way to help you and your friends come home. We'll see you very soon, thanks to his courageous efforts."

"*His* courageous efforts?" Kyril fumes, while Ruskin does his best to look benevolent and smug.

"Never mind about that. We're going home!" Elena throws her arms around me as Aradottir's projection fades out, and we spin like a pair of ice skaters.

"You know what I can't believe? Your bullshit." Kyril shoves Ruskin against the open gate. "You really think you can get away with these lies? Give me that potion now!"

"You might not want to drink it." Ruskin continues to look impossibly smug. He shakes free of Kyril and brushes a speck of invisible lint from his tartan cape.

"Why wouldn't I drink the potion? You think I want to stay here?"

"Go upstairs, and have a look outside."

We follow Ruskin up the steps to the Grand Hall, and with a flourish, he steps unimpeded through the open door. The force field around the castle is gone.

"Look at this!" Ruskin waves his hand at a grassy lawn leading to a familiar forest. Beyond the woods is a shining lake, dotted with windsurfers and tiny sailboats. "We're back in Madison, Wisconsin. Perfectly shielded. Looks like I saved the day."

"You?" I follow him down the steps. "We're the ones who did it. You and your obstructionist friends are going to prison."

He snorts. "We'll see about that."

Elena stares out at the water. Then she turns her back on Lake Mendota, taking in the stone pillars of Arcanos Hall. "How is this even possible?"

Kyril looks around in awe, running his hand along the smooth stone of the stairwell. "It's like we've taken the castle down for repairs, then restored it to its original location."

She shakes her head. "You can't move an entire castle."

"But we just did! And this isn't the first time. Anya and I moved the castle before."

"Oh, I think I finally get it," Elena says, her face lighting up. "So when the castle was taken offline, its representation in the world of perception was removed, but the archetype from which it was instantiated continued to exist, regardless of its apprehended disposition." She pauses, seeing Kyril's dumbfounded look. "What? Don't you Westerners study philosophy?"

They continue speculating, and I step out into the sunlight. The leaves are turning honey gold and ruby red, and a few of them drift gently onto the lawn. A slight breeze stirs. A student passes by, oblivious to the invisible castle only yards away, his head bent over his phone. He drifts along the sidewalk that cuts across the effigy mounds, bisecting the water spirit with two tails.

I've come back to the place that was my home, and I ought to feel a sense of triumph, or at the very least a sense of accomplishment. I ought to feel like I've saved the world. But instead, I feel like a ghost.

CHAPTER THIRTY-TWO

As Dean of The Isthmus," Ruskin declares the next day, pacing in the Grand Ballroom before the assembled faculty, "I want to welcome you all to the new, improved Arcanos Hall. A special welcome to our royal guest, Prince Dominic of the West."

This is met with enthusiastic applause. Kyril looks politely pleasant, despite have made no attempt to dress for the occasion. Seriously, he's back in his metallic anti-drone hoodie, and wearing a baseball cap.

There's more speechmaking, and Ruskin's pompous tone makes me want to gouge out my eyeballs. This is all Kirsten Aradottir's fault.

Last night, when we told her about Ruskin's treachery, she didn't even flinch.

"I'll keep an eye on him," she said, with a nod to Elena. "I'm planning to stick around, at least until Elena graduates. Cibrán's threats are mostly bluster at this point, but we don't want to take any chances."

"But what if I don't want to graduate?" Elena asked. "I've been in college for *years*."

"A diploma could come in handy. Depends on what you're going to do for a career."

Elena caught her breath. "A career?" When she was a princess, she never could have dreamed of choosing a profession. She'd never had that freedom.

"Sure," Aradottir said, as if the new future opening up to Elena were no big deal. "Why not?"

"But Ruskin can't be allowed to run The Isthmus," I protested, ignoring Elena's happy smiles. "We can't trust him!"

"Of course we can't trust him," Aradottir agreed, handing me a canvas bag containing my passport and my mother's precious shawl. "That's why we're keeping him on staff. It's always useful to have someone on the faculty that you can't trust."

That made no sense to me, but Kyril seemed to think Aradottir was on to something. "Standard military procedure," he told me afterward. "Keep your enemies close."

The Ice Captain is currently stationed in a position of honor next to Ruskin, draped in her brilliant crimson Regent's cloak and appearing vaguely amused. It takes me a moment to realize that with Lady Lynch under investigation and Lord Burke on the run, Aradottir is the only member of the Inner Council left. Beside her, looking downright gleeful, Elena is wearing the hell out of a glittering tiara, which she technically shouldn't be doing, now that she's no longer a princess. Jewelry protocol notwithstanding, I suspect she'll never regret renouncing her title. I also suspect that she and Kirsten Aradottir are going to be very happy.

Meanwhile, Ruskin continues grandstanding. "Classes shall resume on Monday, and King Nestor has provided a generous budget to furnish us with everything we need. You all have until tomorrow at 7:32 AM to put in your requests for supplies."

"7:32 AM?" Inez Quissel, Distinguished Professor of Wandcraft and nakedly ambitious conniver, cannot allow this to go unchallenged. "Why not 10:00 AM?"

"Because I need ample time to evaluate your budget requests."

Quissel folds her arms across her décolletage, golden bangles jumbled together like gauntlets. "Why should you get to evaluate the budget requests? And why should you be the dean? I was made Acting Dean after you disgraced yourself on the Isle of Arran."

"Disgraced myself?" Ruskin draws himself to his full height. "Let me refresh your memory. While you were in thrall to the treacherous Lord Burke, I helped uncover his evil plan, saved Princess Elena from his clutches, and enabled my talented protégé, Miss Winter, to restore Arcanos Hall to its original, glorious form. Besides, when I tendered my resignation as Professor of Alchemy, the Regents appointed me Dean."

Kyril leans close. "This place," he whispers, mordantly amused. "It's a circular firing squad. It's like they've forgotten we have *real* enemies."

I'm still rolling my eyes at the toxic infighting, wondering which of these bloviating academic yahoos would make the worse administrator, when a familiar voice booms through the Ballroom, causing all the crystal droplets on the chandeliers to tremble.

"Enough! I am the Dean." Leaning on an onyx cane, his silver hair cropped close to his scalp, Dean LaMarche hobbles into the ballroom.

Inez Quissel makes an awkward bow, while Ruskin freezes in place.

"Dean LaMarche! Sir!" Ruskin is pale as flour, completely done with stirring the pot. "We thought you were dead. Worse than dead!"

"As you can see, my condition is quite tolerable. Thank you for your faithful service in my absence." He rests both hands on his cane and looks about the room. "We are here today, back in our old home, thanks to the efforts of Professor Anya Winter."

"Bravo!" Captain Aradottir says, as she and Kyril and Elena clap their hands. A few members of the faculty reluctantly join them, resulting in some decidedly tepid applause.

Dean LaMarche clears his throat. "I would like you all to know there will be some changes here at Arcanos Hall. We've seen the dangers of relying on the less fortunate for our magic, and we'll no longer base our curriculum so heavily upon hedge-produced charms. We shall divest. From now on, students will focus more intensively on creating their own charms and magical objects."

"What?" Inez Quissel looks like she has a burst appendix. "How utterly backward!"

"Professor Quissel, thank you for your exceptional efforts during this crisis. Going forward, you will teach the students to concentrate their power by crafting their own wands. Wand-making will now be part of the regular curriculum."

"I don't know how to do that," she scoffs. "That kind of work is entirely beneath me."

Dean LaMarche offers her a thin smile. "Well, I suggest you learn quickly." He clears his throat. "We also have a new faculty member on campus—the very accomplished Rocco Carrara, our new Professor of Alchemy and Potions."

I gasp in delight, but Ruskin is beside himself. "What? That fool can't even speak!"

"Rocco can speak perfectly well," LaMarche says, shocking everyone once more. "He's also an expert alchemist."

"But I'm the Alchemy and Potions professor."

Dean LaMarche lifts a single eyebrow, unfurling a scroll. "Really? I believe this document contains your resignation."

"But I resigned only because I understood I would be elevated to the position of Dean." Ruskin appeals to Inez Quissel and Captain Aradottir, but they both look completely puzzled and blank.

"Well, as you can see, we already have a dean and thus no longer need you to act in that capacity," LaMarche says with a sardonic smile. "But since you have tenure, we are obligated to find another position for you, and I'm happy to say there's an opening in the steam tunnels."

"The steam tunnels?" Ruskin is at a loss for words, and I can't help but laugh aloud.

∽

"You wanted to see me, Anya?" Seated at a gleaming enameled table, Dean LaMarche pours three glasses of sherry. His new office looks like a luxurious warehouse, with rolled-up ikat rugs and bouillotte lamps with black metal shades. Several large oil paintings lean against the south wall.

"You're redecorating, I see." I don't want to mention his greatest and most profound loss: the huge oil painting of the red leather gown.

I'm reminded of Aradottir's report that Lord Burke's portrait disappeared from Fortress Burke when he fled. More than ever, I believe that art can be used to crystalize a mage's power, even to transform or conceal the self.

"I'm making some changes," LaMarche says in his casual way. "And I imagine you are as well."

This provides me with the opening I need, so I decide to just blurt it out. "Sir, I'm leaving. Madame Olann has agreed to continue teaching in my place. Please don't think I'm ungrateful. I appreciate everything you've done to restore my reputation, really I do."

He waves a languid hand, passing me a glass of sherry. "I understand completely, Anya."

"You do?"

"Absolutely. I'll do what I can here to clean house, but change takes time. Besides, I'm the one who is grateful. You've saved this college, and shown us more about the lost knowledge of the Elders than we'd ever hoped to learn. Still, I hope you won't leave before someone has a chance to say goodbye." He nods in the direction of the door, and I turn to see Rocco lumbering in. His huge hands are gripping an enormous rectangle wrapped in brown paper, but when he sees me, he leans it against the wall, his face breaking into a smile.

"Rocco!" Rushing forward, I'm completely enveloped in his hug.

"Look at you," I say, admiring Rocco's crisp linen jacket and Tattersall shirt. "Dressed up so fine!"

"If I'm going to be a professor," Rocco says in a sonorous voice, a hint of the Snowy Range in his accent, "I've got to dress the part."

"You got your voice back." I'm smiling so wide that my cheeks feel sore. Remembering the ghostly chorus I heard when Kyril crushed Burke's voice-stealing chain, I seriously think I'm going to cry.

Rocco smiles in return. "I did."

Dean LaMarche takes a sip of sherry and pushes himself away from the table. "It's about time, I say. Time for you to show everyone what you can do. I'm just sorry I didn't have the courage to advocate for you before—when it really mattered."

Rocco just shrugs, and it occurs to me that the integration of this gentle giant at Arcanos Hall will probably change more hearts and minds than we will ever know.

"I saw Madame Olann," Rocco says, extracting a card from his massive shirt pocket, "and she asked me to give this to you. Someone sent it to her yarn shop."

It's a cheap tourist postcard from Rock City, Kansas, featuring a nondescript grouping of round granite boulders. Addressed to The Narrow Gauge. No return address. In block letters, it reads, "Your back."

"Well, you *are* back," Rocco says mildly, reading over my shoulder. "But it should have an apostrophe *RE* after the *you*."

"Very good, professor of punctuation," I tease. But I'm hearing a voice in my head. Always watch your back.

I'm pretty sure I'm going to see my father again, no matter what happens next.

"Okay, next order of business," says LaMarche, shuffling forward with his impressively carved cane and pointing it at the immense rectangle Rocco brought in. "Hanging new artwork."

Rocco pulls away the protective brown paper, and I see at once that it's a familiar oil painting: the unseen woman in the red leather gown.

I'm so astonished I can't even speak. *The woman in the red dress.*

"Rocco rescued it from the castle while you were in the dungeon," LaMarche says, leaning heavily on his cane as Rocco hangs the massive painting on the wall.

There's a catch in his voice, barely concealing the depth of his emotion. He claps a hand on Rocco's shoulder, and the two men—aristocratic wizard and quiet half-troll—both gaze solemnly at the painting.

"Well," Rocco finally says. "It's good to have her back where she belongs."

"I'm so glad; I really am." There's really nothing else I can say, but it occurs to me that I should add one more thing.

"And I want to say I'm glad Madame Olann will stay here to replace me. She's a mysterious person, and it's hard to know what she'll do, but she's incredibly powerful."

Rocco and the dean turn, their faces confused, as if surprised by the change of topic. "Indeed she is," says Dean LaMarche, "but what do you mean?"

"You know Queen Marguerite is restoring democracy to the Scottish isles. What you may not know is that Lord Burke entrapped her for six months in the chaos of Faerie. Using a magical weaving, Madame Olann was able to set her free."

The dean takes a quick breath. Beside him, Rocco is still.

It's Rocco who finally speaks. "So it is possible to escape the Realm of the Fey."

"It is." And that's where I leave them, still gazing up at the painted canvas.

"You look like you could use some ice cream." Kyril comes up behind me, bearing two sugar cones topped with salted caramel custard. I'm sitting on the dock behind the Memorial Union, gazing out at Lake Mendota. A pair of sailboats race north toward Portal Point. I accept the ice cream and the undersized napkin, but I don't respond.

We sit quietly for a while, busy with our ice cream cones, and then Kyril tries again. "I hear you resigned from the faculty."

"Madame Olann was happy to take the job. She probably wants to radicalize the students, and she'll do a better job than I would."

"That's not a reason to quit. You've got to have a better reason than that."

I consider this, allowing the last of the ice cream to melt on my tongue. "I want to go after Burke, even though I don't know where to begin. But it's also that I don't feel like I belong here. I look at the castle I used to love, and I don't see anything that feels like home."

"Home? That's an *ignis fatuus.*" Kyril extends his hand, pulling me to my feet.

"A what?"

"A false fire, a will o' the wisp. Something you can never stop chasing, something you'll never find."

"Oh, you're doing a great job cheering me up."

"I bought you some ice cream, and I told you the truth. What more do you want?"

"I want to make a difference in the world, and I want to belong somewhere."

"Belonging is overrated," Kyril says, making his way past the sailboats and windsurfers crowded against the dock.

"You can say that only because you've never really been an outsider."

He comes to a stop, his face so solemn that I wonder if he's

275

taken offense. Then he opens his hands, conceding. "I'm sure you're right. I didn't think of that."

I smile in response. "It's hard to see the world with eyes other than your own."

"Very true," he says and flashes a grin. The silver streak at his temple gleams in the bright sun. "All I know is that security can be a trap. It can keep people from seeking change. So why not work with me? There's injustice to fight, ancient secrets to uncover, an evil mage to hunt down. Didn't you say you have relatives in Scotland? We'll see the world, and we'll make a difference, just the two of us."

"The two of us? A hedge witch and a prince?"

"For the record, I don't particularly want to be a prince."

"Makes sense. I wouldn't want to be a princess."

"You? A princess?" Kyril raises a perfect eyebrow, lightly punching my shoulder with his fist. "Let's not get ahead of ourselves."

I do my best to suppress a laugh. It continues to be unfortunate, how handsome he is.

"Royal life can be a royal pain sometimes," he continues, coming to a stop at the end of the dock. "But I'm willing to take advantage of certain privileges relating thereto. Like this royal yacht." With a sweeping gesture, he pulls away a lapis blue tarp, revealing a beat-up and faded fiberglass canoe.

"Kyril, that's not a yacht. Seriously. It's a canoe."

"No matter. If you aren't willing to drive with me to an airport, this boat will have to take us where we need to go."

"And where is that?" I ask, watching as he unties the boat from the dock.

"Portal Point. As you know, the portal has been unsealed."

"So?"

"So, Kirsten Aradottir tells me you have a passport. And I have a royal letter of transit. Once we step into that portal, we can go anywhere we choose."

"Anywhere?" It occurs to me that I could really do it. I could just tug on the string and see where it leads. I could unravel my entire life and start again.

Almost giddy, I slip into the canoe and drag a slightly chipped wooden paddle from under the seat. Kyril joins me, shoving away from the dock. The water splashes around us, dark and cold. We paddle steadily, and the marshy green grasses of Portal Point grow near. I can see the fire pit at the very tip of the peninsula, and the picnic grounds where King Cibrán held his council. The hidden portal lies just beyond the green picnic tables.

I think about the narrow sliver of land we glimpsed outside Elena's castle, with its blocks of sun-bleached marble, twin harbors, and turquoise sea. That place, with all its secrets, was out of reach, and maybe it wasn't even real. But it *felt* real, and more than anything, I want to find it again.

Kyril drags his paddle against the edge of the canoe, turning us toward the shore. Our boat knifes through the marsh, and my paddle catches on a glistening hank of enchanted sea grass, perfect for spinning into yarn. I lean over the edge and grab a handful of grass, then another.

Kyril wrinkles his nose as I wring the sea grass dry. "Please tell me you're not keeping that stuff."

"It's not stuff: it's magical fiber, and I most definitely am. You can't complain because you still owe me a ball of yarn."

He tries his best not to smile, and all at once my dream of finding a place in the world doesn't seem so impossible after all. "Bring it along then," he says. "Let's go ashore."

ACKNOWLEDGMENTS

This novel traces a number of threads weaving together textiles and computer technology. My friend Kelly McCullough first got me thinking about computer languages as forms of magic, and his novel *Webmage* was a major source of inspiration for *Arcanos Unraveled*. Thanks, Kelly!

Special thanks to my faithful beta readers Naomi Gjevre and Jonathan Christopherson, as well as the gang in Colorado: Jack, Jeff, Kim and Floyd. Thanks also to my sharp-eyed copy editor, Jean-Marie Dauplaise. You all made this novel better in so many ways, and I'm lucky to have you on my team.

My editor is the brilliant Kat Howard and I would like to sing her praises from the rooftops. She helped me identify critical issues that I never would have seen on my own, and she respected me enough to tell me when I'd gone astray. Thank you, Kat.

I'm truly fortunate to have Stewart Williams as my book designer and the amazing Kathleen Jennings as my illustrator. It's been such an honor to work with them both, and I adore the exquisite cover art they created for *Arcanos Unraveled*. Thanks, Stewart and Kathleen, especially for the enchanted sheep!

I grew up very happily on a sheep farm in northern Minnesota, and I want to thank my parents for having the wisdom to surround me and my siblings with the best possible ingredients for a happy childhood: music, books, and sheep. Thanks to my whole family—I love you all.

My husband Steve is my first reader and my very best friend. He's also the sort of man who gleefully buys yarn in Icelandic supermarkets, which is just one of the many things I love about him. Thank you, Steve. Always and forever.

Arcanos Unraveled is dedicated to the memory of Michael Levy. Endlessly generous and kind, Mike encouraged me to write fiction, and he championed my work. He introduced me to a whole world of writers and ideas, and without his influence, I wouldn't be the author I am today. I miss you, Mike. This book's for you.